SECRETS

the secrets of a girl

Laura Ross, Laurie Ross

Staten House

Staten House

Printed in the United States of America

First Printing, 2022

ISBN 979-8-89778-339-7

Contents

Part One

Protostar

My last name is selfish
And conceited my first name
When it came to matters of heart
I'd forever play the blame game
He directed it though
And allowed it to race
But he pushed this little birdie
And compelled it to partake...

1

Staying in the dark

My mother always told me to stay away from boys. Boys were the pitfall of evil and had my worst intentions at heart. Despite her loving warnings, I found that guys tended to flock to me. Not for the reasons you'd think, however.

I was always the skinniest and shortest in my class. I developed later than most girls, and was convinced that was the reason they hated me. I wore loose t-shirts and baggy jeans while my hair remained in a tight high ponytail. True to form, I was a tomboy. My first best friend was male, as most of my friends were, and we met in the fifth grade. Devin Cooper was actually quite popular, which made our friendship entirely accidental. Every girl in our school loved him, because he was a pretty boy with a smooth caramel complexion. He never wore the same sneakers to

school more than twice which always made me wonder how well off he had it.

His family owned the local dry cleaners in the urban
D.C. area, but I always begged to differ when regarding
their lifestyle. They took expensive vacations and had
a few homes in the islands. Rumor had it that his
stepdad, Quincy, was heavily into drug dealing, which
I never wanted to believe. But there just had to be
a separate, more realistic, explanation behind all of
that ostentation. I knew a reasonable amount of truth
about them from my mother, though, who was very
close to his. Even when I asked her about the drug
money she'd just make a funny face and avoid the
question. As the years passed my curiosity height-
ened, though I was careful not to express it. As I said
though, our friendship was completely accidental.

It was the first day of fifth grade and a simple mis-
understanding. Our science teacher was an old, blind
man named Mr. Huck. Or at least that's what I thought
his name was. Though that part was a little hazy, I had
no trouble at all remembering Patrick Newton.

Mr. Huck decided to pair the class up into year-long
science buddies, which the class typically choose their
partners themselves, yet the old man thought it more
productive to loudly assign each of us a random pair-
ing. This made me panic. What if I was to be paired
with one of the tall, curvy, mean girls? I relatively
excelled in science—in every subject really—but I was
particularly fond of astronomy. The mere idea of

another universe outside of my middle school hell hole was fairly attractive, and whenever I stared up into those stars a familiar comfort rushed through me. I even made my parents buy me one of the most expensive pieces of equipment last summer and that cost me a month's worth of allowance check with-holdings. The Star Gazer. It proved to be beneficial though, because I now had the ability to star gaze on my balcony as opposed to stealing glances with the Star Gazer at my middle school, Eastway Junior High or through my ordinary binoculars.

Mr. Huck ran through the attendance list of names to pair us students up, and I began to notice that there were about four people left to be paired: Me, Sasha Kersey, Latisha Millard, and Devin Cooper. Oh lord, this was not looking good for me. As the process of elimination goes, Sasha Kersey was one of the perfect-ly shaped mean girls, her Caribbean accent drawing in more attention alongside her beauty. She never did anything overtly rude towards me, but tended to glare whenever we made eye contact. That made me uneasy.

Latisha, on the other hand, was the bold, sassy one who no one could believe was in the top tenth per-centile of her class each year. She hung with the hoodrats of the fifth-grade girls, and rumor had it that she carried brass knuckles with her everywhere. Not only was she brutal and intimidatingly curvy as well, but also Devin Cooper's ex-girlfriend as of a few months ago. That made the mouthwateringly attractive boy her territory and completely off limits. I was caught between a rock and a hard place, trapped, frightened and intimidated. I was aware that my random pair would only abuse my knowledge and love of science to their advantage, and I was fine with that. But there was no way I could pair with either of these girls, it'd be a living hell.

"Okay class," Mr. Huck said with a sigh. "There are only four of you left to be paired...let's see here." My heart nearly fell out of my chest when he took the extra-long minute to study his roster. A strange silence fell upon the classroom, and I took that time to inwardly pray for a miraculous outcome. If I paired with those girls I'd be used, and socially tortured. But if I were to pair with Devin, the torture would be far from social. Please work out in my favor, just once... I silently prayed.

"Miss Millard you'll be paired with Miss Kersey," he paused once again to reconsider his notepad. "And Devin, you'll be with Mr. Patrick Newton. Right over there, in the big green jacket."

I frowned at that. Patrick? Well if he was supposed to be paired with this Newton kid then, that meant Mr. Huck sympathized with me. He probably looked at me and figured my worth and decided I should work alone! God was so good, but I was still mildly jealous of this Patrick kid. I scanned the room for the lucky bastard.

"I'm talking to you, son. Get in your pair." Mr. Huck pointed and spoke directly to me.

"Me?" I chirped, frightened.

He winced, agitated. "Yes, Mr. Newton. Now follow instructions—or else!"

The class roared in laughter as the tears coursed furiously down my face. My hair was in two thick braids to the back, and I wore large baggy sweats and a tee shirt. The ensemble was completed with my dad's old army jacket and combat boots. I guess the old man thought I was Patrick Newton, instead of Patrice Newbern.

I was mortified.

Mr. Huck tried in earnest to calm the still-roaring classroom to no avail; I barely gave a damn at that point. They were all blurred entities through my crying eyes, I just felt so alone and trapped again. I needed to be under the stars, because it was their gazes that didn't intimidate or frighten me. At that moment I wanted time to speed up and to blend with the stars into that night sky. Why can't they like me? I wondered internally as I stood, readying to leave the room.

Then, out of nowhere, the students went silent. I turned to face them to find the source that could have been so effective, but my mouth only dropped at the sight. Devin walked proudly across the classroom to eventually occupy the lab chair beside me. I looked down at him, still fully in shock. Did he come all this way to torture me, too? I whimpered and rushed to gather my books.

"Hey," he said. Though only twelve, his voice was the deepest, sexiest music that could have graced my prepubescent ears. "We're partners, right?"

I stared dumbly at him, as did the rest of the class. "Y-Yeah, I guess." I whispered.

He gave a small, encouraging smile as his big hand took mine to slowly reseat me. "Well sit down, and let's get to work. Okay, Patrice?" He said my name with menacing emphasis, as if daring even the boldest kid to challenge him. With my hand still in his, he tightened his hold on me. For reassurance? I didn't know.

Mr. Huck fumbled over himself with apologies, and even offered me the rest of the class period to spend in study hall.

If Devin had asked me to smack my mom that fateful day, I would have done it.

It was love at first sight...

2

From the other side, with love

"You shouldn't let people call you anything they want." Devin said as he reached for a lunch plate. We were in the school's cafeteria for lunch hour and the special today was gross enough for me to skip school: meatloaf. I didn't trust any meat that jiggled and moved on its own accord. Devin looked towards my direction with a questionable expression.

My eyes almost instantly lowered from his gaze. "What?"

His eyes darted from me, to the stack of lunch trays, to the angry line growing behind me, and back.

"Oh! Duh, sorry." I quickly grabbed a tray and proceeded down the assembly line of prison food. Devin waited patiently at the end of the line for me as I paid for the school slop. I couldn't seem to pick my gaze up from the ground because I could feel his stare. Those brown eyes were just...burning through me. I snuck a couple of glances and attempted to play it casual and cool, just like Devin. I failed as soon as he touched my shoulder. "W-where did y-you want to sit?" I asked in order to try to ignore the sensation he caused.

Devin laughed. "Chill, chill. I know a place, mami. Come on." He guided me towards the middle of the cafeteria and I assumed he was joking when he stopped in front of the popular table. Was he for real?

"Hey, D! Lil honey on ya arm, huh?" One of them barked.

"Who the hell is she?" Said another.

"That he-she from science class..." The crowd was roaring.

"Ain't no room for you, boo!" Came a final snicker.

I wasn't sure who was who and who said what but each insult thrown rang out crystal clear. I didn't belong here and it was obvious his friends had no room for me either. In that moment, everything began to kind of move in slow motion and all I could do was stand there, petrified. Devin's firm grasp of my hand brought me back to reality.

He scoffed. "Man, whatever y'all trippin. You ready?"

He was talking to me, I'm sure. "We're not sitting here? Aren't they your friends?"

"Uh...I guess. But I was stopping by to talk to my boy, Ty. Sorry for that, I heard what they was sayin to you, mami." There was that little pet name again, mami. Were we on a pet name basis already? I made a mental note to bring that up to him later on. I looked around and almost didn't notice where he was leading me. I grew a little nervous when we walked through the cafeteria lunch doors and out the school's side door that kids usually skip school from. Regardless of the terrible food, I was never the "let's skip school" type of girl. It seemed as though one might need friends to skip with and that was one of the credentials I lacked.

Once we reached outdoors, I halted.

"Where are you taking me?" I questioned, suspicious now.

Devin looked down at me with those beautiful, brown eyes of his and whispered, "The Spot..."

I inched away from him and those words. "Why? I'm not that type of girl, Devin." Everyone knew where The Spot was and what it was used for. The Spot was actually a small clearing behind the school that was almost like a blind spot. It's shrouded by two big, thick trees and underneath I watched many other couples disappear into the darkness.

"Well if you're not comfortable then...you will be." He confessed with so much seriousness in his tone it made me shiver. Devin proceeded to walk closer into my shadow until his breath warmed my cheeks. I was in shock and was in no position to argue with this version of him. Dark Devin. Mysterious Devin...

I tore my gaze away from his. "I—uh—"

The bell for the ending of lunch rang right on time. It was what I needed to shake this spell I was in. I don't know what was faster; me running all the way to my third period or that scary/awkward/supernatural moment I shared with Devin Cooper. Everything was so quick, in fact, I questioned whether or not it happened at all.

"There's a method to my madness, you know."

It'd been almost a week since my swift encounter with Dark Devin. I decided that the whole moment was real and it was this decision that empowered me to do as much avoiding him as possible. Until now.

I didn't even bother to look up from my science textbook to respond. "Hello, Devin."

He leaned all the way back in his lab chair and lazily tapped his nails against the table. "Did you hear me?"

I lied. "No, what was that?"

He scoffed.

"What are you talking about?" I took the bait and decided to engage in his pouting. Funny, a week ago if he had just randomly spoken to me I would have been tongue tied, had about four internal conniptions, and possibly forgotten the English language. "I was reading about genetic sequencing for the project, so..."

"You've been duckin' me, yo. That's not nice, mami."

I shifted in my seat. "Okay, so I've been wondering who this 'mami' person is? Where did it come from?"

"That's not your name? So what?"

"I mean, you know my name. I don't go around calling you daddy or anything."

"You can if you want." He winked.

"Ugh, Devin!"

"I thought I was daddy now?"

I couldn't help but smile at his charm. This didn't solve the problem, though. Where did this pet name come from? "So—"

"So why can't you do this next time to people who call you everything but your name?"

We spoke at the same time but his question held much more weight. I unknowingly held my breath from the panic. It was a great question; why didn't I correct others who called me Patrick, Patricia, or anything else crazy? I was speechless, but overall afraid to answer.

Devin finally sat up and leaned in towards me. He placed his head in his left hand with his long hair falling behind on the table. His grin vanished and was replaced with a look of significance. "Hm, mami?"

"Patrice!" I snapped. "It's just...Patrice. Please." This action caused a couple heads to turn in our direction. I inhaled and tried to gather myself. He nodded slowly.

It was silent for a while before I felt his hand slowly touch my breasts.

Instinctively, I slapped his hand away from me. "What is your problem?"

"Why couldn't you do that last time? At The Spot?" He seemed as if he were studying me, and that made me all kinds of uncomfortable.

And irritated.

"Because I didn't, alright?" I retaliated.

"A'ight, then. Don't let people do and say stuff to you, Patrice. I wasn't going to do anything to you, so chill. Stand up for yourself sometimes, okay? I'm not going to be here all the time to help you."

Help me? What had he done so far to help me? "Is that so? I see you've remembered my name, all of a sudden." I said, crossing my arms.

Devin closed his eyes and sighed. "I can see that you're tough, Patrice. It seems so. I can see that muscle right behind all that shyness. I know just what you need, too."

Dread slammed straight into me. "What's that?"

He snapped his fingers, as if he had an epiphany. "The one thing tough people have in common in the first place. You know, a street name. Hmm...Tris? Nah, nah nah. Pat is lame as hell, too. Hmm...I like...Trice."

"Goodness you're unbelievable." I laughed. "Okay, I give. That's fine. What about you, tough guy? Hmm—"

"Yeah, you right. She'll like that too." Devin grinned slyly.

"She who?" This guy was confusing. So there was a mami after all? Devin subtly turned his head to the right and signaled for me to look in that direction. It was Latisha with all of her glory, glaring daggers at us. Devin turned back to me and stared for a while before he gave a good natured smile.

"Oh you thought Tisha wasn't watching us at The Spot? That was the main reason I took you there,

Trice. Messing with you and stuff was extra!" I laughed so hard Deaf-Mr. Huck had to give us warnings.

I shook my head and shoved him playfully and did my best to pretend to concentrate on the theory behind genetic matter besides the wild pounding of my heart.

3

Judging the book, reading the cover

"You're coming to my game tonight, right?" Devin asked me playfully, but seriously, one day. An entire year of friendship had passed between us and as soon as I knew it we were sixth graders. I was still considered Devin's frumpy tomboy friend who had the audacity to wear trench coats with Chuck Taylors on a sunny day. Standing next to him was a blessing and a curse at the same time. I was thankful for his companionship but the stares could sometimes be too much to ignore.

Considering I went to all of his football practices, I stared at him with a 'duh' face.

"You want me to?" I asked.

We were standing by the lockers minutes before class, and there were students rushing here and there to get to class on time.

Since it was game day, Devin sported his school football jersey with a pair of Stacy Adams designer jeans. Even though he was only thirteen he still looked like something that fell off the page of a magazine.

He flashed that brilliant white smile and scratched his neatly braided hair. "Now this is why I knew I had to ask. Hell yeah I want you to be there."

"Are you sure?" I hated to ask.

But I figured I bothered him enough at his practices this year that we were giving people the wrong idea. We caused enough attention already merely standing beside each other. He was the only friend I had and I wanted to do my best to keep him around. Plus, the bleachers were normally empty at his practices so I had no worries when it came down to being seen as sappy or in love with him. Though I was...

"It's been an entire year, Trice. You should know by now that I stand by what I say." Leaning his weight on the lockers with his forearm, Devin zeroed his face so close to mine our noses touched.

I wish I could've controlled the slow heat that crept from below my neck. Instinctively, I shoved him away from me. "Creep!" I chirped.

He recovered and laughed good-naturedly. "For real, though, Patrice. You're my friend and I want you there. Game starts at seven..."

"But what if people think—" I began.

I couldn't have seen it coming if it hit me, but Devin interrupted my protests with a quick peck on the lips. The remaining students struggling to beat the late bell whispered and gasped at the public display of affection—the unlikely display at that.

I was panting and he met my doe eyes and flamed cheeks with a confident smile. "Fuck what other people think...this game means a lot to me and so do you. Like I said, the game starts at seven." He jogged to class after that.

I hated how he had the ability to keep so cool while I could only stupidly stand there as several mini bombs exploded inside me. I made a vow to myself when we first spoke to avoid falling in love. But when he did things like that I could practically see my resolve weaken right before my eyes. Even though we grew closer with each passing day it was always in the back of my mind that he was deemed a playboy. I couldn't, for all good reason, endanger my heart to such a guy, no matter how false that reputation could be.

Once my breath and temperature returned, I glanced at the clock on the wall. I had only a minute to get to class at this point, and the panic that set in was immediate. I couldn't risk my perfect attendance record, not even for a minute, or my parents would kill me.

I took only one step before a pair of arms encircled me from behind. The action wouldn't have startled me so badly if I was sure it was Devin, but the fragrance of strawberries hit me just as strong as my shock did. Devin smelled solely of Old Spice.

"I saw that little exchange between the two of you just now, here—" The female voice shoved a piece of paper in my hand. Each time I tried to turn to face her, her stronger arms impeded me.

"What's this?" I demanded.

"Read it later and tell me what you think. I gotta go."

In an instant the stranger disappeared, leaving me even more flustered and pissed off. Just where the hell was this day taking me?

I received my first tardy that day. Screw it.

***

I returned home to find my mother in the living room, counseling one of her patients. She was an older white lady, badly bruised and silently weeping between words. I knew better than to disturb my mother during a session, as the last time I did ended in a very harsh grounding and loss of allowance for a week. With that in mind, I crept inside and tiptoed up to my room. With each step to my room I could feel my excitement rise. This was what I looked forward to each day after school. It was one of my most pleasant constants of the day, and that was stargazing.

Well it wasn't technically stargazing due to the daytime, but watching the clouds pass in the gentle D.C. breeze was so gratifying. I found myself fixed behind that telescope for hours sometimes, as it was hard to focus on reality. As I sat behind the scope this afternoon, I reflected on the events of the day.

I didn't want to love Devin; loving him more than the greatest friend than he was sounded tremendously endangering. I was a virgin who never had a boyfriend or even been within more than three feet of a guy since Devin Cooper, so I chalked this butterfly feeling in my gut for him as nothing more than nerves. That was it. Guys didn't find skinny little me attractive, and even if they did...yeah, I'm sure they wouldn't. I went to every one of Devin's practices and sat in that familiar bottom bleacher that gave me just the right view of him. He was number seven, and lord knows my eyes followed that jersey number all over the field and still would, come this game tonight.

He was so sociable and accepting, I had come to realize that. Even though my best friend had the money, status, and popularity he was unafraid to be himself and hang out with whomever he wanted. I noticed that, even though he tended to date bitches, he made sure that any and every one in his company was comfortable. Gosh...was there anything wrong with this boy? Even though he meant that kiss he gave in the hallway in passing, I couldn't help the butterflies that went to war in my gut.

"That note!" I yelped aloud to no one in particular. When I thought of that frightening kiss from earlier, invariably, that weird encounter came to mind. Whomever it was that grabbed me like that smelled like too much cheap strawberry fragrance spray and had a familiar voice. I knew she was shorter than me, simply by the way she restrained me. She sounded like someone I shared a class with, no one popular, but maybe one of the wallflowers? When I turned to face her she was long gone, and I just jammed the note in my backpack to read later before running to class.

Without further ado, I took hesitant baby steps toward my backpack. Almost as if the note was an actual living thing, or a bomb.

My jaw dropped once I finally read the note:

Hey new girl,

Give me a call, 555-0326, if you still want to go to the game tonight. We need to talk. This isn't optional, be sure to call.

What the hell? I knew being Devin's friend would haunt me sooner or later, but threats? What in the world could she want to discuss? I'm not even sure if whomever-she-is and I have ever even had a conversation, and now we needed to talk? Maybe it was one of Latisha's girls, rumor had it that she was crazy. But if that was the case, then that would have to mean she saw me as a threat. And I knew that just wasn't the reason. My body was on autopilot, it was it that drove me to my father's office and picked up his desk phone.

Surely, I wouldn't dial this girl's number to see what was up.

"Hello?" She answered on the second ring, whomever she was. I hesitated, my mouth feeling dryer than ever.

"Uh, yeah, a girl gave me this number to call. So here I am..."

She hesitated too. "Oh! Patrick, what's up girl?"

That dreaded name. At the mention of that pseudonym, anger and recognition filled me. I sighed. "Biology Class?"

She laughed, a real throaty sound. "That's right, I was there. And I see how close you and Devin have gotten..."

I narrowed my eyes in suspicion, she was fishing for info. "We're friends, yeah. But is there a reason you assaulted me in the hallway?'

She cleared her throat, as if realizing her purpose. "Oh girl my bad, that's just how I am. But I heard you're going to the game, right?"

"Maybe...what's it to you?" I asked meekly.

"I want to help you...what's your address?" She asked in a rush.

My address? "Why do you need my—"

"Look, if you want to stand out and look good then let me help you. By the looks of it, you sure do need some fashion sense."

I thought of Devin, of course. He liked me just the way I was—trench coat and all. He was the only friend

I had, the only one I cared to impress. Then I thought of...me. Looking down at my dirtied Chucks, I decided it worth it to at least hear her out.

"So," I began. "You want to dress me up for tonight?"

"Exactly," she responded.

"But...why? It's only a football game." I reasoned.

"It isn't, and you know it. It's the first time the entire school will see you at Devin's side, on his side of the bleacher. Don't you want to stand out? Dress up for a little bit?"

She took my hesitation and ran with it. I didn't know how to respond to that, or that she had been paying so close attention to me all this year.

"You like him...right?" She said softly.

"We're friends." I sighed, perturbed at this point.

She laughed out loud. "You deflected that with excellence. It's so obvious how much this boy is feeling you."

I gulped, excitement and dread filling me at once. "He's feeling me? Really?"

I could practically see her giving me the duh face. "Uh, yeah. So what do you say?"

"313 Toronto Boulevard." I answered hastily.

She gave that throaty laugh again. "It's Nora by the way. I'm Nora Albert."

"Oh." I said, shocked. I was right, Nora was partly popular but cool with all the cool kids. She was an average sized girl with dark skin and could have any guy she wanted, though rumor had it that she was into girls. Each time I saw her, though, she was alone. A combination of those things undoubtedly concerned me, but I wasn't getting any weird vibes from the girl. She seemed like she had my genuine interest at heart. For some reason.

***

"Oh...my...gosh!" I breathed as I stood face-to-face with the beauty before me in the mirror. Her hair fell in curly black ringlets that cascaded down her back. The only makeup she wore was a light gloss on her lips that accentuated her pale pink cardigan that hung loosely over the fitting white tank. Her jeans were light blue and hugged her curves nicely. Curves...she had curves. I had curves.

"What do you think?" Nora asked me.

"Amazing..." Was all I could say, not sure if I was responding to her or not. I couldn't help but think of a few things. I was certain my mother would not allow me to leave the house like this. She was a very avid feminist and despised anything that perpetuated gender specific stereotypes, including suggestive clothing. And these jeans that Nora leant me hugged me a little too intimately. I also thought of how beautiful and confident I felt, two things I severely lacked since the beginning of puberty. I tried to avoid any thoughts of Devin...because I reminded myself of how all of this was for me. Patrice Newbern.

No, not Patrice, but someone unafraid to be bold and girly at the same time. Someone who, from this night, would determine her own future instead of letting others run all over her.

"Hey, Newton." Nora interjected my inner antics, her voice snappy and concerned. "The game starts in thirty minutes, we gotta get going."

"No," I insisted with an attitude as I stared at my new self. Patrice Newbern was dead. "Call me Trice."

"Huh?" She asked, bewildered, her hand on her hip.

"You heard me..." I stared back at her now with conviction, Devin's advice whispering in my mind. "From now on, call me Trice."

Nora raised her hands in defeat, her brows lifting in shock. "Yes, ma'am. Trice it is."

I strode out of my room surely, confident, and inwardly daring someone to call me Patrick again.

4

Maneater of destiny

For some odd reason I didn't care to analyze, Patti LaBelle's song "New Attitude" rang through my mind as I strutted (or tiptoed) out of my big brother's Ford Focus. I tried to convince myself that this surge of courage wasn't just a temporary adrenaline rush brought on by my latest look; Trice's debut, but something everlasting from here on out. I felt a hand grab me and hold my wrist before I was almost completely out of the car and turned towards the driver's seat with my droll stare prepared. "What is it this time, Manny?"

My brother Manuel Nicholas Newbern was a tall, lanky, darker-skinned sixteen-year-old computer geek who took after our father in height, but many have commented on his distinct facial similarities to our mother. Though abnormally shy, he was ever the most annoyingly overprotective brother to boot and currently the newest licensed chauffeur for the night.

He frowned, hard. "Don't give me that look, little girl. I'm not scared of you. I'm going to Bruno's house so make sure you call me when you are ready for me to pick you up—" He grunted and scowled the length of my apparel. "I still don't like what you're wearing..."

"Okay, so I'll call? Bye!" I yanked my imprisoned arm free from his grasp, slammed the door and walked swiftly from the car towards the stadium steps. I hated when Manny got like that. He treated me worse than my own father, and he wasn't even home that often enough to treat me like a toddler.

"Patrice, wait! Come here." Manny had gotten out of the car and stood by the door. I walked back with as much attitude as I could force into my awkward strut.

"What?" I fired back.

He looked at me closely, seriously. "Be careful, sis. I don't know about this chick."

"Bye, Manny! Don't ruin my night before it even starts, okay?"

He smirked. "I miss my little brother. Why you dressing like this, anyway? I got some new jeans if you want to borrow them."

I rolled my eyes and walked far away from that idiot.

"Slow down, Patrick! You're killin' me!" Nora exclaimed somewhere from behind me. I almost forgot about her and didn't even remember her getting out of the car. I turned around and that action startled her.

"It's Trice! Oh my gosh how many times do I have to say that?" I barked. My hand immediately flew to my mouth as the words escaped from me. Nora's hands were up in the air as if she was being held up by a mugger. Her next reaction startled me.

She laughed. "Girl, chill! I was just playing. You were walking so fast my short ass legs was doing double time trying to catch up!" Nora placed both of her hands on her knees and panted for breath. "Besides, Trice. I was just teasing you, that's what friends do. La-duhh!"

I apologized despite her weird reaction. "Nora, I'm sorry. My brother just gets on my last nerve with all his macho crap. I take my name and its pronunciation seriously because it's so closely spelled like my dad's—Patrick—and I don't want to be compared to someone I hardly know. Someone who barely acknowledges my existence." I didn't plan on the sudden venting, but the words vomited out of me. A moment of silence befell on us and at this time I thought about what Nora had confessed.

At the mention of that word—friends—I inwardly paused. I'd never had too many of those before and warm feelings of delight and overall belonging washed over me. In that moment, I allowed my pompous brother's antics and the reaction it always got out of me to dissipate. Nora extended her hand towards me. "You ready? A certain somebody is waiting to see the Trice."

"Yearbook committee! Smile!"

A familiar voice bellowed from behind us. Neither of us managed to glimpse an inch of the school photographer's face before we instinctively held our hands up to the flash of the camera. I sighed. Nora grimaced.

"Ugh, you freak!" she muttered loudly. It was too late though because as the retort left her mouth he continued through the gate and into the stadium, his shutter sounds fading in the distance. That was weird, was my remaining thought as we followed the crowd into the field. For some reason, that song wasn't playing as loud as before in my mind.

***

Two hours later, I was sure of two things:

One: I was not as knowledgeable on the sport of football as I thought I was. Whenever anyone scored a goal or a point, touchdown I believe it's called, I wouldn't know it. I'd just stand up and cheer with the crowd and try to blend in. The announcer was nice enough but mostly threatened many who refused to stand up and partake in the howls and cheers. Two: I was not as confident as I envisioned my new self to be. Each time Devin made a touch down or ran near my section, it seemed he'd look everywhere but where I sat. I couldn't help but feel slightly less than confident that he'd go out of his way to ignore me.

"Whoooo! Trice, girl, your man looking like a whole snack out here!" Nora roared along with the crowd.

She jumped up and down with delight as our team made another goal.

Automatically, I smacked my hand against Nora's mouth. "Nora, please! Shhhh! Anyone could have heard you yelling like that." Or worse, Devin.

Nora looked up at me with wide eyes, chuckled from beneath my hand, and shrugged. I sighed and plopped back down on the bleacher, defeated.

"Trice, who cares? What happened to Ms. New-look-new-me a few hours ago? Stand up! He's running over here! Devin!" Nora waved and pushed me up towards the fence.

My face was red hot, fueled by embarrassment. My hands covered areas that weren't accustomed to being exposed and suddenly wished that I had packed a bag with my denims and Chuck Taylors.

Devin stood extremely close to where I sat, so close I could hear his deep gulps as he drank from his water bottle. He scanned the crowd with a smile: the top section, the top left, the middle section, the top right, the bottom right, and once his gaze settled close to the front row he yelled, "Nora! What's up, girl?"

My mouth went from a shy smile to a huge 'O.'

Nora appeared to have not noticed my reaction and sudden frigidness.

"Hey hun! Great game! Whatcha doin' tonight?" Nora replied. I could practically hear the wink in her tone. Why was she flirting so openly in front of me? My heart was racing so fast I thought it would burst through my chest. My fists clenched and unclenched uncontrollably. I looked up as I felt tears sting my eyes.

I was mad.

Nora, finally, looked over at me and glared down the length of my body along with a sarcastic smirk and said, "Tisha said what's up! She said last night was fun..."

Devin's face formed a question mark. "Tisha said what?"

Nora looked back at Devin and smiled sweetly. "She said she's sorry she couldn't make it and wanted you go to her house afterwards to—"

I shoved Nora and forced my way through the crowd towards the exit. I couldn't listen to anymore of that. I was so enraged that I didn't notice the huge sob that released on its own. Was this her plan the whole time? Of course, this day was too good to be true. The kiss from Devin, the huge makeover, the promise of a girlfriend, and an interested response from the person I've been in love with for the past year?

The next thing I heard was the sound of thunder as the sky cracked nastily with fat globs of raindrops.

I was standing outside in the parking lot, drawing attention to myself in the tight dress I had on and mid-heels, complimented with tear stained face. I hated crying in front of people. It made me feel ugly and vulnerable.

The sound of a camera shutter made me gasp and look around.

"Oh, what did you want?" I asked, sarcastically. It was the camera boy from earlier. Why did he show up now of all moments? Jeez.

He walked up to me, slowly, as I recovered from the camera flash. Did he get a kick out of taking pictures of girls crying in empty parking lots? The creep.

"It's dangerous out here, you know?"

I tiptoed away from him, steadily, and watched the camera boy give a sorrowful smile as he reached for his backpack.

"Come here, Patrice."

5

Natural isn't so Normal

The roar of thunder and clash of lightning forced me to believe that I was struck down by this weather. If possible, the rain poured down even harder from deeper, more shallow buckets from the thick, ominous sky.

My eyes were glued shut as I stood there, shivering, head down. I had almost forgotten about the mysterious camera boy reaching for something—probably a gun—to finish me off with. I stood there petrified and shocked at the sudden turn of events from today. Is this the end for Trice? I at least wanted to have a boyfriend before I went. I wanted my life to begin, and after the events of the day, I was convinced it was dead over. Even though I now questioned the power of Trice, I still wanted a chance at life—far away from here. This just can't be the end of it.

A sudden pop made me shriek.

"Open your eyes, Patrice." The boy said.

Suddenly, the familiar pelts of rain on my back and shoulders subsided and replaced with warm hands. I peered up at the umbrella that the camera boy held over us. I inwardly released a huge sigh of relief and mentally wiped my brow.

Phew, to live another day, I thought.

"It's the umbrella; Sorry for scaring you." He gazed down at me and I was met with crisp, bright blue eyes. Eyes so blue, in fact, they shined with a unique bleakness. His long, black hair covered most of his face and was mostly matted strings due to the rain. His stare was pensive and...reassuring?

"Th-thanks. It's okay, really. Thank you for this. Thanks." Gosh did I always have to be the babbling idiot?

He grinned. "Three times. You thanked me three times."

"Sorry. Um—no, I meant...I don't know what I'm saying. Ugh, sorry."

He chuckled lightly. "Twice. You apologized twice. You are so predictable."

I was so drained. I didn't care to analyze whether his last statement was an insult or not. I just wanted to go home. Heartbreak and disappointment had a unique way of sucking a girl dry. I opened my purse and fished around for my phone. "Ah ha!" I muttered when I found the little yellow Motorola Sidekick.

I watched the last bar on my phone flash three more times before it died.

"Shit!"

I threw it back in my purse and stomped. What else can go wrong tonight? If I stood out here any longer I'd have to ask for a ride from Devin's dad, and that was not happening. I'd walk the four miles first.

The camera boy pulled me tighter, so as to keep me under the protection of the umbrella, after I had my little tantrum. It was only then I realized how close we were under the large plastic shield.

"Mum, where are you?" He clipped out, annoyed. "Okay, cool. I'm outside with a friend. Is it alright if we take her home? Cool, bye."

I hadn't even noticed him take his phone out. "You didn't have to do that, uh, what was your name again?"

"Never gave it, Patrice." He said simply, smugly even, as if there was a joke he wouldn't let me in on.

Okay. "Okay...well how do you know my name so well?" I asked, my voice dripping with suspicion.

"Look, I'm just trying to be nice." He sighed. "You look like you had a rough night."

I sighed. "You're right. I just wanted to know your name, 'kay?"

"It's Kale. Kale McAllen." He sighed again and looked in the opposite direction with an expression that was difficult to translate. Was he irritated?

"So, uh, your accent? Is it Scottish?" I blurted.

"No, definitely not; I'm from Dublin. Though, that's not the first time I've been asked that." He was looking back down into my eyes again, and giving me that same pensive stare from before in the rain. It took a while to notice that he was smiling due to those eyes telling a story on their own. Kale leaned down, so slow I wouldn't have noticed it if I weren't so still, to the point he was inches from my face.

Everything went silent.

He allowed me into his world as he peered closely into my soul. It was in this quiet, breathtaking, moment that I realized that it did just that; he literally snatched my breath away.

His mouth was moving, then. I was still caught in his unending trance and could only...stand there.

It was the blaring car horn that made me jump.

"Patrice, Mum's here. Did you hear me talking to you?" Kale asked as he guided me towards the bright lights of the black minivan.

"Y-yeah. Alright, I'm sorry." I stammered, climbing into the back seat.

Kale slid into the seat beside mine and never took his eyes off me while he fastened his seat belt. "Three times, now. You've apologized three times now."

***

That's how my dreams ended every night since then.

That was over a week ago.

I sat up in bed and looked around my room. The yellow marshmallow pillow posters on my wall were shimmering in the reflection of the moon. The little stuffed canaries were hidden away in the chest next to my video game shelf. There were sneakers sprawled haphazardly on the carpeted floor. Lipstick, mascara, eyeliner, and brushes were mixed with the madness that had become my floor as well. My gaze finally settled on the vanity mirror in front of my bed. I stared at my reflection and wished it had the same effect as the moon; to make the ordinary shimmer as if it wasn't dull in the first place. I pulled my knees up to my face and buried myself there. My life had spun out of control and my room was proof of it. I pushed myself up from the fuzzy, yellow fur that was my bedding set and sat on the chair facing the vanity. I picked up my brush, twirled it, and ran the bristles through my straightened mane. I sighed and allowed my mind to wander around the events that had taken place since that awful game night.

"Damn, sis. Who whooped yo ass?"

It was Friday night, and I just came home from Devin's football game and, quite possibly, one of the worst days of my life. Kale's mom, or mum I think he called her, was very lively throughout the duration of the car pool. She'd constantly think up some sort of a story to get me to smile. She and Kale were like a comedy duo who kept each other laughing with each other's wisecracks. His mother was very sweet and, regardless of my shitty appearance, never asked any questions.

I scoffed and kicked my shoes off once I got to my room's threshold.

"Don't wanna talk, Manny. Seriously." I grumbled. The door slammed with a moderate bam before he rolled his eyes and pushed away from the wall. I wasn't in the mood for the "I told you so," that was sure to come from him.

Once I heard the familiar click from the lock, I shrugged out of my drenched clothes from tonight. I scrambled around my room for a towel and my huge yellow marshmallow t-shirt with holes in each armpit. The rain continued its heavy onslaught as I tied my hair in a high, frizzy bun at the top of my head. It continued as I found my blow dryer and gave my whole body a once over with the warm air. It left remnants of its presence on my window and threatened it with winds so harsh the whipping sounds pushed against the glass.

The gentle tap on my door caught my attention as my head whipped around.

"Baby? It's mom. Did you just get in?" Monica Newbern asked worriedly from the other side of the door.

I was tempted to remain silent, but I knew how my mother could get when she was being ignored. Her last rampage left my father in the hospital for three days.

"Yeah, but mom I was sleep. Can we talk in the morning?" I feigned a drowsy accent that said, "go away."

She sighed. "Well, alright. I wanted to know how the game went with your new friend. Anyway, I'll talk to you tomorrow. Goodnight, baby." I head her footsteps shuffle away to the top of the steps until it was silent.

"I don't even want to go tomorrow. "I muttered. School sounded like the most unappealing place in the world to spend the next eight hours.

I walked over to turn the light off and caught a glimpse of the note from...her. It was the same one that I had left on my dresser when I was preparing for "Trice's "debut. I quickly scooped the note from the dresser and tossed it into my trash can. All sorts of thoughts had returned to my mind again and proceeded to let those bitter feelings well back up.

I grabbed my purse and searched for my phone that had gave out on me in the parking lot with the camera guy. At the thought of him I began to feel warm despite the cold chill in my room and heart.

Could he have been in on it, too?

The nasty thought entered my head faster than I could catch it and lingered there. Just like that, I was disgusted all over.

I lay down on my side and plugged my phone to its charger. Once it powered back on, I told myself not to expect anything from Devin or anyone else. I told myself to not feel anything when I heard the familiar vibration of a missed call or text.

That vibration never came.

I placed my phone down on the nightstand beside my bed, bawled up my body, and did something for the second time since Devin became a constant in my life.

I cried.

I cried as hard as the relentless rain outside my window.

Part Two

T Tauri

6

The Center of the Universe

An entire month passed before Devin and I spoke. Ever since that horrible game night I did my best to avoid him in the beginning. It was just too awkward to confront those problems, and it seemed like we never could get private moments together like we used to. In the end, my avoidance of him fostered a normal distance that grew between us that officially put an end to our prior "friendship." Any time our eyes met either of us frowned in guilt and turned away. I was so disappointed in him for treating me this way, for neglecting me, and there was a part of me that would carry that forever. However, out of the tumult blossomed a flower, because my relationship with someone else turned into something beautiful.

After Dad dropped me off, I entered the west wing of the school building. I did this habitually, since I knew Devin's locker was on the complete other side.

My hair flowed in the morning breeze as I finally walked inside and made my way to the lockers. The crowds were thick; however, his warm stare instantly found mine in the morning madness. I approached him and offered a huge smile to my accidental friend.

"Top of the morning, Kale." I greeted.

He was in the middle of conversing with another boy we both recognized from Drama class when he addressed me. "That some kind of cruel Irish joke, lass?"

"No, lass," I mimicked his Irish accent perfectly. "Just a wee bit of humor for you before the big exam today." I never even realized Kale and I shared the same Drama class until he told me. Our Drama teacher, Ms. Ja, was a bit of a nutcase but relentless when it came to exams.

Kale excused himself from the conversation with the guy and stopped to stare at me. He had a huge grin on his face.

"What?" I asked. The attention was making me blush.

"Nothing. Just thought this was a perfect photo opportunity. You look so interesting mid-laugh." After ruffling around in his bookbag, he produced a small digital camera. "Stay like that!"

I laughed and turned away, embarrassed. "Kale, no! I look sleepy and haven't had anything to eat. I don't have the patience for this."

He snapped a shot then. "Don't worry, we Irishmen don't run out of energy, so I'll be your strength."

"Oh, shush!" I urged. "Now let's get to class."

***

"Now, class." Ms. Ja addressed, "Your exam will consist of an improvisation piece for whichever scene you are assigned. I hope you have read well."

Ms. Ja was a soft-spoken Korean woman with really long hair. She also wore thin glasses that sat on the bridge of her nose that made her look saner than she was. She could be a tall intimidating lady when it came to theatre, however.

Ms. Ja walked slowly through the room, her small eyes peering into the soul of each of us. She looked Gail Mulligans dead in the eye.

The poor girl trembled under the older woman's gaze.

"Yes, Ms. Ja?" She stuttered.

"Kale McAllen!" She screamed in Gail's face while the attention in the room shifted to my adjacent friend, Kale.

Kale's curly hair bounced in the direction of his whiplash as he looked at our insane teacher. "Ma'am?"

"I want you!" She proclaimed. "To go first. I want you to improv a love scene in which the woman you adore, hates you."

Kale gave her a blank look. "So, will this be a one-man show?"

The teacher sauntered towards him, a determined look in her eyes. "Patrice, join him."

"Me?" I squeaked. Everyone looked at me and made teasing noises. I hated the attention. I hated it.

"Yes; you will be the scorned lover. Stand and deliver!" Ms. Ja commanded.

We sat for a clear twenty seconds, just staring at each other, Kale and me. After a minute he squeezed my hand gently before standing up.

"Don't worry, you got this. I won't make people stare." He assured. This is why I appreciated Kale, my dearest friend, my Irish Prince, in all the world right now, because he considered things like this. He knew I hated attention and promised me an ineffectual performance without saying it out loud and at the risk of his exam grade.

I followed Kale to the center of the classroom without further complaint. He took a long breath before turning to me, sorrow in his eyes.

"I found the letter, Patrice." He began.

Just go with it, Trice. I had to warn myself before running out of the classroom. With my heart pounding in my ears, I took the plunge.

"I meant for you to find it. I've been meaning to tell you this for some years now." I countered.

A small smile tugged at the corner of his mouth as he stared carefully at the pretend letter in his hands.

"How could you do this to me, Patrice? After fifteen years of companionship, two kids, and a nearly-paid mortgage you decide to leave me for the one man I considered a brother—Stephen. Where did we go wrong?" His voice broke.

Damn, Kale, I thought. He was really selling it.

I turned away from him. "We were always wrong for each other, Kale. You slept with my twin sister, for Christ sake!"

He huffed. "But you said we'd work through those issues, woman! I love you, you know that."

I shook my head.

He grabbed my shoulders in each hand, pulling me to face him. "Look me in the eyes and tell me you love me, damn it! I came all the way from Ireland to be with you!"

The atmosphere grew thick, and I surprised myself by how enveloped into the character I became.

"So?" I said indignantly, "I don't care about that now."

Kale's face was as red as a tomato. "Tell me you love me, Patrice. I have a right to this, your love for me. I've worked hard for it."

I slapped him, the entire room gasped. "Get your hands off me! My feelings for you are my right, damn it! You don't own me. You know what—" I pulled off the pretend ring and threw it towards the crowd. They jeered. "Stephen's outside waiting for me. We're leaving tonight."

Kale got real close. "Where? I won't let him take you from me again."

I crossed my arms, smirking. "He isn't holding me against my will, I want to go. I want to be able to smile again—to laugh genuinely!"

Kale brought his hand up to caress my cheek, making me for-real blush and smile a bit. "I miss your smile already. You know I love it when you're mid-laugh. That same laugh I've photographed for years. Those same photographs that adorn my office."

He sank to his knees while wrapping around my middle. "Devin left you before, don't let him hurt you again, Trice. I'm good for you, not him..."

I was so flustered I could only stare at him. The tension in the room got so thick anyone could stab at it with a pencil. Our gazes remained trained on each other for a few more seconds until our crazy teacher interrupted.

"Scene!" Ms. Ja screamed, wiping her eyes. "That's an A minus for you, Kale. Even though you sullied the name towards the end, there wasn't a dry eye in the house. Bravo!"

Looking out into the crowd I saw it: some of the most popular girls in the class were sniffling and wiping at their eyes. I think I was even more shocked to see Mike Lakewood's face, the stoic linebacker for our school football team, blotchy and red.

To my surprise, we received a standing ovation.

7

On Fire and Drowning

"I—I have to use the bathroom. Sorry, could you just—"

I couldn't handle the pressure. I shimmied out of Kale's tight embrace and, like the coward I was, briskly paced to the door. On the way out, I heard one of the guys in the class yell, "Damn, man. She ran right back to that Stephen guy..."

What the hell happened back there? Was he trying to throw that incident in my face? I felt stupid enough already. My heart was beating drums in my ears as I tiptoed to the girl's bathroom down the long, winding hallway. I surveyed the length of the room for any witnesses before I stood before the mirror. In increments of five seconds, I closed my eyes and took deep breaths.

Why did he make me think? With Devin, things were easy. I just had to play the "ugly tomboy" who followed him like the lovesick duckling. Kale, on the other hand, encouraged me to dig deeper into myself than I ever wanted to drill.

I opened my eyes.

There was a thick, bristled, wooden hair brush near the sink with blue and pink paint on the handle. I stared at the brush for a long time, hard, before my hands decided to pick it up, feel the weight of it, and smash it into the long mirror that housed my reflection.

I screamed as I hit it once more and threw the hair tool to the tiled floor. My labored breaths forced my chest to rhythmically jump up and down. At the sound of the creak in the door with voices, I panicked and ran into one of the stalls and sat with both feet on the toilet. I wrapped my arms around my legs and buried my face in my lap.

"What the fuck are you? Stupid or something?" I heard one voice demand, nastily.

Someone laughed. "Bitch, you lucky she ain't send Ronda over here. You gettin lucky right now!"

The other girl said that last remark. I don't know who they were talking to but I felt sorry for this girl. They were so busy arguing no one noticed the shattered mirror and glass on the floor.

"Devin won't talk! He ghosted on everybody. What the fuck else she want?"

At the sound of the last voice my head snapped up. I recognized that high pitched tone anywhere.

It was Nora.

Despite my better judgment, my heart beat faster for her and I couldn't help but be worried. From the sound of things, unless she had some silent squad, the odds of her getting physical were in the "bitch run," category. I breathed in a muted sigh once my face snuggled my knees. Nora was trouble and I tried my hardest over the past month or so to distance myself from the drama.

My mind drifted a bit and traveled back to the events that took place after the incident at the game.

* * *

"Baby?"

My mom's voice broke me from my fixed trance on the television. I was sprawled out on my bed in my canary pajamas playing video games. On a typical day, I'd wander in my brother's room and we'd play together online with many other guys in the chat room. We'd make a whole session out of it with snacks, beer (Manny would sneak some of our dad's stuff) and play until we both pass out from exhaustion.

This was not a typical afternoon, however.

I sighed. "Yeah, mom?"

There was a soft tap on my door before she cracked it slightly. "Baby, your friend is here to see you."

My heart stopped momentarily.

I pulled the door open slowly. "Devin's here?"

My voice broke when I whispered the last word. It had been two days since that awful night and he hadn't responded to my messages.

I looked up at my mother with hopeful eyes as she said, "No, that girl is here."

"What?" I shot back.

My mother's apologetic smile transformed into an eye roll as she nodded and moved to the right.

There stood Nora Albert, standing almost like a looming presence behind my mom. The one person who I deliberately didn't hesitate to delete from my phone and life. Once I reassured my mom and we both heard the faint clicks of her heels reach downstairs, Nora looked up at me (confidently?) and crossed her arms.

She flashed a sarcastic grin. "So...you were my ride the other night. I also didn't forget how you shoved me."

She blinked deliberate blinks and took deliberate steps toward the entrance to my room.

I moved back, unintentionally, glaring daggers at her each step she took. Nora looked around the room in disgust and threw her backpack on my bed.

I finally spoke up. "Nora, what the—are you crazy or something? Stay away from me! Do you not remember what happened?" My controller fell on the floor and permeated the awkward silence she created after my outburst was left lingering in the atmosphere.

"Trice, look, I think you're cool or whatever it's just..." She paused as she looked around my room. "What happened in here? Only boys play video games. I thought I did a better job cleaning up in here! What happened to all that new stuff we got?"

I sighed and looked around the room. I did a pretty decent job at scrubbing away all the Nora from my room. I threw all the new clothes in the bottom of my closet and went back to wearing my basic loose denims, Chuck Taylors, and plaid over shirts.

"Nora, that doesn't—"

She slammed the door closed so loud it scared me.

"Where the fuck is all my make-up? Trice, I've been trying my best not to slap the shit out of you, little girl, but you tryin' me. Where is it?!" Nora started tearing my room apart searching for the cosmetic products. Where the fuck did this attitude come from? She just snapped!

I opened my drawers and threw all the cheap concealers and palettes on the floor/at her. She wanted to play crazy? Let's rock.

"You're so crazy! Take your shit and get out my—"

"You don't even know what's going on right now. I'm trying to help yo sorry ass. Don't throw my damn makeup it's the real shit!" She slapped my hands away and dumped the contents of all of my small drawers in her backpack. She went back to my vanity and ripped some posters off the wall along with some of my favorite books. Nora looked at me, we looked at each other, and both at the video game console. We both jumped for it.

I got to it first and pushed her to the floor. I held my console close to my chest and looked at the open window next to my T.V. and had a hunch she'd be crazy enough to throw it out to the front lawn.

We regained our balance simultaneously and each poised for our next attack.

We started at each other but stopped when the loud bang ensued at my door.

"Baby, you need me to come in there? I'm with a client and I heard something, and it was pretty loud. You good? That Nora girl still here?"

Nora pasted on that wicked grin again and yelled, "We're good, Mrs. Newbern. We were just playin and the video thing fell on the floor. Oops!"

I whipped my head in her direction from the door, with a look of shock.

"Yeah, mom, she's on her way out now. No worries." I said, two could play the crazy game right?

Nora gathered most of the makeup from the floor and threw it in her backpack. When her things were gathered, she shoved past me, gave my room another once over and spat, "Change up this ugly ass yellow color, too. Ugh, it's making me sick. Okay, so...good talk?"

Nora threw open the door and walked, deliberately, downstairs and slipped out the front door. On the way out, her little dance on the rest of the lipsticks and powders left on the floor made more than a lasting impression in my room. She cracked my beautifully rare yellow flip phone. The same phone that housed the last remnants of my friendship with Devin.

Psychotic bitch.

I sat back on the floor with my game and prayed it wasn't scratched or broken. Thankfully, it wasn't. With a sigh of relief, a solemn promise to cut off all things toxic from my life, and my controller, I grabbed hold of my destiny and seized my typical day.

8

In Truth, We Lie

"You're a dead bitch, you know that?" One of the angry voices stated outside my stall to Nora. I felt bad for my almost-friend as I spied, but the anger in me just couldn't help her, or maybe it was the punk in me that couldn't. Either way, I needed to get out of this bathroom, but was concerned as far as the mention of my friend went. What did Nora want with Devin? Why were these girls bullying her and trying to locate him? As annoying as it seemed, my suspicion won out.

"Listen, y'all, tell Tisha to chill alright? I'm good for the money." Nora negotiated. "All I need to do is find him, and he's as good as hers."

Find him? I thought, bewildered. What the hell was going on? It appeared this girl was more manipulative than I thought. Even though we weren't on the best of terms I figured this was just cause to text Devin, he needed to know there were possible dangers in these cold hallways waiting for him.

I reached for my phone and felt only a flat pocket; I completely forgot about the situation earlier when Nora went Rambo and destroyed my little yellow side-kick. Shit. I was still reeling over the phone business when I overheard my name.

Somebody laughed. "What you planning to do about Patrice?"

"Who?" A girl demanded.

"You know," The laugher explained, "that manly looking bitch he used to hang out with all the time."

While the insult stung, it didn't distract or assuage my terror.

Nora started talking again, boiling my blood. "I'll get her, too. Don't worry. We'll be friends soon. Close friends."

They all began laughing and then there was the sound of the door opening. Once their voices became a faint mute I walked out. Nora wants to get me? What the hell could that have meant? This was the main reason I swore off friendships in the first place. Social drama couldn't exist in a group of one, and I lived by that loner policy until Devin and Kale, two of the most important people in my world, rocked me out of that complacency. And loneliness. There was something rotten in the state of my world right now, and her name was Nora. Now it was up to me to figure out just what the hell was up. I vowed to myself that day to keep them safe, my Devin and Kale, and to do that took brevity.

It was time to wake up.

***

The day Devin came back to school could be something described as a celebrity event. He was absent for about a week and his return brooked so many rumors and confusion: the first being the most famous, that he impregnated his Mexican maid (yes, he was that well off, but did not actually have a maid). The next, expulsion. And the final one, juvie. I didn't believe the hype though, as needless as it was to say. I was standing at my locker as I watched the depleted thirteen-year old trudge down the hall. His usually maintained braids were fuzzy and unkempt. His clothes were obviously unwashed and un-ironed. And the most devastating was how the infectious pride with which he walked was replaced with a slumped-over saunter. The entire morning crowd paused to gawk at him and exchange whispers. His eyes remained trained on the ugly linoleum floor and the anger rising in me was really hard to withhold. What did this to him? It was like somebody sucked all the soul from him and spat out...this.

One of the preppy kids named Greg, kids he used to be really cool with, snuck behind him and yanked his thick plaits. The momentum forced him to fall on his back with a grunt.

Fed up, I stalked over to the rich boy to tear him a new one, but halted after Devin stood with predatory quickness to loom over the skinny white boy. The kids in the hall got closer, roaring for them to fight. I remember Devin telling me once that most idiots solved their problems with violence, as his mere presence often posed a threat to others. Devin demanded respect wherever he went, something I always admired about him, but not today. Not now.

Devin moved closer to the cowering freshman. "You wanna try that again, pussy boy?"

Greg trembled, his voice shaking just as much. "No, Devin— I'm sorry! Sorry, sir, I mean."

I watched, breathless, in blank terror anticipating his reaction.

Devin wrapped his large hand around his neck to choke him. The boy's face turned pinkish. "I could kill you right now, know that?"

"I-I...please, Devin." Greg choked out, his small hands pushing against the brute strength of Devin's unfairly larger ones on his neck.

Some of the students chanted for Devin to kill him, others just laughed.

"Fuck you." He grunted as Greg's faced turned a lobster color. He lifted his little body from the ground and several students yelled "finish him" around us. I was mortified. Disgusted. Afraid. Petrified. I opened my mouth to stop this, knowing I had the power, but I just couldn't. Was I about to witness my favorite person murder someone? Tears filled my eyes when Devin's head snapped around to scan the crowd. His indecision hung limply in the air, but when our eyes met he looked as if he was caught. Devin dropped Greg, who was flailing for his life, to the floor like his skin was made of acid.

Devin cupped his hands on his face and hollered his anguish. The once jeering crowd silenced.

Once Devin finally looked at Greg struggling to breathe on the floor, he mumbled an apology and stormed off down the hall. Something propelled my body to follow him.

"Devin, wait!" I yelled the first words to my best friend in weeks. He didn't stop, if anything, he sped up. I knew where he was heading, to study hall. Study Hall was a fancy term for library time, and the school kept the library on high security because it housed expensive collections for the school. Study hall was situated right next to my drama class with Ms. Ja, so I could run straight there after I was finished forcing my friend to hear reason. Each student had an identification card that was to be swiped to gain entrance inside the study hall but could only enter during the student's designated study hall times. Since I didn't have study hall for my first period, then I wouldn't be permitted entrance.

Devin almost reached the study hall when I screamed. "Devin, stop!"

He wasn't stopping and had the door to the library opened by the time I reached him. I hugged him from behind with all my might, as if the remaining bits of my Devin would slip away if I didn't hold him in a vice. My thick tears coated his strong back, but I didn't care. If this was what it took to save him, then it was necessary.

"Let me go, Trice." His voice was coarse, distant.

I shook my head, aware of the line of frustrated students forming behind us to gain entrance to study hall. "I can't, I won't. Why are you treating me this way?"

"Trice—"

"You're my best friend, Devin. Please, just talk to me. Are you in danger?"

His body stiffened even more at that. "We can't talk anymore. Just leave me alone."

"No, Devin." I blubbered. "I need you! Don't leave me. I-I love you."

He released a hard sigh and turned around in my arms to face me. Staring me deeply in the eyes, he cupped my face gently and for a second I saw the old Devin.

"Devin?" I whispered.

His lips were warm and soft as they met mine. The kiss was brief but left me shaking all over. "Trice, stay the hell away from me."

"But, Dev—"

"I hate you, okay?" He blurted out suddenly, making me flinch. He peeled my arms off of him then. "Besides, I don't need love. Not now. Maybe not ever. See you around." He turned and entered the library after that. The students gave me sympathetic looks as they walked inside the room. I didn't care.

I just stood there, numb. Unsure of what to do next, of how to even move again. My first love, and only love, hated me. What was a girl to do?

My class a few feet away, the late bell rang, and I stood in the hall alone.

Or so I thought.

"You need him, huh?" Came a cold voice from behind me. I didn't move. I couldn't move. But I knew who it was immediately, causing more tears to fall down my brown cheeks.

"What about me, Patrice?" Kale continued, the question seeming to bounce from wall-to-wall yet falling on deaf ears. "See you in class."

"Kale, no!" I choked out but was met by the sound of a door opening and closing. He left me, as did Devin. I was alone. This was what I wanted right? My heart stomped on my reasoning to provide the answer to that question and the fuel behind my next stupid actions.

"Patrice, dear, are you coming to class?" Ms. Ja's soft voice permeated the silence in the hallway. My body shook with such intensity it affected my speech.

"N-No, ma'am." I said. "I have to go."

Her soft hand on my shoulder, for some reason, triggered my anger. In a flash, my fist connected with her jaw. There was blood on my aching fist which jolted me to face my future reality: expulsion.

I punched my teacher, Petty Patrice, mousey Patrice, invisible Patrick Newton, assaulted a school official and didn't care.

For some reason my mouth was dry.

***

So, I know what you're thinking: This story sounds a little too exciting to be true, right? As I walked to the Principal's office, my head hung low, I wished that single doubt into fruition, too. Because if this story was untrue, then I could re-spin it to a happy ending, where the heroine gets the guy and rides off into the sunset with her curls in the wind. There were a few inconsistencies in that fairytale, though. For one, I didn't even know what guy I'd ride off with, as they both hated my guts. Second, I hated the sun and the light, as they are overinflated symbols of fake happiness. The dark was where it was at: the moon and stars held their own beauty and secrets to the past. And, lastly, there were no horses in D.C.. Only cars and pavement-pounders.

However, Principal Justice wasn't too thrilled either about my teacher-punching antics. I sat across from the fuming little white dude and attempted to plead my case.

"Ms. Newbern, I'm so disappointed in you."

"Sorry." I said lamely.

"Sorry doesn't cut it, young lady. Do you understand the repercussions of your actions?" He demanded.

"No, sir." I played dumb.

He stood up, then sat down. "I have a hard time believing the current seventh grade valedictorian has difficulty comprehending this. You could get expelled!"

"Sorry." I supplied again, still lame.

He sighed harshly, as if the situation would plague his dreams that same night. He picked up the phone receiver, shaking his bald head. "Well, regardless, I'll need to contact your parents."

I thought of the deep slack and ass whipping I'd catch from this, then the desperation came. "Sir, no! Okay, I'm sorry. I won't do this again."

He waved his hand, as if waving my words away as the phone hummed to connect to one of my parent's cell. "Patrice, this is serious. Ms. Ja may press charges if she feels the need. Your future is on the line here. So, you better start talking."

My heart raced, this was it. It was all over for me. "But, Principal Justice, me and Devin were fighting, and I just was disoriented from all the emotion! And—"

"That won't be necessary, Henry." The serene voice of Ms. Ja came from the threshold as she addressed our principal by first name.

I could feel the heat rush to my cheeks by the sight of her tissue-corked nose. It was probably bleeding from what I did to her. She entered the room with a kind of hushed resolve, like she had a surprise waiting for whomever she looked at.

She occupied the chair next to me and I kept my gaze trained to the floor.

Justice hung the phone up, bewildered. "What was that, Ms. Ja?"

"Expulsion won't be necessary, nor charges. After all she's an excellent student, Henry."

Principal Justice blushed from her repeated use of first name. "An excellent student who punched you, LeAnne. That is unacceptable, and she will be punished."

"Oh, I agree. But it will be me who doles out the punishment for Patrice." She kept a cool smile while my face burned with hot shame.

"But, why, LeAnne?"

She never answered him but turned to me. "Patrice, is this Devin fellow real?"

Now I was confused as I returned her stare. "Y-Yes?"

"Hm." She said. "Interesting."

Justice was bemused when he stood up, then sat down again. A weird habit for a weird little man. "LeAnne, what would you suppose?"

"This is the kind of emotion I've been trying to pull out of you this year!" Her excitement was unbridled, she wriggled in her seat.

Both the principal and I shared the same suspicious looks.

"So, I'm off the hook?" I blurted out, not intending to sound so relieved.

She smiled at me. "Hell no. While I give you an A plus for your performance in the hall, you broke the rules. No hitting. So I came to propose her punishment as community service." She spoke to Justice. "I want her to work for me the rest of the year."

"I agree completely." Justice agreed without hesitation. "The less lawsuits the better. I'll just have to let her parents know."

He reached for the phone and I lurched for his hand, holding it to pause him. He looked at me pointedly. "Now, I thought we discussed the no-touch policy already?"

I composed. "Sorry, sir. But my parents can't know."

"Too bad," he said. "I'll need to let them know about this. Not only about the serious offense, but they'll need to sign the community service forms to fulfill your punishment."

"I'll tell her parents, Henry. Don't worry about it." Ms. Ja assured him.

His face got pink again. "Oh, well...okay. I don't see a problem with that."

I sighed in relief. At least I had a little time to talk to mom and dad first.

Shit.

9

The gooey center

I was released from the hellish situation in the principal's office to return to class. The course of the day went as usual, apart from Ms. Ja's class, who did her best to exclude me from the group activities of the day. Kale avoided me, too, but that was to be expected. I never addressed his feelings for me since that weird day he confessed them during improv, but I did confess to Devin right in front of him. Sheesh, I was such an ass.

I was completely alone as we transitioned to our final classes of the day. I committed both Devin and Kale's schedules to memory, so I knew where they'd be and how to not step on their toes. I was minding my business and walking to my final class, gym, when I felt a firm slap on the ass. I was so shocked I just paused.

"That ass looking jiggly, baby. Holla at me." The voice was deep, menacing, and a little too masculine for a middle schooler.

My mouth hung wide open as I caught the hungry stare from Jack Burn, a known bad boy and Devin's fellow football teammate, when he walked past me in the crowd. He licked his lips as he cast me a final glance but kept it moving.

I felt disgusted and flustered as I stormed with haste to Kale's locker. I stopped, dead in my tracks, when I realized he wouldn't be receptive to listening to my problems and fears as I wanted him to be. I fought the tear that threatened to fall as I walked idly to the gymnasium. There was still a lot of time left before class officially began, about five minutes or so, but at that point I just wanted to escape those poisonous hallways. Unthinkingly, I slipped inside the large gym and paused, yet again to see two guys, unsmiling and serious, playing basketball. The white boy had dark hair and came to be a little shorter than the boy with long braids. My heart couldn't take the surprises that day, and it almost stopped when realization sunk in.

It was Devin and Kale.

"I just want to keep her safe, man You're the only guy who I know she trusts." It was Devin speaking, and I prayed my disguise near the coat rack was successful as I ear-hustled the conversation.

Kale faked right with the ball and artfully dunked it. "Yeah, well, you're the one she loves, bro. Can't you do it? You got her into this mess, you get her out."

Devin stole the ball and dribbled like a pro. "I'm not gonna believe you think like that. If Trice was in trouble, I know you'd have no choice but to help her. You love her too much for that, yo."

"You, too." Kale huffed.

Devin made a face and evaded the accusation. "Just keep her safe, man. That's all I'm asking you."

My blood went cold at their words. What the hell could they be talking about? And as far as I knew, they were strangers to each other with totally different classes.

"You need to have more faith in her, D." Kale replied, competing for the ball. "She's tough."

I smiled at the compliment, as it was something he never voiced to me.

"She can be tough, I know she can." Devin said. "But the Trice I know needed me. Still needs me. I can't trust that she'll know what to do if Tisha got her hands on her. I'm mixed up in some bad shit, man."

"I know..." Kale said, voice lowering. He groaned. "You don't need to ask me to protect her, I'd kill for that girl. I'm just pissed at her right now, is all. She keeps running from her feelings."

Devin held the ball and gave Kale a hard look. "I ain't got nothing to do with that, Kale. Just let me know you can keep her away from me. I need you to tell me you'll do it."

Kale cupped his face before answering. "I got you. I'll do it."

"Thanks, brother. You know what?" Devin began while throwing the ball at him with finality. "You're all right."

Kale caught and held it as he retorted. "It's not for you, I'm doing this for Trice. Remember, I'm doing what you should be doing yourself—protecting her."

A look of pure anguish crossed Devin's face before students piled in. He jogged out of the room with Kale following suit soon after, to get to his science class, I knew.

10

breathing

"First, you got to say 'I need your help, Jack Daddy'"

Jack Burn teased with a high-pitched whiny voice, mocking me. He was staring down at me with a huge grin and somehow was oblivious to the odd stares being thrown our way in the hallway. I found myself looking up and feigning one of those smiles in return as if to say, "Don't mind him we always joke like this" while shooting a baleful glare at him really screaming "Shut the fuck up now, you idiot."

"Jack, I wouldn't ask you if it wasn't important. I know you dated most of the popular population of girls here. What do you have on Nora Albert?"

He snorted and scrunched his face. "Nora Albert? That short girl with the red hair? I mean, we dated in the fifth grade but that's it. I'm no one-woman man."

"Ugh, okay; noted. Wait, isn't that a little young to have a girlfriend?" Elementary school was no highlight in my academic history; my braces and overalls were a part of my regular rotation in my wardrobe and served as relationship repellant in those days. However, the six-foot two blue eyed football player standing before me with a devilish grin and dimpled cheeks didn't appear to have the same struggles in any grade.

Jack leaned back into his open locker. "I mean-nn...sex appeal doesn't have an age limit. So—" he crossed his arms and lifted a brow, "—you gonna say the magic words or are we done here?"

I shifted, uncomfortably. "I just need some information!"

"Nothing in this world is free, Newbern. So?"

I sighed and cleared my throat. "I need your help...Jack Daddy."

"Hm...I couldn't hear you." He stopped to high five some of his jock friends that walked by and promised to meet up with them later. I gritted my teeth then.

"I said, I need your help, JACK DADDY!" I said this with a full-on whisper/shout. Loud enough for his jock friends to pause, turn and howl/laugh in our direction.

"Tell her, J-man! She knows who her daddy is!"

My face turned beet red as I swiftly spun on my heels and away from this scene. I power walked to the media center and didn't stop until I reached my favorite area, beautifully tucked away in the corner of the building: Astronomy. I could hear the drums in my ears pounding away as I gathered myself. Thankfully, this section was frequently vacant so no one saw me pacing like a mad woman. What was I thinking? It had been a whole week since I spoke to either Devin or Kale, since seeing them on the basketball court balling like old pals. Their whole conversation replayed in my mind daily. How long had they been cool like that? Why did they talk about me like some child they shared custody over? And, more importantly, what did I need protection from?

I never knew if these questions helped calm me down or frighten me more. Either way, I decided to opt for solitude. I could get to the bottom of the simmering scandal and imminent drama on my own. I scoffed out loud. So why did you let your first lead run you away, Patrice? Toughen UP, already!

I reached for one of my favorite books and winced when I felt the familiar vibrations of a text alert in my pants pocket.

I gulped as I unlocked the device and felt a cold shiver as I read the daily dose of hate from the unknown number:

"You can't hide forever, dumb bitch! WATCH YA BACK."

***

Something was burning. Hmm.

I jumped at the sight of smoke prowling from the kitchen.

"Shit! Shit! Shit!" I shrieked.

I grabbed an oven mitt and yanked the oven's door open and coughed at the onslaught of heat that hit my face. I held the cheesecake pan midway in the air before fully pulling it out and sitting it on the cooling pad on the counter. I groaned. Thoughts of yesterday's spectacle may have had something to do with the product of my mother's decreed "Mommy and Me Mondays."

My mom ran into the kitchen screaming before unleashing the contents of the fire extinguisher all over.

"Ma! What in the world?" I screamed.

"You okay? I heard you screaming, and I saw smoke so I ran from the bathroom. Come here." She walked over to me with a look of worry all over her features. My mother was dressed in an all-black pants suit and her hair pulled back into downward ponytail. Her red lipstick was half applied and slightly smeared. Her cat like eyes were said to be one of the reasons she was often mistaken for Sade. "There was a timer...did it not go off? Where's Maisey?"

I rolled my eyes at that. "She's in the yard playing with her dolls. Mom, she was just making more of a mess without you here so I said she could go." We both looked outside at the seventeen year old smiling with two dolls in either hands, oblivious to the whole Patrice-letting-everyone-die-in-an-accidental fire event. My mom ran her psychiatric practice from our home and this often meant some of her patients would have some exposure therapy here as well. Maisey was an intellectually disabled young woman who'd been a patient of my mom's for three years now. She was very sweet and quickly became a regular around our home with her warm energy.

My mom placed a hand over her heart and sighed in relief with her eyes closed.

"Thank goodness. Patrice, you have got to be more careful. I know we don't have many Mommy and Me's these days and it really shows."

I grinned at her failed attempt at trying to get me smile. She could be so awkward sometimes. "I'm sorry, mom. I was watching Maisey and must have lost track of time. Plus, we haven't had one of our get togethers like this since I was nine."

"Ah, well, shame on me then. My daughter should know how to bake a simple cake." She placed her manicured hands to her hips and surveyed the warzone of exhaust all over the floor. "I'll get Manny to help with clean up duty. I was just trying to cheer you up, Poo."

"Mom, please." I grimaced at the nickname.

"Well! I can tell something is going on with you. You come home lock yourself in your room playing those video games for hours. You've barely said a word to anyone in weeks. What's going on, daughter-of-mine?"

I shrugged and walked outside to the patio. My mom followed and sat across from me at the table near our garden. I placed my cheek in my hand and kept my gaze on the hydrangeas. Next to stargazing, smelling flowers were high on the list of self soothing techniques for me. There was a huge gust of wind that fanned those botanical smells in our directions and sent shivers down my arms as I looked at my mom's question mark of an expression.

"I kind of...broke up with someone. Well, not really. It's Nora. Remember her? We haven't been speaking." I blurted out finally. This was partially the truth. I couldn't tell her about all of the drama: Devin's ignorance, Kale's insistence, Jack's stupidity, and the threatening texts. Nah, that'll prompt her to pull me out of school tomorrow.

"Oh no, Poo. I'm sorry. I didn't like her all that much if it makes you feel any better. She's very...loud."

"Mom!"

"Okay, you're right. This is about your feelings. How does this all make you feel? You've been blocking out the world so I assume...you've not been dealing with these feelings."

Damn, she's head shrinking me. "I guess you're right. I'll try reaching out more."

She was slowly nodding with that tight smile she got while she was in one of her sessions. "That's a good idea. Maybe she's going through something she feels she can't tell you about? Remember, everyone goes home to their own realities. No two families are identical, and neither are their dynamics. Reach out. She might need that right now."

Maisey squealed and ran into my mom's outstretched arms.

"I got flowers!" she exclaimed and flashed a smile decorated with braces with colors of the rainbow. We both smiled. It was hard to have any intense moments with her energy around.

"Maisey, Patrice isn't feeling well. Can she have some flowers too?"

"Yeah! Here ya go!"

It was my turn with the quarterback tackle of affection that was Maisey. She was armed with the hydrangeas I was gazing at earlier. I grabbed the flowers and chuckled.

"Can you put it in my hair, Maisey? I wanna look like a princess." I said.

Maisey squealed and tangled the flowers in my hair so that it sat on top like a nest. It would take some serious detangling to undo this crown.

"Aw, look at my girls! Now, who wants some cake?"

I shot my mom a droll stare while Maisey cheered, "Yay!"

***

"You must really like stars, huh?"

Those words seemed to puncture my comfy solitude. I was sitting in the public library in one of my
favorite seats. My face was near sniffing the grainy
pages of one of my treasured constellations books.
Typically, I devoted this portion of my day to day
gazing into the huge star in the sky during the day but
decided to take a day trip to one of my favorite places
in town. It was easy to lose myself doing this, since the
stars I urged to see were scientifically inaccessible, and
this did little to my ever-wondering brain.

I blinked in the direction of the voice and sighed,
wearily "Are you following me?"

Jack Burn crouched down and stared directly in my
eyes.

"I could say the same to you. I mean you were the
one who cornered me at my locker the other day." He
said this with his usual smirk and mischievous glint in
his eye.

I exhaled harshly and rolled my eyes while gather-
ing my books. Why was he such an ass? I decided to
get to the bottom of things on my own. Trice was an
independent woman after all.

Jack grabbed my wrist– locking me in place.

"Get off of me, Jack. Just forget it." I yanked my arm
slightly.

His expression turned to stone, "I'll help you."

"Huh? What do you mean?" I was genuinely lost and
slightly nervous at his sudden change of personalities.

He stood to his full height then and reached into his denim pockets.

"For the record, I'm here to grab a few books for my kid brother—not following you." He unlocked his phone screen and placed it on the table in front of me.

He sighed. "I think I know who's sending these text messages, Patrice. I've been getting them, too."

11

Inklings of sun

Between the shock of Jack's confession and sudden willingness to help me, my brain decided to go on autopilot. I realize this because there are several aspects about my surroundings that change, as they did typically with the passage of time: for instance, the library, usually packed tight with the hustling bustling college kids, turned quiet. It seemed as though everything stood still, even the air itself as I regarded the tall jock.

His pale fingers snapping caught my attention, brought me back to the here-and-now.

"Trice?" Jack whispered curiously.

I blinked twice. Three times. *I'm fine,* I replied inwardly to the boy.

Without hesitating, he pointed to his small android phone before grabbing it. He swiped at the screen a bit before presenting it to me.

"See?" Jack adds, indicating the one-sided text thread with his eyes.

I stare at it dumbly, forcing the dry lump down my throat as I repeated the deranged words in front of me. "You better stop fucking with Patrice before your balls get clipped, pretty boy." My voice trembled.

His jaw flexed in irritation as he pocketed the phone. His huge arms crossed his chest as he regarded me now, with a glint of determination in his eyes.

"Fucked up, I know, but I think I might know who it is. And I'm gonna confront that fucker." He growled.

I gasped, cupping a hand to my mouth at his idiocy. "What? Jack– no! That's stupid and, quite possibly, suicide."

He emitted a noise between a grunt and a chuckle. "Right. Just as stupid as getting involved with a known drug dealer. How stupid of *me*."

His words send me backwards, making me frown. "A known drug dealer? What are you talking about and how am I involved in it?"

He shot me a skeptical look. "Don't lie to me. You can keep up the charade with everyone else, but not me. I can smell bullshit from a mile away and, right now, something's stinking."

Fury replaced fear real fast as I placed my hands on my hips and pointed at him. "You better talk, Burn. Are you trying to tell me you're a..." I glance around us nervously, hissing my next phrase... "drug dealer?"

He sighed, a weary look of defeat crossing his face before responding. "Devin Cooper, stupid girl. He owes Latisha's brother some serious dough and they are looking for him. You knew that...right?"

I blink slowly again. Once. Twice, before hissing, "Is that what this is about?"

It was Jack's turn to look confused. "Huh?"

A blanket of realization enveloped me as I stared fiercely into his ocean blue eyes. For some reason, I kept hearing the class laugh at me as I nearly ran from the room that day. The day Patrick Newton happened. Small Patrick Newton felt like a small alter presence since then, a frail little thing in the back of my mind feeding on all of my tears and fears.

Fuck this, Trice suddenly leapt to the forefront of my subconscious, the badass alter ego birthed from my newfound confidence. No way could I shy away from this fight, not with this dude egging me on like this.

I squinted angry eyes at him, "This all a part of the game, Jack?"

Another sigh, then he says, "Patrice, no. I literally came here to help you—"

I slapped him with every ounce of force I could muster.

"You liar!" I roared, the librarians now more than a little concerned as their gazes snapped to the scene we were now making.

I disregard them as I confront this bully. "You came here to plant doubt in my head, during a time like this? Devin is not a drug dealer! You're spinning this to make him the villain."

Jack nursed his pink cheek as he looked down at me, shocked. "You're either hopelessly in love with this drug dealing boy or really as crazy as they say."

I grit my teeth, using all the restraint I had this time to keep from delivering another smack.

"Stop it." I say.

He shook his head, causing his blond hair to bounce with the act. "Hey, I'm not lying, okay? Come on."

He reaches to grab my hand, and I resist but he doesn't release.

"Devin is not a drug dealer!" I squeal ineffectually as he pulls me towards the doors.

His hold is firm and voice resolute when he says, "Nope. You're about to see what I'm talking about."

Confusion cuts through the furious head fog just then as I take in his words. "Where are we going?"

"To see your darling, Devin." He says bitterly.

I wanted to protest. I wanted to scream my outright refusal to this blond maniac as he shoved me inside the passenger side of his electric blue Ford Flex, but the words didn't come. I couldn't resist the urge to check on Devin, to see his smile again. I hated how my heart danced at the notion of seeing the boy who vowed to never see me again.

Gosh, was I becoming *that* girl?

One of those girls who were gluttons for the embarrassment involved in another public rejection? Entangling myself with boys, I thought, my mother's words reaching my ears again as Jack sped through the D.C. streets and into the hood opposite of town. Boys really were the root of all evil.

The once sunny day seemed to disappear into the gray skyline of the notorious lower east side. The side of town plagued by the most drug and gang activity, so apparently dangerous that permission slips became a necessity for inner city field trips. Looking back to when it all ended, I wish I turned back. I wish someone warned me that it'd all end here that day.

Jack pulled the car to a stop at an open part of the street that neared an alleyway. An abandoned house with faded white paint and hanging shingles was situated near it, one that looked just as ominous as the darkened alley it seemed outfitted to.

Jack's hard blue eyes darted around for a full minute before he spoke again. "All right, we need to be quick. You ready?"

That was a good question. Was I truly prepared for what would happen next?

I managed a nod in the darkening car. Evening was now upon us as we climbed out of the car.

"This way." Jack said as he approached the ugly house.

I gulped as I followed him like a lost puppy in the hood. I guess I truly was the lost puppy in the hood, since this white boy seemed too familiar with this dangerous area of town.

He knocked on the varnished wood door, where an emaciated black dude answered. His lips were so chapped that I knew the dryness would not be attributed to the cold dry winds of D.C.. His yellowish eyes flitted between Jack and me suspiciously.

"The fuck y'all want?" He rasped angrily.

Jack's voice deepened to an unfamiliar tone when he replied, "Looking for Coop."

'Coop' I realized was Devin. The thought of my Devin being associated with such a place made my stomach turn.

The chapped lip man widened the front door as he regarded Jack's request. He wore a thick sweater with threadbare jeans I knew was way too thin to sustain the cold weather. Shaking my head to focus on literally anything else, I peered inside the obviously unrented house to see several people laying on the floor.

Several men and woman lined the dark wood floors, and there was even some singing coming from inside. Two people hovered in one of the farther corners where remnants of a kitchen used to be. One a man in similar attire as the chapped lip door man, except his black long sleeved shirt stretched really long down his legs as if it were a dress. His dingy socks were surrounded by heaps of garbage. The woman he spoke to had dark brown skin that seemed to be dry as well. She scratched her neck furiously as she began to wrestle the shirt-dress man for something in his hand.

Their bickering soon reached my ears by the time the shirt-dress man reared back to punch the half-naked woman.

My heart stilled when his fist connected with her face, immediately immobilizing her.

"Hey!" The chapped doorman yelled over his shoulder. "Give the bitch her hit and shut the fuck up."

Groans and a desperate yet familiar voice responded from behind the man.

That's when she came into view.

"No..." I whispered in abject horror. It couldn't be, I thought as my eyes squinted into the dark house to pick apart the scene again before me.

The half-naked brown skinned woman reached up suddenly, snatching the small object from the shirt-dress man with a triumphant squeal.

"Daddy said I can have it!" She purred, before subsequently jabbing the object into her inner forearm.

"Helen?" I called out, incredulous and frightened by the sight of Devin Cooper's mother half naked in a crack house.

A dreamy look masked her face before she turned slowly to the front door, where Jack and I stood.

She squinted her eyes at me, as though trying but failing to recognize the girl who'd been best friends with her son for the past few years.

A brief glint of remembrance hit her then, I knew, because her horrified face mirrored mine.

"Coop in the back." The chapped doorman answered. jerking me out of the terrified stare down between Mrs. Cooper and I.

I fought, really hard, to choke down the tears that threatened to come. This couldn't be real. I thought in a haze as I gawked at the woman who befriended my own mother now slumped in the same corner she'd been previously punched into.

The delight on her face was one someone may call peaceful had the needle in her arm not jutted out as a glaring reminder of the reality I couldn't face.

The mere thought of Devin with the same look on his face, that same needle in his arm, was too much for me to bear.

My weight suddenly proved too much for my own legs to bear, as they wavered before I staggered into Jack's chest.

He caught me before I could tumble down the concrete steps and gave me a hard look.

"Hey," he grumbled. "Straighten the fuck up. This ain't the place for that weak shit. Come on."

He pulled me into a stand before dragging me to the alleyway.

I froze.

"No." I said, my voice small and depleted of its previous fire. Trice was gone.

He ran another stiff hand through his blond hair, turning to face me. "I told you. This is the real Devin.

Plus, we're confronting that fucker about these text messages since he's the cause of them."

I shook my head, my brain now truly a mush pancake at the mere thought of Devin with the needle in his arm.

He sighed in agitation, as if my horror was a mere action of a petulant child. "Patrice. Let's go. I'm now involved in this mess and I really don't want to be. I was more than willing to help you with this, but the person behind these texts is threatening to expose some shit that would tank my chances of getting into Rutgers."

Expose what shit? I wondered inwardly. There were so many questions and not enough answers in the air lately. So many that my pancake brain was mushing even more as I adjusted the backpack I forgot I was wearing. I had to face this, I realized as the doubt cloud eased some. Trice, I plead my boss-alter internally, please move my feet forward. I was begging for her strength as opposed to weak Patrick Newton's insistence to jet back to the car.

Expelling the breath I wasn't aware I'd been holding, I confirmed my answer with Jack before we began the dark descent into the alleyway to no-man's land.

Crinkling from underused pipes from the crack house and chittering from the alley rats surrounded us. My fear of rats was severe, but it paled in comparison to the scene I was afraid of stumbling onto.

I slammed into a thick wall before realization hit me. I was so lost in thought that I didn't notice Jack's abrupt pause. The 'wall' I slammed into was his huge back.

If I'd hurt him he did not relate it to me, as he began to speak in a curt whisper to a dark figure just ahead. The figure turned to look at him before inching closer to him– to us!

I decided hiding behind Jack's back to be the best option as Jack finally addressed the shadow. "Oz said you'd be back here."

Oz was the chapped lip doorman, I summed as I squeezed my eyes shut. The shadow's heavy footsteps made clunking noises I recognized. He was wearing boots.

"All right." The man spoke. "What you need?"

A brief second passed before the shadow man spoke again, his tone lighter as he said, "Burn? That you?"

"Yep," Jack retorted. "It's me."

They exchanged friendly claps before the shadow spoke. "Wassup dog, you need some more work?"

Jack bunched his shoulders. "Nah, man. I still got some left from the last one you gave me. It's good shit."

"That's wassup." Shadow said. "What you need?"

"Looking for Coop." Jack supplied evenly.

A brief pause before Shadow spoke. "For what?"

The man's voice was laced with suspicion as Jack spoke.

"I'm looking after his girl while he's away. I need to clear some shit up with him real quick."

Was he talking about me? I gripped the back of his school jacket tightly in frightened anticipation.

"You ain't with Saint and them, is you?" His voice turned grave as he asked that, making my chest tight with worry.

The next minute, the sound of clicking pierced the tense silence. "Because if you is with Saint and Tisha and them, this gonna be the last bag you cop."

Before I could stop myself, a loud gasp escaped my mouth.

"Who that behind you, nigga?" He demanded, his gun fully brandished and aimed at Jack.

I felt Jack tremble underneath my hands. "Come out here, Trice." he said nervously.

With wobbly legs, I stepped from the protection of Jack's back.

"Please don't shoot. We're just looking for Devin..." I pleaded, then whimpered as Shadow turned the gun to me.

"We're not with Saint and Tisha." Jack said with his hands raised in apparent horror. "Ty, you know me. I don't bang."

"Ty...?" I said in wonder as I gawked at the shadow presence. "As in, Tyrone Zelman?"

He looked around in panic at my words just before he closed the distance between us. "Girl, you better not use my government name out here. How you know me?"

Tyrone Zelman was one of the silent, stoic dudes Devin hung out with. Since Devin had been popular amongst all the school crowds, I had always assumed him an acquaintance or one of the jocks. Looking at Tyrone up close, I realized he was every bit of monster I feared Devin might be right now. Paranoid and high on a little something.

"It's me!" I cried, my hands raised the same as Jack. "Patrice. Um, I'm the girl who went to all of his football practices. I remember you were at some of them, too. Just please don't shoot!" I begged him, hot tears running down my cheeks.

"Yeah, man." Jack affirmed. "We come in peace."

I would have laughed at Jack's lame peace offering had there not been a gun in my face.

Tyrone looked between the two of us before a large smile cracked his lips. "For sho. I remember you was always watching that boy like you wanted to suck his dick or something."

Boisterous laughter rolled off him so thunderous he had to clasp his chest in restraint to keep from falling. After tucking the gun back into his hoodie, he relaxed his shoulders and turned a look at us.

"I...I..." I was so flabbergasted that's all I could manage out.

Jack didn't look any better, as his cool face was now blistering red with anxiety.

"No need to deny it." Tyrone said, recovering. "But yeah, he left north of here."

"North where?" Jack asked.

Tyrone shrugged, digging his hand in his pockets. "I think he said he was heading to Brooklyn or some shit to live with his pops."

"To live?" I choked out. "But that's his mom in there." I said, indicating the crack house to the left of us.

His eyes followed my thumb before flexing his jaw. "Yeah, uh...she's paying off a debt right now. Why, you want me to hook you up?"

Devin's menacing words from fifth grade I didn't quite understand at the time floated back to my consciousness.

"I'm not going to be here all the time to help you."

I stumbled back, my legs feeling that forbidden weakness again as the weight of his words set in stone. Helen was doing drugs. Jack's words were true: Devin was in serious trouble with Latisha. And Devin was gone.

Devin was gone.

Devin...was *gone!*

Part Three

White Dwarf

I
Can admit to being
Selfish and *I*
Know in my heart of
Hearts that the right thing
Is in front of me
Yet *I* close these eyes
I hold you close and have
The nerve to sympathize your
Plight
Though it isn't fair or—
Or right
But when *I* look at
You, *I* cry and
Through these oceans
I see the best of me
In you but
I wish to tell you what hurts
And *I* cannot
Because to do this is to
Hurt you instead so
I cover it up with
Makeup
And flat iron my hair
To pretty the lies and
ugly honesty
That wants to burst
Inside of me.
I love you, and to

DEDICATION

Admit this is to dishonor that
Ugly pride that lives in me
And to dirty my hands is to
Dirty what's right and
When you peel off the skin
You'll see the barest part of
Me and
I admit this verse
Has saved me

12

Forget-me-knots

Easton Rogue High School - Freshman Year

The Protostar phase in a star's life cycle occurs before it takes shape. It is considered its infant stage due to its rather unformed nature, but there is a hidden element of beauty to this stellar phase. The element is simple, pure, and untouched. I found myself missing this phase in my own life, the life that happened before...drama. I was the mousy little meerkat with her head in the books and eyes in the stars. Now, I can't even remember the last time I stole a glance at my formerly treasured telescope. In fact, I kept my windows closed whenever I was home. Mostly out of disgust with myself at having abandoned my truest parts.

I blinked away the stray tear that threatened to fall as I adjusted my faux eyelash in the bathroom mirror.

"Babe, you almost done in there?" My boyfriend called from just outside the door.

Eyelash secured, I reached in my Gucci mini purse to grab for the mascara case. Once reapplied, I spent an extra five minutes ensuring my makeup was flawlessly applied just as my bestie taught me.

"Come on, Trice." Nora Albert urged me from the adjacent sink.

I must have been lost in thought or something, because Nora typically consumed an hour or two applying her makeup, but when I stole a glance at her I saw her waiting impatiently by my side.

I cleared my throat before addressing my best friend.

"Oh, right. I'm all finished."

A bright smile spread across her face which, combined with her hair dyed in multiple shades of purple, made her look like the Cheshire cat.

A pit formed in my gut, one bred from anxiety. What if this wasn't enough? I ran out of the typical shade of tan I used for my foundation and was forced to go a shade lighter. Would I look like a fraud if I went out there?

"You look perfect." She supplied the answer to my unspoken question.

I flashed a weak smile as I ran a hand through my flat ironed tresses. "Thanks, Beach."

"You're welcome, Beach!" She jeered excitedly, grabbing my hand and leading me towards the bathroom exit. "Time to go, though. Your blond knight is waiting outside the door."

I rolled my eyes as a small laugh escaped my chest. "Blond knight, huh?"

She grinned devilishly before pulling us out into the halls. Students were rushing to class, and in the midst of the frenzy, I spotted him.

His blue eyes lasered into me, hard and unapologetic. My heart did its usual dance at the sight of him, all six feet of him, in his black hoodie and joggers.

He approached me with predatory focus, almost daring any one of the hurrying students to collide into him.

"Patrice." He said, still staring into me.

I gulped. "Hey, babe. Sorry to have kept you waiting."

He shrugged easily. "All good. You ready to go?"

"Yep." I chirped nervously, looping my arm through his.

After pitching a quick goodbye to Nora, he and I strode easily down the hall and around several corners before reaching my first period class, Calculus.

We turned to face each other then.

He went first. "All right, baby. Text me when you're all done with classes and I'll pick you up."

I glanced around before replying. "Sure."

Before I could dart into the classroom, he grabbed my arm to stop me.

I looked up at him curiously.

A small smile tugged at his lips before he answered my confused expression. "Where's my kiss?"

"Oh!" I exclaimed, blushing furiously before reaching up to place the briefest of kisses on his thin lips.

His hand at the base of my neck glued me in place. His tongue shot through the barrier of my lips to lace itself with mine.

I met the intensity of his kiss, wrapping my hands around his neck and squeezing.

We ignored the confused stares of student passerbyers as we molded ourselves to each other.

Keep going, Trice. I told myself.

The chime of the tardy bell rang, causing him to release my now weak body.

I laughed when I pulled back to stare at his lip stick stained mouth. "Nice look, Burn."

A confused furrow of his brows formed on his face before he seemed to follow the direction of my humor.

"Ha ha." He half laughed before wiping the pink smudge from his face.

"I'll see you later, okay Jack?" I affirmed.

He nodded, turning away and waving. "Yes ma'am. Text me when school's out and either me or Nino will be by to give you a lift home, okay?"

I did my best to avoid the lurid stares as I found my seat in class. Ms. Montez decided to make an example out of my tardiness that day by assigning me an extra pop quiz. I took the punishment in stride, and before too long, I found myself doodling in my leopard note-book as I awaited the dismissal bell to ring.

Nora and I sat side-by-side in our final period, Health Sciences. Funny, science used to be my fa-vorite subject in school, and now the sound of the teacher drone on and on about the marvels of the human body only made me want to puke in boredom. Even still, I was good at it. I memorized the subject by studying the material myself at home and working on my EGP Project, the project I considered my magnum opus, and this was how Nora cheated her way though this class– through me.

I felt a jab at my side, causing me to jerk my body in its direction.

"Hey Beach." She whispered playfully.

"Hey Beach." I returned the greeting, glancing ever so often in the teacher's direction to make sure she didn't catch us talking. "What's up?"

"You got last night's homework?" She asked between bites of her cherry flavored gum.

I rolled my eyes, waving her words away. "Girl, bye."

"Trice, come on!" She groaned, squeezing her small hand around my wrist. "I swear this is the last time I ask. You know I be busy after school with Luther and all."

"Busy?" I asked incredulously. "You call those meet-and-fucks you got going on with Luther, 'busy?'"

She glared daggers at me. "Don't be hating 'cause we in love. We just real passionate is all. Plus, we don't just be fucking. We date occasionally, too."

I snorted. "Sure."

"Trice....please!"

I expelled a huge breath before responding to my best user-friend. "Fine. This is the last time though. Okay Beach?"

She smiled joyfully at my use of our nicknames for each other. "Thanks, Beach. I promise I'll leave you alone till you leave for your trip."

I winced as the memory of my mother's business trip to New York crept to the forefront of my mind. She had an American Psychological Society conference in Queens coming up next week. She just about begged me to attend with her. I hated traveling these days, as all my free time was consumed with either studying, hanging out with Nora, or hanging out with my boyfriend, Jack Burn.

My heart twisted at the evolution of Jack and mine's relationship, too. I felt mildly responsible for the path he chose; instead of studying hard and staying in sports, he merely gave up on school. Since dropping out, he got jumped in to the 590's, the dangerous street gang that made my entire body shudder in cold fright at the mere thought of them. He told me not to worry myself over it, that it was his path and his decision to take the route he did, but my guilty conscience couldn't help but make me feel partly responsible. For everything Devin's absence and actions put him through. Since his departure, Jack did his best to protect me from the vicious words, stares, and overall treatment from our class and peers. Devin had apparently stole a hell of a lot of cash from the 590's leader, Saint, and the subsequent bounty on his head still lingered today, but no one knew Devin's whereabouts at all. Saint had promised to make his entire family pay for his betrayal, including Helen and me.

Helen had paid enough, I thought. Though I hadn't seen her since that day in the alley, I had heard through rumors that she was strung out bad and still living in the house she inherited from her dead father.

"Trice is my girl." Jack had stated to Saint, when Saint demanded our presence at one of his "meetings."

I shot him a look that surely mirrored the panic inside of me. I had hoped this would be enough to stop him from committing to something stupid, but to my dismay, it didn't.

"Your girl?" Saint said, chuckling in disbelief.

Jack nodded, his back straitening with his seriousness.

"Yeah, my girl. So nobody better fucking touch her. And I want in."

Saint stood, rounded the large oak desk in his basement office, and stopped in front of us.

"Just what the fuck do you mean, you want in?"

"I mean what I said." Jack reemphasized while coldly meeting his stare. "I want in. With the 590's."

"You do understand that this here is a family? And that the only way out is six feet under...?"

Jack's icy smile matched his stone cold eyes. "Hell yeah. And when I see Coop, I'll be sure to tuck him in when he takes his dirt nap. I got you, Saint. I'm solid."

My eyes squeezed shut at the memory of Jack's beaten and bloody body. Despite my protests, the 590's jumped him "in" that night. They'd beaten his pink body so badly he was unrecognizable for the weeks following.

I hated myself for putting him in the middle of this. For signing himself to pay off my debt, the debt that evil bastard placed on me to pay before he fled to heaven-knows-where.

"Girl, I can't wait to party tonight!" Nora exclaimed as she jiggled in her seat.

I blinked, forcefully withdrawing myself from the memories before responding to my bestie.

"Yeah, girl." I said agreeably. "I'll be over at your house at, like, nine o' clock. Cool?"

While nine was considered early to attend a party, I had to prioritize an adequate amount of time to my EGP tonight.

"Yessss..." She said, continuing to dance in her seat with her tongue out. "We gonna get fucked up! Party at my house whoop whoop!"

"Ms. Albert!" the science teacher snapped. "Be quiet, or you'll be partying in detention."

"Bitch." She mumbled defiantly before going still in her seat.

"Excuse me?" the teacher challenged, standing up to face her now.

"Itch!" I said for her. "She said she got a bad itch. That's all."

The class erupted in laughter and she slapped me playfully at my outburst.

"Sorry, Beach..." I whispered, smiling at her apologetically as she rolled her eyes.

I did my best to blend into the laughter of the raucous crowd and avoid the chilling stare from the only unsmiling guy across the room: Kale McAllen.

13

Give her something

"Jack wants to see you."

Nino, Jack's Hispanic, normally silent, goon told me once I slid into the back seat of the sleek new model Dodge Charger.

I nodded gingerly. "Okay. Where is he then?"

"At the house." He said, terse and formal.

"You mean...the House house? Or his parent's house?"

Nino, being Nino, answered my question with mere silence. He usually had a social limit, I noticed in the past weeks since Jack got a personal driver. Jack, from my limited understanding, did very well to please Saint. He'd gone from walking me home every day to sending drivers to take me anywhere I wanted to go after school. Even though he no longer attended school, he made sure I went and got home safely. I appreciated him more than words, but Nino's chattiness brought my inner alarm sensors on.

The drive to Woodley Park, an affluent suburb in D.C., took only thirty minutes, as the sky began to transition into an evening dusk. I forced the questions down my throat as he parked the car outside the large colonial style house. Two grand pillars lined the front porch and the familiar shiver shot through my body as I watched Nino exit the car.

"Out." He commanded.

I inched apprehensively out of the car, my face burning. He nodded for me to follow him to the front door. I could barely make out the sounds of the birds chirping in the distance my heart thudded so loudly in my chest, making a resounding crash sound in my ears.

This was the House. Saint's house.

A beautiful, tall African American woman answered the door. I choked a little at the sight of the familiar girl.

She glowered at me as she spoke. "Why the fuck is she here?"

Nino, stoic as usual, shrugged at her fury as he answered. "Latisha, tell Saint I've brought her."

Latisha Millard, Devin's ex-girlfriend, Saint's baby sister, and the crazy bitch who formerly wanted to kill me due to Devin's dirty deeds, chuffed. "Yeah, whatever. He's in the office." She jabbed a perfectly polished finger behind her.

Nino nodded as he entered the house.

I followed suit under the burning scrutiny of the crazy bitch who once wanted me dead.

I flashed a weak smile at her as I passed by.

She flipped me the bird before rolling her eyes and stomping down one of the hallways opposite of us.

Okay, then, I thought awkwardly as Nino ushered me into the elevator at the end of the hall.

"I thought you said I was meeting with Jack?" I hedged as the doors closed.

A grunt was his only response as the doors opened minutes later. He walked towards the large oak desk in the center of the room. The large office chair was spun facing a large, Harlem Renaissance picture. Smoke fogged the air as the stench of marijuana filled my nose. There were several other men in the room hovering against the walls with their guns on display at their belts.

I gulped in fear, my heart dreading what was soon to come.

"I got her, boss."

"Nice work, Nino." the gruff voice I knew to only belong to Saint Millard, said. "Wait for her by the elevator. I'll let you know once we've finished."

"Yes, boss." He answered, nodding his respect before disappearing at his boss's wishes.

The chair turned to reveal Saint. His smooth brown skin was covered in tattoos of various shapes and words. He seemed to keep a menacing smile on his face, even when dangerously angry, which served to heighten my terror.

"Sit." He instructed me, indicating the white chair in front of the desk.

I obeyed, sitting awkwardly in the plush seat.

"I bet you're wondering." He angled his head. "'What am I doing here?' Right?"

I nodded timidly, avoiding his eyes.

"Oh, Patrice, You are such a pretty thing. You'd do well as my bitch."

The terror lump in my throat appeared, making me choke in shock at his blunt words.

His laughter filled the large room. "Calm down. Didn't mean to startle you."

With a bravery I didn't own, I spoke. "Where is Jack?"

"Ah," he said reverently. "Burn. He's one of my best runners. He moved up the ranks quickly, you know. If he keeps on the track he's on, I could easily see him making lieutenant one day soon. That one's got potential."

I nodded, the large goon's compliments making me even more uneasy, as I sensed a "but" or "however" coming.

"However," he said, just as I figured. "We're here to discuss you."

I straightened my back, steeling myself. "Okay...how can I help?"

His smile was boyish, as if he didn't casually kill people for a living.

"See, that's the kind of mentality I like. Always willing to serve at a moment's notice." He leaned back in his chair before continuing. "I hear you're going to New York next week for some trip."

I chewed on my lip anxiously, reason dawning on me.

"Yes." I answered evenly.

He nodded, matter-of-fact as he cracked his knuckles. "Now, you wouldn't be going to see that Devin of yours, would you? Last I heard, he went to New York where no one has seen him since."

I frowned at his implication. "Saint, please trust that I would never betray you, or Jack, or anyone in the 590's. I don't know where he is."

Several, long minutes ticked by before he spoke again. He seemed to be studying my face for deception.

"Don't worry, girl. I trust that one of my best soldier's girls ain't dirty. She's loyal, been loyal these past few years, and understands the risk involved if she turned out to be a rat."

I swallowed my grief before speaking. "I'm going to Queens for a conference. It's for my mom. I really didn't want to go, but she's insisting we go and have some mother-daughter time before I leave for college."

He frowned, still smiling. "Got proof?"

My thudding heart just wouldn't ease up as my mind scrambled. Proof, proof. Where do I get proof?

"N-No." I stuttered. "Please believe me. We're going to a conference. That's it."

"Hmm." Saint scoffed throatily. "Well, then you wouldn't mind it if I sent some soldiers with you on your little girls trip. Right?"

"What?" I yelped, fear filling me at the thought of some armored goon tailing mom and me all the way to Queens.

"That a problem with you, my loyal girl?" He asked, mocking me, daring me to challenge him.

I thought and fought hard inwardly at defying him. I also thought of all the trouble I'd be bringing to Jack if I did anything less than comply.

My shoulders sagged with defeat. "Okay, that's fine."

The boyish smile returned to his tatted face as he raised a hand.

Nino materialized beside me then, making me shudder at the surprise of his presence.

"Then it's settled. Nino, get her home safely."

"Yes, boss." He groused as he grabbed my arm. Not forceful, but firm as he guided me to my feet and towards the elevator.

"Oh, and Patrice?" Saint called from his throne. "Not a word of this to Burn, you understand?"

"Yes." I nodded vigorously as the doors to the elevator closed, effectively ending our conversation and igniting a new fear in me.

***

I stepped out of the shower a few hours later, feeling the greatest I'd felt in days. The pounds of foundation I wore every day felt like a physical weight, like an actual presence I couldn't live without these days. I reveled in how much more bold and beautiful the colors made plain old me, little Patrick Newton, appear to the world. While I loved the look of it, I adored the feeling of it sliding off in the shower much more. The sensation was like a mask that constricted my breathing, but kept the real me inside. My ultimate suit of armor.

I ran my wet, toweled body to my small bedroom at the end of the hall. The calm that usually flowed through me didn't quite come, as a hot rage filled me in its stead.

My room, the usually organized mess it was, hadn't a piece of laundry anywhere on the floor. The desk, typically littered with notebooks and papers devoted to my secret EGP project, was bare. Even the telescope, my formerly treasured thing, I left right by the bedroom window, was gone. Who could do this? My room was as spic and span as a room could be. There wasn't even an ounce of dust floating through the air.

After donning on an extra long nightgown from the closet, I turned to wreak the much needed havoc in this house.

"Mom!" I scoffed when I entered my parent's bedroom.

She looked up at me passively, her large glasses hanging low on her nose as she completed her crossword puzzle at her desk.

"Is something the matter, Patrice?" She asked casually. As if she didn't just violate my space.

I crossed my arms indignantly. "Um, yes! My room?"

"Hmm...?" She didn't bother to meet my glare this time.

"Mom, please respect my space. Did you have to clean my room while I was in the shower? My EGP papers are all spread out and scattered."

"Girl, those showers of yours last so long it's a wonder you're just now seeing it. Your room was cleaned about an hour ago."

"What?" I demanded, edging further into the room.

"Watch that tone, missy." She commanded softly. "Mind that temper before it gets you in trouble. Now, I'm sorry he invaded your space, but it needed to be done."

"He?" I asked. "Who's that?"

She gave me a 'duh' look before answering. "Your brother cleaned your room. He said he couldn't stand the smell that was coming from there."

"And you didn't stop him?"

"Not my business." She said, shrugging. "Plus, I agreed."

"Ugh!" I screeched, leaving her room to search for my traitor of an older brother in earnest.

"Open up!" I roared while banging on his bedroom door across from mine.

When no answer came, I grit my teeth in frustration. This wasn't like Manny to invade my space in this way. We never had the typical sibling relationship fueled with animosity. We were tight, always looking out for each other and protecting each other's secrets. Concern blanketed me as soon as the anger did, and before I knew it, I twisted the knob until it crackled. The ring that encircled the knob made a jingling sound as I pushed the thick door open, deciding to invade his room just as he did mine. Manny's room was always in tip top shape. Since he was taking college courses from home online, he was always in his room that doubled as a study room. Manny was, for all intents and purposes, my parent's Golden Child, the spitting image of our father and with similar interests in politics. He was on track to becoming mayor someday, we all knew he was capable, knew it was in him. My brother was typically so honest and upstanding, allowing me to play his video games to near destruction just to make me happy. So this odd behavior was sign enough to check in on him (and get revenge).

"Patrice, get out!" He yelped, chucking a pillow at my frozen body.

"Manny?" I mumbled in bewilderment. No way I was seeing what I thought I was seeing. No way my brother was this careless. No way my brother was nakedly spooning a smaller built guy in his bed. Just...no way.

"Patrice! Out! Now!" He growled low, forcing the covers over the other man's naked body to shield his face.

"Um..." Was all the sound that came out of me. I was literally shocked and motionless.

He sat up in bed. "Patrice, please, shut the door before Mom sees."

I remained there, the door hanging open as wide as my mouth did.

At my lack of movement, Manny wrapped a sheet around his middle and stood up in one quick motion.

"Patrice...please." He pleaded.

The desperation in his voice snapped me out of the fog.

"Right!" I stammered before darting out of his room. Once in the safety of my own, now spotless, room, I fell to the floor. What the fuck was that? Manny openly boning in the middle of the day? That surely didn't fit his personality. The stress of Saint's menacing stare and promise to withhold a few truths from my protector, Jack, coupled with the sight from a few seconds ago, brought about a shudder from me.

What literally *was* my life?

14

Hindsight, insight, and foresight

I waited for the familiar white noise to emanate from my parent's room once eight o' clock struck. The familiar claps of the ocean sounds played through my mother's surround sound system, giving me the invisible signal to sneak downstairs. Dad was out of town on business, thank heavens, because trying to sneak around him was damn near impossible due to his bionic hearing. While he was blind as a bat without his glasses, he always said his ears overcompensated for the uselessness of his own eyes. My mother was usually just as astute, too, but after taking her seven o'clock AdvilPM's, she was as good as dead to the world.

My room was in such pristine condition, courtesy of Manny, it took me a while to find the outfit I'd carefully planned to wear for Nora's house party tonight. A tight fitting black crop top with baggy silver Jeanie pants. The pants clung tight at my waist and ankles and sagged in the limb area, providing ample view of the butt Nora frequently called "dunk in the trunk." It was difficult to believe that anyone could find the rear I'd tried to hide for so long in tomboy attire attractive. Trusting her hopefully honest compliments, I went with this getup for the night as I stood on the front porch under the street lights. My house was on the corner, so our neighbors were situated on our left while trees nestled us on the right. My heart fluttered as I caught sight of the beauty above me, the one I tried so hard to ignore since Devin's departure.

The stars.

They shone so brilliantly, causing my body to thrum with excitement and wonder as a mild breeze carried in the air. I allowed my curls to hang freely, and the feather caress of them against my back brought forth a shiver from me.

Even under all this makeup, the stars shone right through me.

Before I could catch myself, my feet began to move to the noiseless tune of Maxwell's Pretty Wings, playing its smooth rhythm in my mind and heart.

My traitorous heart shot an image of a boy with long cornrows and shiny full grin to my mind. I remembered how he had a way of flirting with me while making me feel so protected and empowered.

I thought of Kale, of his companionship and healing powers to mend the broken parts inside of me. How

I treated him could only be described as unfair, and for that, I understood his decision to hate me. After Devin left, I should have been there for him more than what I did. His father made major news after he was found guilty in the murdering of Devin's little brother Michael. Thinking of the little boy's constantly sunny demeanor whenever I visited the Cooper residence burned in my chest. I mourned for them, for all involved in the careless violence of it. Kale turned into a ghost of who he used to be, his angry eyes that occasionally lingered into mine making his disgust for me blatant and clear. Nobody messed with him.

A stray tear streamed down my face at Maxwell's inwardly sung verse, making me mournful all over again at the amount of pain birthed at the death of my relationships. They were two of the closest friends I'd ever had.

I had to leave, he sings, I had to leave, I had to leave...

The sight of a sleek black Ford Explorer purred to a stop in front of my house, ripping me out of the sorrowful reverie I wallowed and danced in.

Nino exited the driver side to stand beside the rear passenger side. He cast an irritated, expectant look my way.

"Coming." I called/whispered, wiping the tears from my face as I creeped to the SUV.

"Baby, hey." Jack greeted me warmly as I slid into the back seat beside him. He pulled me in for a kiss, and I forced the lump down my throat to return it.

"Hey, boo." I said, my voice weak.

"Hey..." he said, his wide smile disappearing to reveal a concerned frown. "Everything okay? Somebody do something to you?"

"No, no." I placed a hand to his chest as I faced his worried glare.

He calmed visibly. I could only catch glimpses of his profile under the passing street lights as the car weaved easily through the D.C. night traffic.

A few moments passed before he spoke.

"You'd tell me if someone was bothering you, right?"

"Yep." I squeaked nervously, willing my forced smile to conceal the lie. Saint was bothering me, but I couldn't tell Jack anything about it if I wanted to keep him safe. It was finally my turn to protect him, to protect somebody I loved the way they always seemed to do for me.

Determined not to fail him, I cleared my throat and stared at him through the shadows.

"Yes, Jack. Everything is just fine."

A lazy smile returned to his jock-handsome face. Even though he'd shaved the long blonde hair he used to rock as a football player, he'd still looked every bit as gorgeous. His shaved head and new tattoos made him look ruggedly attractive, like something from a mafia film.

He tightened his strong arms around me while placing a gentle kiss to the top of my head. "I'll always protect you, Trice. I got you. So, loosen up. Party night, right?"

I chuckled, wrapping him in my arms and squeezing him just as tight.

"Oh lord." I giggled. "Don't get too crazy tonight. We should all have some good and safe fun."

His laugh rumbled through his chest, sending vibrations to my...well, down there.

"You're the only person I know who'd put safe and fun in the same sentence. Still the same old bookworm nerd, huh?"

Though he only teased, his words sliced through me. The mere mention of my old life hitting me like a Mack truck and making me dangerously aware of my current reality.

"I guess so." I laughed through my makeup mask.

Before he could speak again, the car came to a stop in front of a quaint one-story house. I recognized the blue craftsman home as my Beach's, Nora Albert.

"I'll text you when to pick us up, Nino." Jack told the stoic driver.

He nodded, and peeled away from the curb after we got out of the car. Jack looped a possessive arm around my shoulders as we walked towards the front door riddled with teenagers scattered about. Most of them I recognized like Sasha Kersey and Dustin Newport from Calculus. The rest of them looked to be way older, with beards and beers in their hands as they conversed casually on the porch.

"Finally! You're here, beeeach!" Nora exclaimed once we made our way inside. Nora sat at the large dining table with a blunt between her fingers. Nora was actually sitting on the lap of a stoic looking black teen, Luther Noonan. Luther attended our rival school across town, and he and Nora were not officially official, but I could tell Nora wanted to be more with him. He had a reputation of fighting, having been to juvenile detention previously. I feared for my best friend, because I didn't trust the guy's presence or intentions where they concerned her. Every time I confronted her regarding my concerns, she'd laugh and change the subject. It was hard to talk to her about this topic without the surge of hypocrisy tearing into me. I was literally dating a drug dealer. A high school dropout. A guy who Saint Millard even respected as a drug-dealing prodigy.

I pressed my lips in a firm line at the sight of them. "Nora, hey girl!"

"Nope!" She said disapprovingly, shaking her head after parting from our hug. "Don't even talk to me until you get some liquor in you."

I frowned at her, and shouted over the music, "What?!"

She shot me a smirk, extending her huge blunt to me. "Smoke."

"No!" I yelled as panic iced my veins. I'd never smoked a day in my life, and had no intentions of breaking new records tonight.

"Come on, babe." Jack said close to my ear. I had forgotten his arm slung around me. "Loosen up tonight."

His blue eyes indicated the blunt in Nora's chubby hand.

I rolled my eyes at them. "You guys."

Nora reached behind her and grabbed a red solo cup, presenting it to me. "Fine. If you won't smoke, then sip on this."

"Why are you guys so intent on getting me high?" I know it was childish, but a pang of hurt ached in my chest at their blatant disregard for my sobriety resolve. After witnessing Mrs. Cooper in that crack house almost two years ago, it did something to me. Or maybe, it undid something in me, like my lax outlook on drinking and smoking. I couldn't stand it.

Jack squeezed my hand. "Hey, hey. It's all right. I won't let anything hurt you."

You're hurting me, I wanted to say, but bit my lip instead. My hand trembled as I reached for the cup of mysterious liquid Nora presented. Before I could accept it, I pulled my hand back and stuck it in my Jeanie pocket.

I felt around for a few minutes until I found it.

My mascara.

"I'll be right back, guys." I told my bestie and boyfriend's anticipatory gazes. "Gotta pee. And reapply my mascara."

"I'll come with." Nora volunteered as she turned to place the cup on the table.

"No need!" I chirped as I all but ran through the crowd to the guest bathroom at the back of the house. Couples were making out along the side of the hallway, and I squeezed my eyes shut as I brushed past them. The bathroom was miraculously unoccupied, and I thanked the heavens again for the win as I rushed in and slammed the door shut.

The vibration of my phone caught me off guard.

I studied the screen and rolled my eyes at Jack's worried texts:

> **JACK:** Trice, you OK?

> **ME:** I'm all right. Just peeing.

Another buzz lit my phone, and I forced myself to study it.

This time, however, the concerned texts originated from Manny.

> **MANNY:** Sis, got a minute to talk? I want to explain what you saw earlier. I'm sorry if that caught you off-guard.

I fanned my heated face, attempting to fan the dread in my heart too. I didn't want to talk about that right now. I didn't want to add more to my emotional plate today. The pressure from my boyfriend to drink, pressure from Nora to smoke, and now this.

After I applied a fresh coat of mascara and primped my curls, I took a deep breath. I had to ready myself for the onslaught of further peer pressure out there. Or prepare to call a taxi home.

With renewed resolve I only half-felt, I twisted the door knob.

Only to gasp at the guy hovering in the door frame. The guy I hadn't talked to in almost two years. The guy I failed.

"Kale." I breathed in shock.

His expressionless face scanned my body up and down before he spoke. "You done?"

"Done?" I frowned.

He rolled his eyes apathetically before pushing me aside. "I need to piss. Move it."

He practically shoved me into the hallway as he brushed by and slammed the door. I would have been more angered than anything, if the absence of his Irish accent didn't mystify me more. Just who was that?

Though only sixteen, he sported a five o' clock shadow and puffy red eyes as if he'd been crying earlier. I knew him better than that, though. Kale wasn't a crier. If anything, those puffy red bags were attributed to lack of sleep.

I failed him so...so bad. If nothing else positive would come out of this party, then I decided to take this chance to make things right. Kale wasn't a partier, but I saw this opportunity as a gift from above to set things right with him. Maybe if I could just explain to him how much I valued his friendship, or how much

I missed his warm hugs when I had a bad day, then perhaps he'd forgive me. We didn't have many private encounters to do this; where Jack was, Nora wasn't, and vice versa. I was under constant observation from the 590's, too, so I had to seize this moment, in the here-and-now because it might have been our only opportunity for a private moment.

When the bathroom door opened, Maxwell's lyrics came to me again in spite of the blaring trap music that shook the house. Your face will be the reason I smile...the song hummed though my mind as I bore witness to Kale in the doorway.

A smile curled my lips at the sight of him, just as Maxwell predicted.

He froze when he saw me though, as if in disbelief that I still stood there.

"Kale." I greeted.

His jaw flexed as he zeroed his neutral face on mine. The answer I hoped for didn't come. Only silent scrutiny.

I cleared my throat and crossed my arms. "I'm sorry!"

His eyes were mistrusting now as he regarded me. "So?"

"Oh." I chirped, licking my suddenly dry lips. "Um, I just thought you should know. I'm very sorry."

"I don't need your fucking pity, Patrice." He spat my name.

"Whoa, I'm not pitying you! I'm just here to say that I'm sorry for all the hurt I caused."

He chuckled darkly. "All the hurt you caused? You think that solves everything?"

I fought the tears back as I neared him. "No! Well, yes. Well, no wait. I..."

He threw his head back and laughed maniacally. "Don't you see? That's the problem. You think the world revolves around you. All around Trice."

"Kale...I'm so sorry for everything—"

His blue eyes darted around for a moment, scanning the perimeter. "No sign of your boyfriend."

While it wasn't a question, I didn't reply. I couldn't speak past the emotion in my throat to form any words. Tears were flowing freely now as I continued to stare at the broken teen I once loved.

"I'm surprised." He snarled, "Jack's got you on such a tight leash it's hard to see where you begin and he ends. Fucking Jack Burn."

I noted that he spoke mostly to himself, but that didn't lessen the sting. I flinched.

"I promised him I'd keep you safe. And you go and get involved with him. The fuck is wrong with you?" He growled.

"Kale." I sobbed. "I didn't have a choice. You don't understand what Devin put me through—"

"What he put you through?!" He snapped, cutting me off and getting real close to my face. I hadn't realized he stalked me into the bathroom until the door shut behind us.

"You always have a choice, Patrice. Always. Even those texts couldn't keep you out of harm's way."

My mind scrambled at his words as I fought to piece together some understanding. "What texts?"

He swore under his breath instead of answering.

"Kale!" I demanded, standing straighter as he backed away now. "Tell me it wasn't you..."

He paced the small room, his face turning darker shades of red with restraint and obvious frustration.

"Kale..." I whispered brokenly, the ugly text messages flooding back to my focus. Those same text messages, sent to both Jack and I, led us down a path we could have potentially avoided in that alleyway, effectively sparing us heaps of heartache. I could not believe that my sweet Kale, the same guy who held me gently as I cried when we'd watch dubbed J-dramas, was responsible for all that horror.

"I wasn't supposed to tell you that. Fuck!" He roared, punching a gaping hole into the pink wall above the sink.

I leaped back in fear, afraid of what he'd do to me if I made any sudden movements.

When his stormy blue eyes met mine, I could have swore I saw guilt there. Raw and unfiltered, before his eyes hardened and he turned around.

"Don't come near me again, Patrice." Was all he said before stalking out of the bathroom.

I lingered on the wall, panting and ugly crying with the shock of the truth freezing me there.

Flashbacks assailed me then, as the image of Kale's back brought Devin's to the forefront.

"Trice, stay the hell away from me." Devin snarled those cold words after delivering such a tender kiss that warmed my insides. Now Kale. History literally repeated itself right before my eyes, and I couldn't stand reliving that nightmare.

Devin was gone.

Kale was gone.

For good, and there was nothing I could do about it. No way I could pull either of them out of all that darkness.

No, I thought. I refused this information. I refused this knowledge.

Determined not to feel anything else, I rushed to the darkened dining room where Nora remained. Except a slow song thrummed through the speakers, and she was shamelessly grinding her coochie on Luther's lap.

Jack sat at the opposite side of the table, polishing off one of the three cups in front of him.

"Hey," I barked at him. "Come with me."

Surprised at my boldness (I assumed) he allowed me to grab his arm and the huge bottle of vodka before guiding him towards the back of the house. Instead of turning right for the bathroom, I guided him left towards Nora's bedroom.

"Whoa, Trice–"

"Get the fuck out!" I hollered at the teen girls I recognized making out on Nora's bed. They jumped at the sight of my flushed, manic face and eyes.

One of them began to protest before the other urged her to shut up and obey my command.

Once we were alone, I took the bottle and gulped a mouthful of the vodka down. It burned the fuck out of my throat, making me cough a bit, but I didn't care. The pain didn't register as I shoved Jack to the now empty bed.

"Babe, shit, hang on." He said, placing hesitant hands to the sides of my hips. I was now straddling him and gulping huge swallows of the inferno liquid.

"No." I choked out, my head swaying a bit. "I want you."

He looked around, uneasy for a second. "You sure? I mean, we never fucked before. I wanted to at least wait till your birthday or something."

"Ugh!" I threw the bottle across the room, it shattered against the far wall making the room smell like a brothel.

"Stop trying to protect me! I'm not a fragile bunny you have to save all the time, Jack. I'm your *girlfriend*. Your *girlfriend* wants to fuck you. Now."

He tightened his grip on my hips again. "I'm so high right now. I want to make sure you know what you're asking."

Anger surged through me as I peeled my Jeanie pants off. Then my underwear. Then his pants went.

In minutes, my bare pussy hovered over his swollen length.

"Good thing I'm not asking." I whispered, sensuous and menacing before sheathing my virgin pussy on his waiting dick.

15

Writings on the wall

A soft knock came at my bedroom door the following night, somewhat startling me as I finished off the text message to Jack. His response was instantaneous:

> **JACK:** Are you on the pill??

I fumbled with the phone as the knocks made me jump to my feet.

"Hey, Patrice. Got a moment to talk?" Manny's voice carried through the dead silence in the outer hallway, making him sound like a haunting spirit. My eyes searched the room nervously until I saw the new pile of clothes on the floor. I buried my phone under it and scrambled back to my bed.

"Sure thing, bro. Come in." I called.

He entered with slow furtive steps and shut the door behind him. Once he got a look at me, he furrowed his thick brows skeptically.

"You okay?" He asked.

"Yep." I nodded in rapid up and down jerks. "All good."

"You look like you got caught doing something you had no business with." The smile that began to form died instantly as the gravity of words cemented between us. Visions of his naked body intertwined with the lighter skinned guy in his bed materialized in my mind, and I pursed my lips, feeling a tad bit awkward.

"As if I have any right to throw judgment your way." He answered the unspoken question as he sat down beside me on the bed. "Cool if we talk about it? The elephant in the room?"

Raising my hands, I shook my head at him. "Brother, listen. Your sex life isn't any business of mine. I'm sorry if I made you uncomfortable in thinking I judged you for that."

He flashed a small smile and leaned back on the bed.

"I knew you'd say that. Always accommodating my feelings. It's not okay, sis. You're fifteen, still only a kid, and you had to shoulder the burden of walking in on me having sex. Has Mom or Dad even had the sex talk with you?"

I gulped nervously, realizing just how confusing these sudden hormones had me feeling all the time. Without any advice or guidance from our parents, at that.

He seemed to understand my silence and continue. "Dad had that talk with me. Well, sort of. He told me to pretty much screw as many chicks as I could when I turned sixteen, always wear a rubber, and if a girl tried to pin a pregnancy on me, to let him handle it. Not very sound, or moral, advice in my opinion."

A vibration sounded from the corner where the pile of clothes lay strewn. Another text message from Jack, I figured, recalling the cliffhanger I left him on due to Manny's startling arrival.

Manny cast a questioning look at the pile. "I literally cleaned your room spotless and you managed to hog it up again." He shook his head warily. "Only you."

I rolled my eyes, inwardly grateful he chose to linger on my tidiness rather than the phone buzz we both heard.

"You were saying?" I encouraged him as I crossed my arms.

"Right." He winced. "My point is, sex is weird. And I wanted to let you know that it's okay if you have questions or reservations surrounding it. Come to me if I can be of any help, okay?"

My chest squeezed at his endearing offer. He really did care about me, and for that I was grateful. Opposite from our parents, Manny always made his feelings clear for me. Clear in his adoration for me as a guardian more than a big brother.

For that, I figured he'd deserve only honesty. After all, we were each other's greatest secret keepers.

"Thanks, Manny." I breathed, clasping his hand. "You're totally the best big bro in the world."

He blushed and waved his free hand. "Aww shucks, kid. Not all heroes wear capes!"

We laughed in spite of ourselves and the heaviness of the conversation. After a moment of reminiscent light chatting, I paused to study him.

"I had sex!" I blurted.

If possible, his jaw would have fallen clear to the floor at my admission. "Patrice. What?"

I nodded as my cheeks burned bright with shame. "Yeah...last night at Nora's party. I didn't mean to, I was just drinking and got carried away."

The phone buzzed again in the corner. Manny ignored it.

"Are you okay?" His voice was ripe with worry.

I stilled, oddly unprepared for that response. "I...I think so."

He grabbed my shoulders, commanding my eyes to meet his. "He didn't force himself on you did he?"

My mind reeled back to the memory of Jack's hesitant questions just before I guided him in me.

I shook my head.

Seemingly satisfied, Manny released me to settle back into the bed. "Good. Thanks for trusting me with that, sis. If the act was consensual, then there's nothing to feel shame about."

Shame. An emotion I became all too familiar with as of late.

"Do Mom and Dad know?" I probed tenderly.

He frowned before digesting the meaning of my question. "Uh, oh, that. I haven't come out to them, no."

I squeezed his hand again, hoping the small gesture would give him some of my strength. He was so strong. So strong all the time with big-brothering me and managing our parent's expectations as the prodigal son.

"Are you going to tell them?"

"Bruno, thinks it best if I told them sooner than later." He said on a sigh, mentioning the study partner I'd only ever heard about instead of met. "But I'm not sure it's any of their business who I date; sometimes it's guys and sometimes it's girls. I don't know if Dad would understand, so I'm not sure if I will." He cast sullen eyes to the floor that just about killed me.

Our parents' limited old-world conventions of 'holy' love made me grimace at how they'd receive this news from my dear brother. Pure protective rage and sadness filled me as I imagined the sight.

I crawled up the bed and flopped dramatically over his hard chest.

"Ouch, P!" He howled as he wrestled me across the bed. "What was that for? You just about knocked the wind out of me."

I reached over and hugged him tightly around his neck, ignoring his protests. "It's your decision, Manny. I'll love you regardless."

He quieted and stiffened in my hold. "I know, sis."

"That means, I'm here for you too. Even if I am still young and inexperienced. Come to me, too."

An or so passed as we laughed through the rest of the night, the rift between us slowly healed as we regaled more tales and secrets from the past.

I took a deep breath before responding to Jack's back-to-back texts a few hours after Manny departed.

> **JACK:** Are you on the pill??

> **JACK:** We'll get you a doctor's appointment later this week.

> **JACK:** I'm outside. You sleep?

I frowned at the final message. He sent that over an hour ago. Why would he just show up at three a.m.?

I crept to my bedroom window that overlooked the front of the house to see a single black Audi parked across the street. It was the most lethal-looking vehicle on our otherwise suburban street lined with minivans.

I dialed his number, and he answered on the first ring.

"Finally." He said. "I thought you were dead or something."

"Nope." I retorted. "I was in bed, going to sleep. I tend to do that after hours in my own home." I actually immersed myself nose-deep in my secret project, but I couldn't reveal this to him. To anyone.

He snorted at my sarcastic tone. "Trice. Either let me in, or meet me at the car."

"Jack, no. I didn't invite you over here, and it's too cold to go out in that weather in what I'm wearing."

A pause, then he sighed before repeating. "Trice. Either let me in, or meet me at the car, babe. I need you right now."

***

The next few days pass by rather quickly. Several calc tests and now routine fuck sessions with Jack later, the morning of the New York trip was upon us. Well, my mother and I, since we were the only ones attending the conference. My mind wandered to Saint's menacing words about me being a loyal girl, and what the gang did to rats as I stared absently at the conference admission ticket in my hand.

"Patrice?" A voice inquired.

Just what would happen to me if I found a way to ditch out on the trip? Or if I convinced Mom to fly to New York instead of driving? Would there be major pushback from Saint if I casually told Jack about this?

"Patrice?" The voice repeated.

Who was I kidding? Hell yeah there'd be pushback. Jack would end up chicken chow, pig slop, or Saint's favorite analogy, rat cheese. I already had to lie to Jack about the logistics of the trip, telling him we were flying Delta instead of taking my mother's new Hyundai.

"Patrice Anika Newbern!"

I recoiled instinctively at the use of my Swahili middle name.

I met my mother's furiously expectant stare just then, guilt radiating through me at the realization that I'd been too zoned out to hear her words.

She, Manny, and I sat at the dining room table. Since Dad was still away on business in Wisconsin, Mom went out of her way to prepare one of our favorite breakfasts before our departure to the Empire state: Pancakes, waffles, and fruit.

"Yeah, mom?" I asked innocently before stuffing a pancake in my mouth.

She crossed her thin arms in disapproval. "So you agree then?"

I looked frantically at my older brother for support, only to see his face scrunched up in silent laughter. Once he caught me staring at him, he sobered, then shrugged. He'd apparently be of no help to me.

I gulped, facing her. "Um, yes?"

Manny's thin body quaked with more laughter, making me want to punch him.

Mom smiled. "Aww really, Patrice? I always thought you couldn't stand your Aunt Patty?"

I froze. "Oh...no, I don't."

Manny continued to giggle in the seat across from me, next to Mom.

Mom just about danced at my words as she took a small sip from her orange juice. Aunt Patty was my mother's older sister, the one who raised her when she grew up poor on the streets of Camden, New Jersey. She was one of those really mean relatives, and I mean really bitter towards anything modern or new age. I remember one time we went to visit her in her East Camden apartment when I was six and I accidentally flushed her goldfish. It was a long story that I actually sort of blamed Manny for, but long story short, I bore the brunt of the punishment. Aunt Patty, after whom I was named, stormed in the bathroom and demanded I wash my mouth out with the used bar of soap on the sink. I resisted it, crying the entire time she forced me to take a bite and spitting all over the place, until Mom took pity on me and told her it was enough. Since that visit almost ten years earlier, I avoided her. Didn't prefer her company. No, I flat out couldn't stand that bitch. And here I was agreeing to pay her another visit. Oh, no.

I chewed on my bottom lip as the anxiety rode me. There was no way I could see that lady again.

"You want to visit Aunt Patty?" I sought to reconfirm.

"Well yeah. Didn't you hear me tell you about her bunion surgery? I want to stop in and check on her while we're up there— make sure she's doing all right."

"Right." I acquiesced. "But isn't Camden a long drive away from Queens?"

She rolled her eyes and stabbed into another pancake. "Oh, I forgot to mention. She moved to Harlem last year since her building got demolished. They rebuilt and jacked the price up so high she couldn't afford it anymore."

Damn it, I cursed inwardly. Then another ray of hope overcame me at the new excuse.

"What about Angie?" I blurted, referring to Aunt Patty's only daughter I knew lived in New York City. She worked as a Special Ed teacher to middle schoolers.

Her hand froze mid air at my question. "Didn't you already agree to come with me? Why are you always fighting me, daughter of mine?"

"Mom, I'm sorry." I conceded, feeling the daughter-of-mine guilt full force now. "Aunt Patty isn't my favorite company, but you're right. A promise is a promise, and I know this means a lot to you."

"I know the Pierce side of the family isn't the closest." She started, abandoning her breakfast and alternating her focus between my brother and I. "Hell, there aren't even that many of us left due to all the illness and drugs. But I want the two of you to know something."

A beat of silence followed her words as we watched her stand up.

"You two are my everything. And it would give me comfort to know that if I got sick in my old age, that you both would check on me. Aunt Patty is the closest thing I ever got to a mother, so yeah, I'm worried about her. And you don't have to like her, I know she's done some less than redeeming things in the past but she is family. So." Mom looked at me now. "Here's your out. Let me know now if I need to book an extra night at the hotel for you while I stay at Aunt Patty's."

My face burned with emotion as I sensed no manipulation in my mother. I would usually expect her to use one of her therapist tactics to deceive us into doing a chore, but when I could not find any sign of that deviousness I sighed in defeat. She was right, and I knew it, but admitting it out loud was something I didn't feel like doing.

Instead, I stood and hugged her rail thin body. "No worries, Mom. I'll be there."

She released a breath I wasn't aware she'd been holding and wrapped her arms around me. "Really, Patrice. I don't want you to feel forced into this. You don't have to."

Three hours and several pit stops later, the welcome sign to New Jersey appeared on the side of the highway as we passed by in my mother's black Hyundai. We were a little over an hour away from the Luxe Hotel, the bougie hotel in Queens Mom booked with Dad's credit card. Since he traveled so often for business, he frequently gave Mom free reign of his credit cards to compensate for his absence.

The hotel was situated about ten minutes from the conference center the American Psychological Association would convene and the skies were pitch black when we finally arrived at the fancy castle disguised as a hotel. Once we parked the mid-sized car in the crowded parking lot, we agreed to ditch our dinner plans and head straight to bed. Mom and I were originally meant to share a room with separate double beds for the duration of the three day trip, but tonight would be the only night we'd spend there since she already told Aunt Patty to reserve her guest room for us. The dread in my gut mirrored the anxiety in my heart at the thought of interacting with Aunt Patty. I knew, deep down, she was a part of the reason I rejected my given name and opted for 'Trice.'

"Grab the bags, honey." Mom instructed as I exited the car. After a long stretch my limbs lavished, I opened the trunk and expelled an aggrieved sigh at the unnecessary amount of luggage before me. I knew most of those bags were filled with Mom's wigs and jewelry. I had half a mind to protest the task, but nearly choked on the words at the sight of the black man who materialized beside me. He wore a black polo shirt and black fitted jeans. His faded haircut accentuated his strong facial features and jawline, too.

"Can I help you?" I yelped in fright.

"Let me help you with those bags, miss." He offered, already tugging the large suitcases out of the hatchback. Once he unloaded the final bag, Mom's panicked voice whipped through the air as she approached me.

"Sir? You want to tell me why you're touching my property and talking to my child?" Her voice brooked no argument.

He looked oddly familiar before he smiled back at her.

"Sorry about that, ma'am. The Luxe offers complimentary bellhop service. I came to assist with your luggage."

Mom's shoulders sagged with relief, and she reached over to offer her hand to him. "I'm sorry about that! Yes, we would love the help."

He flashed another ruggish smile at us after shaking her hand. "No problem, miss. What room will I be taking these bags to?"

Fear crawled up my spine, screaming at me to not reveal any information to this man.

Mom did so anyway. "Room 216, on the second floor."

The bags that would have given Mom and I twin hernias now covered the man's back and arms. He juggled the heavy items with rapid ease.

"I'll lead the way." He offered as he walked to the front entrance.

I made a mental note to report this suspicious man after we made it safely inside, as he sported no branded uniform like the other hotel employees who occupied the lobby. I wondered if Mom picked up on it too, but if she did, she didn't seem like it.

She collapsed dramatically on the bed when the three of us entered room 216.

"There is a God!" She moaned as she curled around the plush white pillow on the bed nearest the window. "Patrice, pay the man."

I could feel the color drain from my cheeks at her request. She wanted me to pay this creepy stranger?!

"No need, ladies." The bellhop insisted after he lined the bags neatly in the corner. "This is a complimentary service."

"Mmm..." Mom hummed sleepily from the bed. "Okay...so tired."

An awkward silence hung in the air as we watched my mother practically fall asleep within the few minutes she made contact with the bed.

It was only the two of us.

I glanced his way, the fear heightening at his waiting eyes on me.

"So." I muttered. "I guess that's it?"

"Yeah." He replied. Another tight smile crested his face as he strode to the door.

Relaxation began to flood me as the distance widened between us. Until he reached for my arm and grabbed it with a chilling force.

"Boss told me to watch your every step. So don't try no shit, girl." The calm and casual tone of the bellhop disappeared, in its place was sheer danger. A threat.

Realization dawned on me from his whispered words. This explained the misplaced clothing. This was Felix the Terrible, one of Saint's goons who guarded his home 24/7. No wonder he looked so obscure, because this dude never smiled in the small amount of time I'd seen him.

"Get off me!" I hissed, wriggling free of his grip and glowering between him and Mom's sleeping form.

His lips twisted in a sinister smile as he retreated a step. "We're watching you. Remember that shit."

"I got it!" I exclaimed, but it came out as a whine as the attitude I'd intended to lace into my tone was overshadowed by the terror.

He scanned my face momentarily before scoffing and leaving the room. His footsteps made no sound as he left, but I wouldn't have heard it either way over the thunderous heartbeat in my ears.

16

Love grows here

"Dr. Monica Pierce Newbern, we welcome you to the stage to share a few words of intrigue." Dr. Hange Gustappa, a fellow psychiatrist and presenter at the American Psychology Association, announced before a round of applause erupted from the packed conference room. I smiled proudly and cheered my mom as she took the stage in her tasteful violet colored pantsuit. She obsessed all morning over which wig to wear to the event she'd looked forward to every year, and I assured her the mid length wavy bob was best while she argued the long straight made her appear more dignified. Two extra wigs to consider and one hour later, I was pleased she selected my choice, as the wavy tresses framed her caramel round face perfectly.

Mom spoke with captivating grace, capturing the crowd of professionals with a brief monologue about her background and what motivated her to spend the last of her savings to apply to Yale. By the end of her speech, there wasn't a dry eye in the house as we stood collectively to award her with another round of applause.

"Good job, Mom!" I gushed when she rejoined me at our small table.

She gave a modest smile while fanning her hand at me. "Oh, that's the same story I tell every year. But thank you, sweetie."

Guilt toyed with my heart at that, realizing how often she invited me to these yearly conferences and my abject refusal. Felt like I was always failing someone I loved, and to remedy this, I made a decision to support my mother. In all things, just as she did me and Manny.

"You hungry? Thirsty?" I inquired as the crowd thinned. The conference was at the tail end, and I knew, from reading the admission ticket, that only the closing remarks remained until dismissal.

Mom's brows lifted as she observed me through suspicious eyes. "I am, actually. Thought we'd get some hotdogs from the street corner."

"Nope." I said with gleeful conviction, shaking my head. "Let's go downtown. I saw a cute little cafe on West Ave we could try."

"Hmm." She breathed contemplatively. "I like the sound of that, Trice."

I almost choked on a breath hearing my otherworld nickname leave her lips.

"Trice?" I queried.

She giggled at my nervous expression. "Well, I heard all your little friends call you that. I'm your mother, can't I call you Trice, too?"

I only stared at her, not sure what to say.

"What? I'm cool, I'm hip, right Trice?" She asked, destroying my bemused silence. I laughed so hard it sent pains to my sides.

"Really, Patrice?" She grumbled, folding her arms in dismay. "I'm really that lame?"

Recovering, I met her eyes square on. "No, Mom. I'm sorry. You're hip. So hip."

The look she tossed my way brought another fit of laughter from me.

The hurt in her eyes sobered me. Before I knew it, I extended a formal hand to her.

She eyed it curiously before clasping it in hers.

"Name's Trice, ma'am. Pleasure to meet you."

A warm smile spread across her face, endearing me to her even further.

"Pleasure getting acquainted, daughter-of-mine. Now let's blow this joint and get some food!"

We giggled impishly and stood up. I couldn't help but notice the only incongruous tattooed man dressed in all black and occupying one of the obscure tables in the corner of the room as we crept out.

17

Ozone and Nebula

We decided on going to the quaint little cafe on West Avenue called The Stream. The rich scent of vanilla and patchouli assaulted our senses as the kind black woman with dreadlocks seated us. Mom and I laughed and chatted a good deal on the five minute walk from the conference center, making the emotional atmosphere not so tense for a change. I guess the air was a little too calm, because my eyes bugged at her request from the waitress.

"Ma'am." The waitress responded almost teasingly. "We do not serve alcohol here."

My usual anti-drugs-and-alcohol mother pouted. "Not even wine?"

Cynthia, the name the placard on the waitress's chest read, shook her head as she glanced between us. "I can give you a few more minutes to decide, if you like?"

"Nope!" I chirped, slamming closed the thin menu. "I'll have a latte as well as a ham and cheese croissant. Mom?"

I stared her down expectantly.

She seemed to battle with a notion before conceding. "I'll have the same."

"You feeling all right, Mom?" I asked once the waitress left. It was hard to conceal the worry in my tone.

The joy seemed to drain from her face as she sagged into the booth across from me.

She nodded. "I'm feeling a little anxious about seeing Aunt Patty again."

I nodded in understanding, reaching for her hand and squeezing. "I thought you were excited to reunite with Aunt Patty?"

"I am." She answered hurriedly. "I just don't want her to think I've forgotten about her. It's been quite a while since I was able to visit. Work has been so insane, and now she's experiencing all these health problems..."

"All?" I asked, my nose crinkling in confusion. "I thought it was toe surgery."

Her mouth lifted in a small smile. "Bunion removal surgery."

"Yeah. That." I waved my hand. "That's not all, is it?"

"Nope. Doctor diagnosed her with Type II diabetes, hypertension, and arrhythmia, or irregular heartbeat."

I squeezed her again, edging closer to her in my seat. "Mom, that's kind of a big deal. Aunt Patty's like, sixty-five now?"

"Sixty-seven, come this December." She replied in mild defeat.

"Gosh." I breathed fretfully. "I never knew she was dealing with so much."

"And all by herself!" Mom said, inhaling sharply before a single tear slid down her brown cheek. "All this time she'd been telling me that Angie was living with her as her full time caregiver. She lied right through her teeth. I didn't find out the truth, that Angie got an apartment in NYC with her fiancé, until a couple of weeks ago."

"Aunt Patty finally told you the truth about her situation?"

Mom's face reddened. "Angie called to ask if I'd speak to her landlord in Camden. She was apparently fighting the landlord and the municipality about the demolition of the building where she lived. She and a few other tenants tried slapping him with an appeal, but ran out of time and were forced out. I had never been so pissed in my life!"

I shook away the cloud that formed in my head from the information overload I was receiving. That sounded just like something spirited old Aunt Patty would do. Fight tooth and nail about a cause she believed in, and she lived in that cramped apartment for years. I guessed there had been more to the story when Mom broke the news of her move to us, and I was glad to finally get it.

Only, I wasn't truly glad, considering my bitter old aunt was forcibly kicked to the curb from the home she raised her siblings and children in.

We'd long abandoned the food that sat, cold, on the table before us.

Cynthia returned to our table looking just as concerned as I felt for my mom. "Would y'all like the check?"

Mom absently reached for her purse before I slapped her hand.

"Ouch! Patrice?!" She exclaimed.

I reached inside my mini Gucci purse, fingering through the thick wad of bills before retrieving a twenty and placing it on the table.

"My treat." I said with finality.

"Patrice...where'd you even get this money?" Mom demanded after Cynthia took the cash and departed.

I blushed, hating the lie I was about to tell. No way could I tell her that money came from Jack Burn, the boyfriend she didn't know I had.

When he showed up unannounced all those nights ago, I met him at the sleek black Audi he occupied alone.

"Early birthday gift." He told me as ragged breaths raked from his chest. We just finished fucking in the backseat when he reached into his denim pocket and tossed a huge wad of cash my way.

"I don't want this." I threw it back at him. "Plus, my birthday is like three months from now in July, remember?"

"'Course I do!" He defended. "Trice, come on. I wouldn't feel right having my girl traveling alone without some change in her pocket." He tossed it back at me.

"Jack, this is wrong. I'm your girlfriend, not your whore." Hot anger coursed through me as I righted my half-naked body in the seat. "I don't want your money."

After several back-and-forth tosses of the cash wad, I deflated in defeat, growing tired from the argument.

He flashed his award-winning smile in victory before placing a light kiss on my forehead. "Good girl. Use it however you like. And have a good time in the city, okay?"

His words echoed in my mind before I swallowed and said to Mom. "My allowance, remember? I've been saving."

"Sure. Okay." She looked suspicious and troubled. "It better be from allowance."

"It is!" I groaned.

A moment lingered before she began the probing I anticipated. "How's school going?"

"Awesome."

"Really?" She countered with the same suspicious tone. "And the EGP project? Have you made any significant progress—"

"Mother-of-mine!" I cried, interrupting her and flailing my arms for dramatic effect. "I just wanted to treat you to a nice lunch. That's it. Okay? I figured we both could use the extra fuel before facing Aunt Patty, is all."

A haunted look crossed her face at the mention of her sister-mom. I felt ashamed for using that as the subject-change, but mildly grateful the heat was off me.

"Sorry." She muttered, guilt-stricken. Mom wrapped arms around herself before speaking around a sob. "Pat might be in serious trouble, and she didn't even bother to tell me. Her sister! So, yes. I thought a little liquid courage might soothe the soul, I admit. Didn't mean to project those feelings unto you, sweet-ie."

"No sweat." I offered a weak smile, my heart splitting as I looked upon her. "And maybe she withheld the truth to protect you, Mom. Come on, you know you're her favorite child, as she says."

Her chuckle didn't match the sorrow in her eyes. "I'm a grownup. I don't need protection."

I inwardly begged to differ as I witnessed her cheeks pale on the drive from Queens to Harlem. After cleaning and checking out of our hotel room, we packed and began the thirty minute drive to Aunt Patty's place the GPS told us was just off East 42nd street.

"You got this." I whispered.

I gave Mom a tight, yet brief, hug in reassurance as we stood outside the door of the rundown shack of a house. I attempted as best I could to hold my breath as the stench of hot piss assailed my nose. The smell seemed to carry in the breeze from the alley that neared her house.

I knew this area, the condition of Aunt Patty's new home, bothered my mother, but she chose to keep quiet as the thin door swung open.

A corpulent, chocolate toned woman answered the door in a sky blue nightgown that blanketed her toes. Her long gray hair formed a cloud around her face, making it difficult to see her eyes as she was also about a foot shorter than my five foot two frame.

"Mama?" Mom's fearful voice strained to the old woman.

She looked up at her, a deep scowl curving her face. "Monica? That you?"

Mom gulped hard before speaking again. "Mama, why are you walking around all open and free like you ain't just have bunion surgery?"

"Now, listen here." Aunt Patty reared back and jabbed an accusatory finger at Mom. "Miss Monica, I'm grown as hell. If I want to walk around this house with bare ass hanging out, I will. This is my house, and you're supposed to be a guest in it."

Despite her frail appearance, her raspy voice oozed liquid fire as she spat the words to Mom.

I waited for my mother's usual fiery comeback, but none came. Instead, she cowered and her stare hit the ground before she spoke again.

"Yes, ma'am. Forgive me."

Aunt Patty tutted three times before giving us her back.

"Y'all gonna stand there and let all my heat out or come inside?"

We stumbled nervously inside at her subtle command and shut the thin door behind us. There was no gentle way to describe the inside of my bitter aunt's house in the hood. The small shack housed several bookshelves loaded with dusty old books and Knick knacks while garbage lay strewn across the floors. In fact, it was difficult to tell the make of the floors, since getting a clear view of them was impossible. I remembered Aunt Patty as a person who had a hard time parting with her items, but this was on a whole new level of hoarding.

"I'd offer you both some dinner if I knew you were coming this early. Either way, I gave your share to Busta."

She hobbled to the hospital bed situated near the fireplace in the living room.

"Busta?" I implored, my eyes searching the room.

"My dog. Found him in the alley a couple weeks ago and it seems he won't be rid of me anytime soon." She chuckled, and the force of the impact in her chest caused her to cough.

Mom advanced on her. "Mama Pat, I told you I was visiting this week. Remember we discussed Trice and I staying in the guest room?"

Aunt Patty waved a dismissive hand as Mom neared her. "Must've slipped my mind. Here." She reasoned as she reached around the bed and tossed a large brown handbag at my mother. "Order a pizza for dinner. Encino's is good."

Mom caught the bag and eyed her curiously. "Mama, we already ate. It's okay. Is there room for us to spend the night here?"

"Monica." Aunt Patty shot her a pointed glare. "What kind of mother would I be to let one of my own spend a bunch of money on some fancy hotel? Nonsense!"

"Mama, I told you. It's all right and I don't want to be a burden." Mom repeated as she occupied an empty portion of the bed. I remained by the door, afraid of stepping on something with a pulse.

Just then, a multicolored Australian Shepherd bounded into the room making excited yipping sounds. The large animal made an intentional beeline for me it seemed.

I froze.

I wasn't afraid of dogs, per se, but the unpredictability of animals always unnerved me. I was a lover of constants, of science, and animals proved to be opposite in every regard.

"He won't bite you, girl." Aunt Patty relented as if sensing my reservations.

Busta paused his excited yips and crooked a curious look at me.

I had a weird urge to prove an unspoken accusation wrong from Aunt Patty. I knew how she thought of me, as a silly girl without sense or muscle.

I leaned down in spite of the wild beating in my chest and extended a hand to him. I didn't realize my eyes were sealed shut until warm licks coated my hands, then face.

I couldn't fight the grin or giggle that escaped me as Busta pinned me to the floor, showering my face in the doggy version of love.

"That settles it, then." Aunt Patty proclaimed in a light tone I never heard from her. "Y'all are staying. If mean ol' Busta likes you then you're worth keeping around for these next few nights."

***

Mom and I spent the next morning giving the run-down shack a thorough cleaning. Tonight marked our final night in New York, and instead of spending it shopping or hanging out with my cool older cousin Angie in NYC like Mom originally promised I could, I found myself wrist deep in toilet scrubbing.

"Fuck, eww!" I screeched my disgust as the tar-like substance spewed from the porcelain toilet bowl. The sludge covered my face and t-shirt and I'm not sure where the fortitude that prevented me from puking came from. In a rage, I threw the plunger at the demon bowl.

"Watch that language, daughter-of-mine!" Mom scolded me from the kitchen. Most of the house was cleansed besides the trickiest rooms, the kitchen and bathroom, in which we drew straws on which room to conquer. I figured luck was on my side judging by the tiny sized room, but clearly I was wrong.

So wrong.

I apparently got so lost in my fuming, I didn't realize the fluffy canine lapping at my shirt.

"Busta, no!" I reprimanded as I shot to my feet. "You don't want to eat that."

Busta whined and walked sullenly in a circular direction at my tone.

I crouched low to muss his long mane. "You're still a good boy, Bus." Patrice Newbern, the formerly afraid of animals bookworm, now crouched to reassure the intimidatingly large dog for licking poo. I even nicknamed him. If I wasn't so livid at the state of Aunt Patty's living conditions I'd have laughed.

"Patrice, we ran out of dish detergent– ugh!" My mother's revolted tone came from the entrance. She looked horrified as she studied my clothes.

"Patrice, why the hell do you smell like that?" She pinched her nose.

I began removing my clothes in rapid succession at the poopy reminder. "Sorry, Mom. Taking a quick shower then finishing up in here."

I ignored her gag as I hopped in the rusted shower.

"You really smelled like shit, you know?" Mom re-marked as I entered the kitchen. I rocked another Mis-fits t-shirt and skinny jeans, a towel wrapped around my hair from the thorough wash it deserved after the poop assault.

"I'm aware, Mom." I snorted. "Where's Aunt Patty?"

Mom paused at my question, holding a dish she'd been washing in place as she answered. "Asleep. In the living room. She fell asleep watching the gospel channel. I already administered her meds for the day."

I nodded, studying her body language carefully. "Need help with anything on that front?"

She shook her head. "Nope. As long as she takes her meds and rests, then she'll heal just fine."

"Okay."

"I did want to run an idea by you, if that's all right?" The fact that she thought to ask me, well, anything, caused me to rear back in astonishment.

"Sure," I affirmed in a tone that encouraged her to continue on with her question.

"Okay." She exhaled, scrubbing the dishes with more vigor. "I'm thinking about asking Aunt Patty to move in with us. How would you feel about that?"

18

Make a smile for me

Uneasiness and anxiety blanketed my stiff body for a moment as my mind fought to register my mother's meaning. Live with us?

I cleared my throat before responding. "Um, how does Aunt Patty feel about it? She agreed to it?"

The anguished look on Mom's face was sign enough that she didn't ask her.

"What about Dad?"

"We spoke this morning. After I told him about her living conditions, the holes in the walls, the barely-functional appliances and dangerous neighborhood, he said he wouldn't mind it, so long as you guys were on board."

I took the 'you guys' to mean Manny and me, as my father often evaded the responsibility of making important decisions.

"All right." I weighed the idea in my mind. "If Aunt Patty agreed to this sudden move, would there be room for her?"

She faced me, her brown eyes furious. "Of course, Trice! We'll make room for her. She'll have my office."

"Mom, you need your office. You work from home and your patients are familiar with your office. Think of Maisey. She'd be so unsettled at the abrupt change." I hated being the voice of reason, but someone had to be.

Mom chewed on her bottom lip, considering. "I'll move the office to the basement. Done."

"Okay." I breathed. She should have been a lawyer, as her debate skills were subpar. The idea of waking up to my aunt sort of pissed me off, but I knew she was right. The ceiling in this place was near collapsing, and Mom and I spent the most uncomfortable night in her abandoned bedroom. The entire room reeked of urine and mothballs that I was counting the minutes until we were back on the road to D.C..

Still, I despised the idea of waking up to her criticisms, so I chose to press the issue.

I straightened. "There's no way Aunt Patty's agreeing to this. She just lost her home of thirty years to 'big government.'" I air quoted my aunt's choice of words for her previous landlord. "Long story short; she'll fight you tooth and nail on this. There's no use in reasoning with her."

The hurt in her eyes proved to be sign enough that I pushed too far. Too hard. She averted her eyes back to her task before speaking again.

"She's fresh out of dish detergent." She spoke, cold and clipped at me. "You remember where the Save & Go is located, right?"

My heart thudded as I reached for her.

She shrugged my hand away. "It's two blocks from here. Go pick some up for me so I can finish these dishes."

"Mom?"

She waved my words away. "Go, Patrice. I won't talk anymore about this. Clearly your auntie is too much of an inconvenience for the idea to even be plausible. Just go."

I saw the proverbial wall rise before us, the same one that existed before the trip. The one that prevented us from ever understanding each other for all these years. The familiar sinking feeling reemerged in my gut at the sight of my mother's unwillingness to talk this out further. There was no reasoning with her when she got this way.

"She's not a burden to me." I refuted before turning on my heel.

"I'm so disappointed in you." I heard her murmur before I exited the house.

The familiar whimper made me freeze after detangling my curls and adjusting my coat.

Busta crept towards me with the largest pleading eyes only a devil could resist. I almost shooed him away until realization dawned on me. Aunt Patty was nearly bedridden, so when was the last time he even got a chance for fresh air? Went on a walk, even? I was no dog expert, but from what I gathered from television, dogs required outside time for their social and mental development.

After sorting through the packed coat closet, I spotted a leash that matched his dirty blue collar.

"Ready for an adventure, Bus?" From the excited way he jumped and yipped one would think he understood English. I smiled at him before setting off to the grocery store in the hood.

A thought, so brilliant and bright in the hope it created in my chest, came to me as we strode down the busy Harlem streets. While I was glad to be spending quality bonding time with my mother, that discussion reminded me of our differences, of just how damaged our relationship was. There was no way I wanted to spend another uncomfortable night in that hell house, sleeping in a cramped bed beside the mother I desperately needed distance and freedom from.

I fished the phone from my Gucci mini and dialed the number to hope.

"Patrice?" Her baby soft voice lilted through the phone.

I breathed a sigh of relief. "Angie! What's up?"

"Nothing much, honey." She answered warily. "Everything okay?"

"Yeah," I answered too quickly as Busta and I rounded a corner. "Just wondering if I can ask a favor?"

"Of course, anything. You and Aunt Monica fighting again?" She asked a little too knowingly.

"Um, sort of." I admitted. "Listen, is it cool if I spend the night at your apartment? I can't be around her right now."

I knew it was a huge ask, considering we hadn't held a conversation since I saw her four years ago. Angela was always the cool older cousin I looked up to, the badass who never took no for an answer and crushed college so hard she came out with two degrees. It was no surprise when she landed the high paying teaching job in NYC.

"Didn't Aunt Monica tell you?"

"Tell me what?" I asked, confused.

"We're coming over for dinner tonight, me and Ricky."

"Oh." I uttered, my disappointment evident.

She sighed. "P, look, I'll talk to Ricky. But you need to clear this with your mom before I agree to this. You're still a kid."

I rolled my eyes, hating the 'just a kid' argument all over again. "Sure. Thanks Angie. See you tonight."

"Sure thing, love you, cousin. We'll talk about this when I see you tonight."

I ended the frustrating call a few seconds before leashing Busta to a bike rack outside the store. I wasn't well versed on proper dog care in the slightest, so I mentally determined buying the detergent as fast as possible to be the most moral thing to do.

I pondered the day's events as I scoured the aisle for the detergent my mother preferred. Was I being too harsh on her about this? Even though Aunt Patty's demeanor softened several degrees since I last saw her, it didn't excuse her cruel actions she exposed me to growing up. I decided early on that I hated her, and I typically stuck to the constants in my life. Hating her was one of those constants. Except, shame filled me just as soon as the hatred did.

Shaking thoughts of rehoming my sick aunt and the pained look in my mother's eyes away, I approached the checkout counter with my item.

"Five twenty-five." The heavyset black man totaled as I reached for the cash wad in my purse. I fingered out a ten and handed it to him, only for my hand to freeze midair when I caught a look at him.

"Quincy?" I couldn't conceal the astonishment as I gawked at his sunken eyes and oily skin. He looked like a serious mess since I last saw him. Quincy Masters was always so posh, so coiffed in his appearance, that the sweaty man before me made me wonder if I misidentified him.

"Yeah?" He grunted, eyeing me suspiciously. "Who wants to know?"

I nearly choked as I pocketed the change he handed me. I realized two years had passed before he even saw me. My body and appearance changed so much since then, no more tomboy clothes or chucks he'd gotten acquainted with when his stepson and I were friends.

My heart lurched and my mouth grew dry as the thought struck me. If Quincy worked here, at this obscure store in Harlem, then that meant Devin lived nearby.

Devin...

That huge grin and rich laugh occupied my thoughts as I stared dumbly at the man.

"I'm sorry, wrong guy." I murmured as tears fell. Busta and I just about sprinted back to the shack.

19

Late rat gets the cheese...

"Mama, why didn't you tell me you were living like this?" Angie demanded frantically as she entered Aunty Patty's treasured shack. Her hostile greeting overshadowed the jaw dropped reception from us at the sight of her large pregnant belly.

A tall Hispanic man with dark brown curls that made him look like Orlando Bloom offered a timid apology after helping Angie into a chair.

So this was Enrique Reyes, or Ricky, my cousin's smoking hot fiancé.

"Nice to meet you all." He offered, standing rigidly at her side. "What brings you ladies into town?"

I appreciated his attempt to diffuse the tension in the room. I found myself answering for Mom and I.

"Oh, um, we came to attend the APA conference in Queens. Tonight is our last night in New York."

He nodded, genuinely intrigued by my response. "Nice. I'm born and bred from Queens. You should check out that cafe downtown, they make the best sandwiches. It's called The Stream."

"You're right!" I gushed. "We visited that place and the ham and cheese croissant sandwich was so yummy."

A warm smile spread across his face. "My little sister loves their clam chowder."

"To hell with clam chowder!" Angie interjected, shooting her mother a menacing look. "Mama, tell me what's going on here?"

Aunt Patty stubbornly ignored her, keeping her eyes trained on the TV. Busta lay in her lap and she stroked his fluffy fur with absent purpose.

"This is why I called you over here, Angie." My mother spoke from the kitchen door frame. Her arms crossed as she stared at Aunt Patty on her hospital bed. "I knew you hadn't seen her house before either. Should have known you wouldn't let her live like this."

Angie cradled her swollen belly as Ricky assisted her to stand. "Hell no I wouldn't have."

She waddled over to block the view of the old school television from Aunt Patty.

"Are you hearing me?" She asked, her voice filled with emotion.

Aunt Patty waved her away. "Get out of the way, Angie! Forensic Files is on."

"Mama, look at you! You are bedbound and living in a virtual hellhole! Is this why you never let me visit? Why can't you let me take care of you?"

"No!" Aunt Patty finally snapped. "I'm your mother. I don't need to be taken care of. If you're not staying for dinner, then get the hell out."

Mom approached her then, the two women forming a barricade around the old lady.

"Mama Pat." Mom implored. "Please come live with us. You can't live like this. I thought Angie could speak some sense into you, but I see you're just as stubborn as ever."

I watched the scene from the far side of the living room, holding my breath as I witnessed the standoff.

"Back away from me– both of you! Ungrateful bitches." She growled at them.

Neither budged.

"I'll call senior services if you don't make this easy." Angie threatened. "I don't have room at my apartment, but Monica has that big house in D.C. I'm sure you'll be comfortable in. Don't you want to see more of your family?"

"Come on, Ma." Mom uttered in a small voice, throwing her thin arms around her sister-mom. "Please. We're begging you. Don't push us away."

Angie sat beside Aunt Patty on the bed, looping an arm around her, too. "Mom, please. Please let us do this for you."

I saw Aunt Patty's resolve weaken within the confines of her favorite children's arms.

As if sensing the tension in the room, Busta growled from the floor.

"Everybody get the hell out!" Aunt Patty commanded, her voice cracking. "You're upsetting my Busta. And I have a lot to think about."

20

Aftershocks and undertones

Three months passed in the blink of an eye, and before I knew it, summer break was upon us. Since returning from New York, life slowed to a pace that I relished. No drama or curve balls thrown my way which created a stress-free environment for me to focus on finishing up my secret project. I was so close to completing it that I found myself spending heaps of time cooped up in my room, preparing its essential elements before presenting it in a few months. I couldn't believe my sophomore year of high school was soon approaching. Come September, or two months from now, I'd be that much closer to adulthood. To freedom.

The gurgle from my traitorous stomach brought me back to the reality of my life. I stood from my desk and stretched my barely showered body. I had needs that required tending to, no matter how much

I avoided socializing with the fam nowadays since we adopted the bat.

"Want anything from the kitchen, Aunt Patty?" I asked my old bat aunt from the door frame of her basement bedroom. Since she now lived with us (only temporarily according to her blatant protests) she insisted on staying in the basement and out of the way. While I didn't object to the idea that kept her as far from my room as possible, Mom argued and lost to her over this decision. She threatened to move back to Harlem if her terms weren't met, so that quieted Mom from further goading her into occupying her home office.

Aunt Patty shifted her heavy frame in the queen bed Mom insisted on buying her to scowl at me. "Get me some grapefruit juice, saltines, and a pickle. I'm starving down here."

I fought really hard not to roll my eyes. "Sure thing, be back in a sec."

A chubby calico cat slinked towards me from her pillow throne near my aunt's bed.

I reached low and swooped the cuddly feline in my arms, knowing all too well this was what she craved.

"Hey, Rhymes." I nuzzled her wet nose with mine as I carried her into the kitchen. Her purrs sent pleasant vibrations to my neck and chest.

We adopted Rhymes shortly after returning to D .C. and moving Aunt Patty into our home. Busta seemed so lonely, and after taking him along to a pet meet-and-greet at a local adoption event, he and the chubby calico met and couldn't stay away from each other. The rest was history.

We kept her downstairs with Aunt Patty most of the time since Manny was mildly allergic to cat hair.

"Good morning sweetheart." Dad said, his eyes never leaving his phone as he occupied one of the seats at the dining table.

I assembled the oatmeal with one hand while I balanced Rhymes in the other. "Hey, Dad. What are you still doing home?"

"Taking the day off." He said between sips of coffee. He shot me a disbelieving look. "You should too, you know."

The thought of all that paperwork awaiting me brought on an audible whine from my lips. "Ugh, don't remind me. This will all pay off in the end though, right?"

I placed my oatmeal to the side and began preparing Aunt Patty's strange meal request.

"That food for you, or your aunt?" Dad asked.

I paused to stare at him. "Um, both?"

"But you hate oatmeal?" He said almost as a question, yet I understood it as a statement.

He was right. I did typically hate the mushy stuff, but the thought of eating my typical sausage and eggs this morning made me uneasy.

Before I could answer his non-question, he stood and came over to me. After ushering me to sit down at the table, he resumed the preparations for Aunt Patty's snack. "I'll make it for her. You just take it easy and enjoy your breakfast today, kid. Tell me what to do."

My cheeks warmed at the unexpectedly kind gesture. I long since released Rhymes to the floor where she lay contentedly at my bare feet. This cat truly loved us.

"Thanks, Dad..." I muttered in mild surprise.

After instructing him with the meal prep, he disappeared briefly to present the food to her downstairs.

"Is everything okay?" I questioned between bites of oats when he returned to the kitchen.

He made a sheepish look before answering. "Well, yes. I can be nice sometimes, right?"

I frowned at that.

"What?"

"Where is Mom and Manny?" I countered suspiciously.

His cheeks pinked as he checked his phone. "Um, I don't know. How are your studies going?"

I caught the abrupt conversation pivot and glared at him. "Dad, now you know I'm not gonna just roam on by that conversation change. You always know where Mom is."

Another blush as he checked his phone. Was he embarrassed?

"Daddy?" I demanded, rising to my feet and looming toward him.

The sound of his phone ringing interjected my next round of questions. There was something fishy going on, and I would figure it out before returning to my room.

"Finally." He breathed in relief before answering the call. "You got it? Oh, you're here? Okay, babe, I'll bring her."

Wordlessly, Dad grabbed my arm and pulled me to the front door. "Dad! Hey!" I protested as he dragged me outside.

I froze my tirade as I gawked dumbly at the scene before me.

A canary yellow Volkswagen Beetle occupied the empty front driveway. Did we have a visitor? I wondered inwardly as I studied the front doors open to reveal my mother and brother exiting the car with huge smiles on their faces.

"Mom? Manny?" I called to their searching gazes.

"Happy birthday, sugarplum." Dad whispered as he gave my arm a squeeze.

"Happy birthday, Trice!" Mom and Manny sang in unison as I sprinted to the yellow car and wrapped my arms around them.

"You guys!" I blubbered through tears of joy. "This car...is for me?"

"Yep." Manny affirmed with pride. "I bullied Mom and Dad into getting this car for you, too. Can you believe Mom wanted to surprise you with a trip to Sea Land?"

I hackled at the idea of visiting the waterpark I enjoyed as a child.

"Oh, stop it!" She defended lightheartedly. "Your father was worse. He thought an astrology textbook would be the best gift."

We all fell into laughter at that admission.

I turned sympathetic eyes to the old man. "Really, Dad?"

He blushed in humiliation as he ran a hand through his hair. "Well, it was a collector's box set. Sheesh."

Before I could get another joke in, Mom extended the keys to me. "Here, Trice. Take this car somewhere."

"You guys do know my birthday isn't until tomorrow? And I have no place to go." I said, a little embarrassed by the truth in that statement. In all honesty, I was so enveloped in that secret project this summer, the only thing I made time for was eating and nightly fuck sessions with Jack. He climbed into my window every other night or so since I returned from New York, and I found myself craving the sexual release after a long day's worth of cramming.

"Well how else were we gonna surprise you?" Manny inserted saucily. "You're so damned smart, you figure out every surprise we plan for you every year."

This was hilariously true, but I remained quiet as a thought came to me. The mall. I could barely remember the last time I reupped on makeup, and the back to school deals were all over the place in retail. Maybe

I'd call up Nora, my bestie and Beach I hadn't seen since last week to gauge her interest in joining me.

I placed a quick kiss on each of their foreheads before snatching the keys and jetting to the house.

"Thanks, guys!" I called, so caught up in the excitement I hadn't noticed Busta on my heels. "Gotta shower and *drive* to the mall!"

21

Find the golden needle

My mind drifted to the evolution of mine and Nora's relationship as I drove the short distance to her house. I figured surprising her with the new car the best option in lieu of calling beforehand. Better off this way, I thought, as I envisioned the shock and joy on my bestie's face upon gazing at our new ride for the afternoon. Drifting again, I recalled the sorrowful look in her glassy eyes as she approached my locker that day.

"Hey, Trice." She spoke through tears.

Fear slammed into my chest, so hard and raw I considered bolting.

It had been three full days after Devin's disappearance, and there were so many days after that that merely faded to black. I mean it, I remembered being so stricken by the loss of my former best friend I completely shut down. The only reason I'd even shown up to school that day was Jack's insistence that it would be good for me. So I trusted him, and there I was.

"Nora...what do you want?" My voice trembled.

"Trice, please know that it was all a lie! I had no intention of handing you over to Tisha or to make you pay for Devin's mistake. You have to believe that." She grabbed my arm tight, her desperation holding me there.

"I talked to Jack, and he filled me in on the situation. He said there was no need to fear since we'll both be protected from now on. I really like you, Trice. I hope this means we can still be cool."

I ground my teeth in restraint. "Great, so now you only want to befriend me because my boyfriend told you to?"

The audacity of this girl, I thought as I regarded her glum appearance.

She straightened slightly before responding. "Yes."

"Oh..." I couldn't hide the sting and shock effect of her admission. "You want to be my friend...because Jack told you to?" I couldn't resist repeating it.

She nodded. "Yes."

"Why bother?" I yelled.

"Because!" She matched my pitch. "Why not? He said we'll both be protected from any comebacks on Devin's behalf, and besides..."

I waited patiently, mostly due to the devastation of her admission but also out of curiosity.

"Besides, I think you're cool as hell. You dressed like a straight dude all through middle school and always put your love for Devin on full display. You're real. You're as real as any girl would want in a friend, so yeah. Plus, I don't think me lying to you again would get us anywhere. If anything, it made things worse. So," She said, her demeanor sunnier as she pulled me in for a hug. "Let's be the best fake friends we can be, okay? Sooner or later, I'll grow on you, just watch..."

And grow on me, she did. I soon found myself at her house and rummaging through her mom's make-up drawers every day after school. I made note to keep her at an emotional arms length, given her traitorous history, but I couldn't help but love the traitor-turn-Beach after a while. She became the sister I didn't know I wanted, or needed.

In truth, her friendship saved me. Helped repair the gaping holes in my heart Devin and Kale created. So yeah, I was forever grateful, even if it all is just for pretend.

I made a display by honking my new horn as long as possible when I parked outside her house.

Nora came out wearing her bonnet and a long t-shirt that fit her like a dress due to her short stature. "What the– Trice?!"

"Yessss, Beach!" I hollered. "It's me! I got some new wheels and am dying to go to the mall. Come with?"

"Do you even have to ask? Beach I'm coming!" She proclaimed exuberantly before running back into the house with promises to freshen up and return in five minutes.

Nora's five minutes existed along the realm of thirty, but I hid my frustration as she slid into the leather passenger seat.

"Girl, I need details." She urged as her eyes did overtime assessing the dash.

I explained the entire day to her; from my aunt's typical bitchiness to my dad's sketchy behavior in the kitchen that led to the car's discovery in the driveway. I took extra care to omit the details of the EGP project. This wasn't the time.

"It's a goofy color, but girl this car is all you. Congrats, again!"

"Thanks, friend." I sang contentedly as we cruised to the opposite side of town toward CityCenter Mall.

Despite my limited driving experience, the short drive was smooth. We chatted about several topics like school and the latest gossip in the air at Easton Rogue.

"Girl," Nora prefaced with a dramatic clap of her hands. "Did you hear about that sexy ass Tyrone Zelman? Please tell me you have."

I swallowed as memories of him with a gun perfectly poised at my face resurfaced.

"Tyrone keeps a low profile. Haven't seen or heard much of him." I mused.

She fanned herself. "Well, well. Rumor has it he got some babies on the way."

"Babies?" I squealed, overemphasizing the plurality. "With who?"

"Sasha Kersey. You remember that Trinidadian girl we had biology with?"

Sasha's catty demeanor and former status as Latisha's best friend plagued my memory. "Of course I remember. Sheesh. She's pregnant?"

Nora nodded as she gazed out the window. "Yup. With twins."

I had a mind to ask how she became privy to this knowledge, but refrained. Nora was the worst gossip, and while unpopular, she accumulated all the information she could from her fly-on-the-wall status in the crowds.

"Poor Sasha." She said warily as I rounded a corner. "Can you imagine what she's going through? No way I could imagine being a pregnant teenager. Sophomore year is going to be interesting, to say the least."

Sophomore year, I thought as wayward feelings assailed me. I fought hard to conceal the pain that shot through my chest at her words as well as the side of town we entered. I knew this side all too well. Kale's house, the one only he and his mother lived in, was situated about a block away from the CityCenter Mall, a very popular spot for teens to hang out. I remembered preferring to spend our movie nights at his house due to the distance from the shopping center we could easily disappear into for some good food and privacy. There was this sushi and sake bar, Jin-Tama, we frequented after school to play a few rounds of drunk karaoke or watch sappy j-dramas. The place was magical at the time for us, especially with us both being huge drama nerds.

My breath caught as I drove by the white colonial with large rose bushes I recalled Jennifer, his mom, planting with pride. So many good memories mixed with bad ones as I blinked hard to refocus on the road. That chapter is over and done now.

The huge shopping center teemed with people and aimless chatter as I parked my new bug into a compact car space. The space neared the sushi place that brought painful memories rushing to the surface.

"Let's get some food before we hit up the makeup deals at Sephora, okay?" Nora interjected my reverie as we climbed out of the small punch buggy.

I nodded sharply as we began the walk to the food court. I was grateful to my bestie who carefully avoided the sushi place considering what I told her about my painful history that transpired there.

"What's new with you girl?" I asked as I chewed around a slice of pizza. We occupied a small round table at the corner of the food court and I had to practically scream to enunciate my words to her.

"Well." She began, her smile waning. "Not that much you don't know about already. Especially the Luther thing."

"The Luther thing?" I parroted.

She narrowed suspicious eyes to me. "Girl, don't tell me you didn't know Luther got jumped into the 590's last week."

Horror iced my veins at the memory of Jack's body after that gang initiation. I desired that for no one, not even Luther the jerk.

At my confusion she scoffed, "Trice, girl, come on. Don't give me those judgmental eyes. It's what he wanted."

"Wanted?" I could barely process her meaning. "Why would anyone want that? Is he all right?"

She nodded. "Yeah...he's resting up at his mom's house in Baltimore. He asked that I visit him next weekend."

I fought to lift my jaw from the floor as I righted myself. "Nora, I don't think that's a good idea. Just stay away from him."

"Excuse me?" She demanded fiercely. "What did I tell you about passing judgment? Just be a friend and support me. I want to be with him so what other choice do I have? I gotta make sure he's okay."

I grabbed her hand. "You always have a choice." I repeated Kale's cold words verbatim to her. "Always."

She wriggled out of my hold, her stare full of anger. "Choice? You mean to tell me that, if given the choice, you'd be with Jack Burn? Mixed up with this gang shit?"

"I...have a lot of love for Jack."

"But that doesn't answer my question. If it was up to you, where would you be right now if Devin didn't steal that 590 cash and left you to deal with it? Huh?"

I cringed from the venom in her tone. "I-I don't know."

"See?" She said. "That's who we are now, 590 girls. Yeah this life is fucking scary, but we got to suck it up, say 'fuck choice' and back our men, no matter what. And be there for each other, too."

I wanted so many things in that moment, the strongest being to yell, to shout my anguish at the truth she spoke. She was right. This was life now. I was Jack's girl, and I had to admit it. Nora was my best friend, all I had and now the only one who'd understand my plight more than anyone. I had to believe the reality she drew before me, despite my rebellious heart that pounded in protest against it. In spite of our previous agreement to fake friendship, I closed my eyes and decided to trust her with one of my many secrets. The secret I swore to tell no one, but could no longer hide from my gang sister.

I took a deep breath. "Nora?"

"Yeah?" Her tone went from snide to concerned real quick. "Tell me, what's wrong?"

Die Patrick, I commanded inwardly to the pitiful alter ego I worked so hard in shunning these days. Be brave, speak your peace. Trust her.

"I...saw Quincy while I was in Harlem a few weeks ago." I said the words in a rush.

It took her a minute to draw together the weight of this proclamation before she stood to her feet.

"Oh, shit! You found him? You know where Devin is?"

Her excitement confounded me into a mild nod of my head.

"Yes! Fuck yeah!" She twerked her hips, summoning bystander gazes our way. "That's the best news I've gotten all day, girl! Thank goodness you took care of our Devin debt."

"Nora!" I chided, guiding her back to her seat. "Quiet. You never know who's listening."

She frowned. "So? If the 590's took care of Devin, then what's there to be so somber and chaste about?"

I could have giggled at her usage of the vocabulary terms from last semester's SAT prep class. But this was no laughing matter.

"Well, I haven't exactly told Jack about it. I-I don't know why I haven't, but I think it just wasn't the right time to."

"When is the right time, Trice?" She questioned indignantly. "When?"

"I don't know, Nora!" I snarled, emotion flooding me all at once as a mini bout of nausea did. I choked down the nauseous bile before standing and marching down the square.

She fell into step with me, a bit breathless before yanking my curls.

"Sorry, you walk way too fast." She said, angling her hands at her hips. "Beach, I'm sorry. Let me redo this."

I crossed my arms tightly under my mildly tender boobs. "Just forget I said anything, okay?"

She looped an arm through mine. "I got you. I won't say anything to Jack. You're my real best friend, so I promise you that. Like I said before, we've got to be there for each other, through and through."

A smile betrayed my annoyed disposition as we strode, arm in arm, further down the square. "I suppose so."

"You suppose so?" She mocked with feigned indignation. "Girl you better love me."

I threw my head back as laughter escaped me, lifting the tension in the air. "I do. You know I do. Thanks for being there for me, Beach."

We stopped in front of the restrooms where Nora turned an adoring gaze up at me. "Always, Beach. But first."

She poked a finger into my side. "Friend's who are there for each other wait for them as they take a quick pee break."

"Sure." I chuffed in defeat. "But don't take forever. I'll freeze out here waiting for your slow ass."

"Whatever!" She shot back playfully before extending a hand to me. "Can I borrow a tamp? Forgot mine at home."

"You can keep it, actually." I teased as I handed her the pink and purple swirled tampon from my favorite Gucci mini. "No use in returning a used tamp."

She flipped me the bird while laughing and disappearing into the restroom. Warm fuzzies flooded my being at our friendship milestone as I studied three women exit the smelly room. A distant sense of alarm permeated my conscience at a thought, however, one that slowly killed any fuzzy in sight. Our menstrual cycles were unusually synced, a theory we tested by several months of shared tampon runs. Fuck, I cursed myself internally at the period my body skipped for the second time in two months.

22

Stolen and swollen

I stared in abject horror at the solid double pink lines that confirmed my worst fears. I had long since dropped Nora off at her mom's with promises to return to the mall the next day to snag more beauty finds.

"I trust you'll know what to do when the time is right, Beach." Nora encouraged before shuffling into the small blue house.

I smiled sullenly at her backside as the distance widened between us. I was grateful she hadn't noticed the cheap pregnancy test I slipped into my bag at the checkout counter as she was engrossed in the new Fall Revlon collection she swore to buy with her next allowance.

"Shit!" I bellowed as I slammed the testing stick into the trash can near my bedroom desk. How could this have happened? Jack and I were so careful, I thought.

He made it a habit to pull out when he neared his climax, and I was on the pill. He took extra precaution with preventing this as I recalled the clinic visit after I returned from New York several weeks ago. Obtaining that pill was the only way he'd agree to touch me again, and I was so eager to not give up those fuck sessions that melted loads of my study stress away.

The studying. The EGP. That damn secret project I realized was my ticket to freedom I was now regretting. I studied so hard and long I took very little breaks to eat, sleep, and much less remember to take a pill. It was no wonder this happened, since we had sex every other night in his car or quietly in my bedroom these nights.

My phone's vibration stunned me out of my panicked thoughts. I reached inside my pocket to study the screen.

> **JACK:** You up?

Several hours and a lighthearted family dinner passed, leaving me to pace the small length of revealed carpet in my room at midnight. The text thrusted me back to reality, forcing me to reply to him through the numbness.

> **ME:** I'm awake. Want to come up?

The fuck sessions I routinely looked forward to now made me want to puke from apprehension and the prospect of facing him again. Would he hate me if I told him the truth?

The familiar rapping on my window made me yelp in terror.

"What's got you so jumpy?" Jack asked once he was fully inside. "I thought you'd miss me, baby."

He pulled me into his long arms, placing a kiss on my forehead.

I reared back to stare at him. "I do miss you, boo."

"Really?" He growled between kisses. "Prove it to me then."

After an hour of quiet fucking, I curled my body around his as we lay in the darkened room. Neither of us spoke for a long while as he trailed lazy circle patterns in my back while we cuddled.

"I–" we began at the same time.

He chuckled. "Ladies first."

"Right." I replied with a small smile, grateful for the darkness that hid my facial features. "Um, how was your day?"

His chest rumbled with laughter. "How was my day? Since when were you concerned about my day?"

I paused to ponder that. True to form, since becoming a 590, his "work" was never a topic for discussion, and I cursed, forgetting myself.

"Since now." I said with fake confidence.

Another pause, before he muttered. "My day was spent making sure your birthday is all you deserve it to be."

"Oh." I blinked, with all the stress of the secrets I'd been holding onto I forgot about my birthday tomorrow.

"That yellow car yours, in the driveway?" His voice was neutral.

I nodded.

"Hmm. Okay." He broke off, as if restraining himself from saying something else. "I have another birthday surprise for you. Be ready tomorrow night at eight."

Tomorrow night at eight, I thought. While I had to think of a creative excuse to get out of whatever plans my family cooked up, I was filled with a renewed sense of purpose at the prospect. Tomorrow night at eight, I'd tell him about the double solid pink lines. Tell him about the pregnancy I only hoped he wouldn't resent me for.

"Tomorrow night at eight. It's a date." I affirmed, before cupping his cheek.

Before we could slip into another heated encounter, I placed a hand on his chest to prevent him from kissing me.

"What's wrong, baby?" His voice was disoriented from my refusal.

"How come you didn't tell me about Luther?"

"Luther?" A ragged sigh blew from him as he considered my words again. "Right, Luther. That's 590 business, baby. Don't be bothered with it."

I sat up. "Well, he's Nora's guy, so now it's my concern. You could have at least told me, Jack. Not cool at all."

"Nora's guy?" He scoffed. "Barely. Even so, like I said, butt out. It's 590 business."

"But–" I started, but his death grip on my upper arm caused me to groan low as pain shot through my arm. "Jack!"

"No more of this shit, Trice. Stop asking, 'cause I ain't telling. Understand?" His voice leaked promising menace, low and bespeaking a certain danger.

My entire body trembled with fear as I regarded him. The familiar warmth in his tone was gone, and in its place a dark persona. Gone was Jack, my protector.

This was Burn Man, the new moniker he earned after a trail of mysterious trap houses burned to the ground last month.

Not wanting to be on the receiving end of that wrath, I placed a fretful kiss on his lips. "Sorry, babe. I won't ask again."

"Good girl." He breathed in that same tone, kissing me back. "I'll have a chat with Nora later on."

I'm not quite sure how I got any sleep a few hours after that terrifying encounter with Burn Man. I awakened to the nauseating smell of fried bacon, and an empty right side of the bed. Jack was gone. Like usual, he crept out before my parent's awoke or Busta could come mewling at my door.

My nipples and pussy throbbed from the night before as I walked over to study my secret project on my desk.

"Dear god." I mumbled in agony as I studied the cheap pregnancy test strip I previously discarded on my desk. Beside it, a note scrawled on a shred of notebook paper in Jack's distinct handwriting.

Tears coursed down my face as I read the chilling note aloud:

"Change of plans. Meet me at this address tomorrow at four. Don't be late."

I unfreeze my body momentarily to lift the mewling cat at my feet. Rhymes nuzzled her little face into my neck in satisfaction at the action, and I sought to bask in some of that feeling as I headed down the hall with her. Except, no comfort came as I stopped in the frame of Aunt Patty's basement bedroom as I often did in the mornings to check on her.

"You're just gonna stand there without speaking, girl?" Her hoarse voice bellowed from her bed. I noticed Busta laying beside her as she watched the Maury show.

"Oh, sorry Aunt Patty." I snapped out of the daze, realizing my weird actions, before adding. "Want some breakfast?"

She studied me for a long moment before motioning with her finger. "Come here, Patrice."

I frowned at the peculiar request, tightening my hold on Rhymes as I neared her. "Okay..."

She muted the sound from the TV before staring me dead in the eyes. I mean it, her eyes beaded into mine with laser focus I wanted to cringe from.

Her eyes then roamed along the length of my t-shirt clad form with knowing suspicion.

"What?" I blurted out, rudely, finding it increasingly difficult to conceal my alarm.

"Hmm." She scoffed. "You're gonna tell your mom?"

"Tell her what?"

"That you're pregnant, girl."

Dread coursed through me so hard and fast I gasped, dropping Rhymes. Thankfully, she fell onto the bed, but scurried toward Busta in haste.

"How did you know?" I queried, tearing up.

Her brows furrowed in agitation. "Was that supposed to be some kind of secret or something? Patrice, I might be old, but I'm not stupid. And I've had a few babies of my own to recognize the signs of a terrified teenage mother-to-be."

All my strength left me then as I sank to my knees beside her bed. I sobbed into the blankets for a long while, and I found myself oddly thankful for her silence.

"Stand up, girl. Come on." She reached down, tugging on my shoulders until I sat on the bed with her. "It's going to be all right, Patrice."

While her delivery was curt, I sensed no judgment or animosity in her tone. "Are you gonna tell Mom?"

She shook her head. "No, Patrice. It's not my business to tell, but I think you should, and soon."

I nodded my understanding, dropping my gaze to the floor.

She lifted my chin to meet her eyes. "Listen up, girl. I...I know I haven't been the easiest person to deal with. Hell, you have every right to hate my guts, but know this. Your mom went through this very same thing, and I didn't abandon her. So I won't do that to you."

I blinked, barely able to believe what I was hearing from my old witch aunt. "You're...not angry? Not going to tell mom to kick me out or send me away to boarding school?"

She did something I'm not sure I ever saw before. Smile.

"If only you heard the stories of what your mom put me through at your age. Hell no I wouldn't do that to you. Just, um, know that...I'm in your corner no matter what your parent's have to say about this. Okay, sweet girl?"

More tears streamed down my face as I nodded, feeling accepted and comforted from the least likely source.

"Good. Now go enjoy that birthday with your head up, okay? No more tears. I'm not really into hugs, so." She reached for my hand, enveloped it in her aged one, and lifted it to her thin lips. "Go slap that baby daddy silly if he doesn't support this pregnancy. It's all about Patrice today."

I flashed a watery smile, kissing her cheek. "Will do. Thanks, Aunt Patty."

"Damn right!" She sneered. "You weren't named after me for no reason. Us Patrice's are bad bitches!"

I laughed good-naturedly, feeling so thankful for my aunt's presence at that moment and a renewed sense of confidence. I knew what I had to do.

23

Tennessee

I sighed at the text from Nora I read before buckling my seatbelt.

> **NORA:** Sorry, Trice. Won't be able to make it to the mall with you today. Happy birthday.

Peculiar, I thought as I adjusted my mirrors like my father instructed me to during driving lessons last year. It wasn't in character for Nora to not honor a birthday request, since she made it her thing to always show up for me, no matter what. Even if we'd fought, she would still show up, pissed and all, but present regardless. I loved that about her, so her sudden inability to attend the mall with me left me to wonder if Jack had a hand in this.

"I'll have a chat with Nora later on."

His depthless words chilled the air, my body, making me shiver from their intense threat of danger. He wanted to meet me at four, so despite the disappointed looks I received from my family, I opted to spend this day with my Beach until my meet up with Jack in five hours. Yes, it was about time to meet and come clean with Jack, or Burn Man.

Since Nora couldn't come, I opted for loneliness. This was by far the worst birthday, but I made a mental note to do just as Aunt Patty says, by "grabbing onto life by the balls and kicking."

I smiled as I considered the unexpectedly warm encounter with my aunt. She knew about my mistake, my pregnancy. In fact, she could see the sorrow in my face before having to say anything, and the comfort of her words acted as a balm to my aching soul. It gave me the strength to confront Burn Man, the monster, and assert my choice.

Fuck that, I thought, I always had a choice. And my choice was to boss up and keep this oopsie baby Jack and I created. No matter what. Even if my parents disowned me, I took solace in Aunt Patty's support in all this.

I was minutes from the mall when the white colonial appeared in the distance. Kale's house.

I mentally forced myself not to observe the suburban home, no matter how much my heart and curiosity screamed against it. How was he doing? I wondered as I slowed by the house. I considered how much pride he took in his photography, and wondered if he still filmed and took pictures.

All thought and consideration stilled when I witnessed the pale, lifeless body on Kale's front porch. It was a man, I gathered as I screeched my yellow bug to a stop in the front driveway. A man with dark hair and a gray tracksuit.

The closer I got to him, the more the air wreaked with hard liquor. I turned the man's face gently to study him.

It was Kale, good lord, my Kale was hurt. He was so pale, and skinny, that I barely recognized his bruised face when I took him in.

"Kale!" I shook him. "Kale, sweetie, wake up! Can you hear me?"

I released a relieved gush of wind at the sound of his tortured groans.

"Jen...leave me be." He croaked through chapped lips. My eyes searched the small porch for it, then I saw it: three empty bottles of Jack Daniels liquor bottles littered the ground near his feet.

"Kale," I whispered, my futility and shame rearing its ugly head at the thought of not being able to help him. Again. Of failing him. Again. "Please, baby, wake up."

He hiccupped before his eyes peeled open. "Patrice?"

"Yes, honey." I answered, cradling his head in my lap. "Ms. Jennifer!" I called moments later.

"No use." He grogged. "Frosted Flakes..." He grumbled before emitting light snores.

"What?" I yelped at him, shaking him again. The fuck did that mean? I fumed inwardly, then recognition hit. I remember he teased his mom all the time about her job as an executive assistant for the Kellogg Company. He'd always say that her job paid her in Frosted Flakes before the room would break out in gales of laughter, me included.

Sighing at the memory, I felt inside his pockets in search of his phone.

Once recovered, I lifted it to my ear to speak to the woman named Jen in his phone.

"Kale, you're supposed to be in bed." She scolded before I spoke.

I cleared my throat. "Um, hi Ms. Jennifer."

"Wait, who's this? Scarlet, that you?"

I bit back the retort I'd wanted to fire about whoever the hell Scarlet was, before clarifying. "No, Ms. Jennifer, it's Trice. I'm not sure you remember me."

A pause. "Right, Trice, of course I remember you. You were all Kale could talk about a time ago. How's life been treating you?"

I always loved that about his mom, her friendliness. She was always so easy to talk to that I almost gave in to her request about my life before remembering the task at hand. The urgent task. Like, the drunken urgent one.

"Sorry, Ms. Jennifer, but it's Kale. He's passed out cold on the front porch. I think he drank a few bottles of liquor and must have locked himself out."

The concern I expected didn't come. She cursed.

"Fuck, sorry about this, Trice. He's supposed to be in bed resting like the doctor said. Would you do me this favor and get him to bed? I'll be home in an hour to look after him."

"Sure thing." I agreed easily, as if this was the natural next step for me to perform. To care for him.

"Thanks doll. The key is under the first rosebush nearest the porch."

"No problem at all. I'll take care of him." I said, meaning every word of it.

"You're an angel." She said before disconnecting the call. Once I dug the key from the intended rosebush, I fiddled with the automatic lock before dragging his heavy body into the house. Though he'd lost weight, he was no feather, as I collapsed with him into the sofa.

I pushed on him gently to ease to my feet, but his arms encircled me.

"Kale, damn it, let me go! You're so drunk." I growled. His arms tightened the more I struggled. "Kale!"

"Mmm..." He moaned dreamily. "Patrice, stop crying, it's only a movie."

"What?" I shrieked, pausing my movements. "Kale? Come on sweetie, let me up."

His eyes closed, he continued to speak with a boyish grin. "You always get so worked up over J-dramas."

I stilled, becoming eerily aware of the memory he was probably reliving. Tears fell as I watched his bruised face smiling at the memory. I almost felt bad for waking him from a much needed rest.

"Sweetie..." I whispered, attempting to stand again and failing. The guy's hold was ironclad.

I paused, considering a different tactic just then. There was a peaceful way to do this without waking and frightening him. I took a deep breath and prayed this worked.

"Kale," I whispered. "How can you not be sad that Toshinori dies in the end?"

Another dreamy laugh escaped him. "Trice, you're such a wimp. He got what he deserved."

I gulped, praying this reenactment of one of our j-drama movie night dates did the trick. "You don't believe in true love?"

His arms loosened a significant degree, allowing me to slip out of his hold.

"Love's a losing game." He muttered, before sinking back into a deep sleep.

My heart pounded as I regarded his emaciated pale body. While Kale was unhealthy, he was still a growing boy. The ridges in his chest and definition in his jaw proved to be the results of those hormonal changes I was not able to witness by his side. He'd done so much growing, while I felt the same short twiggy girl I'd always been, always in his corner. Loving him from the shadows while everything about him darkened.

After closing and locking the front door, I scanned the state of the living room I hadn't visited in nearly two years. Though clean, I noted several differences since the last time I visited the McAllen home:

First, the large portraits on the walls that framed a happy, modest family of three were long gone. Second, there were no large boots that routinely lined the front foyer and the house no longer smelled like a strange fusion of berries and cigarettes. I knew the meaning behind this change immediately.

The monster was gone.

Kale's dad, Clifford, the tall man with beady, piercing blue eyes no longer haunted the hallways and intimidated the cheery woman and boy in the rooms. I loved spending time with Kale at his home, but we made it a point to never share the same space with Clifford by hanging out strictly during his work times.

I hated the dark fascination he seemed to impose on me whenever I was in his presence. That glacial, calculating way his gaze seemed to linger just a few seconds too long on my smaller-than average breasts. Cold sweat and fear chilled my insides whenever Kale came to school with a new bruise he'd fib about receiving from the blunt end of a broom or accidentally tumbling down a flight of steps. I knew Kale, my Kale, to be a sweet and conscientious person, one who took painstaking care of his photos. I didn't buy his unbelievable tales of how he'd gotten so beat up, but it was almost an unspoken measure we took to never press the issue. To never look deeper. If only we did, I ruminate miserably, there'd be no chaos. No death and destruction.

"Want to see my toy collection?" the distinct, angelic little voice that could only belong to Michael Masters asked. Devin and I sat in the little waiting room of the doctor's office. I remembered the day clearly, as this was one of those weird Masters Family occasions I felt so out of place in. I intended to come over to Devin's house that day after school to assist him with some algebra homework. In the middle of our session, Quincy storms in and demands he take his eight-year old twin siblings to their annual physical exams at the doctor.

"Pops," Devin protested from the desk we occupied to study. "I'm in the middle of some shit right now, see?" He indicated me with his eyes.

Quincy, the burly no-nonsense stepdad sucked his teeth dismissively as he stared me down. "And?"

"I have to study and get this homework done, or they say I won't be able to play football for the season. I can't fail." Devin responded, standing up.

"Study?" Quincy asked, laughing. "You in here, *alone*, with this girl?"

Devin frowned, he and I sharing the irritation in the room. "Uh, yeah. It's Trice, remember? She comes over sometimes."

Quincy sobered and gave a small smile. "Right. Okay, son. There's plenty of time to get your pickle wet, but right now, I need you to take care of your brother and sister."

Devin groaned and rubbed his neck, as if his very words caused a cramp there. "Pops, why can't you do it?"

A brief haunted flash lit in his eyes for a moment, making me very conscious of the double truth in his next statement. "I got a work thing. Washing machines are breaking down and I got a guy in to inspect them. Long story short, Helen is out, so you need to take them."

I recalled the dry cleaners his father owned as Devin begrudgingly agreed to the task.

And that's how we landed in the family doctor's office an hour later. With Yvonne, the quiet more reserved twin, at Devin's side of the waiting room resting on her big brother's arm and Michael chatting the minutes away next to me.

I blinked, mildly confused about what toys he was indicating. "Toys?"

He giggled, revealing his semi checkered toothless grin. "My dinosaurs, duh!"

"What dinosaurs, Mike?" I asked, my gaze drifting to locate the object of the boy's fascination.

He dug around his little denim pocket to uncover three miniature reptile figurines I recalled Devin gifting him for his birthday two months prior. Michael's passion for dinosaurs bordered obsession, and I knew better than to deny him a dino related activity since he had such a nasty habit of temper tantrums.

"See?" He ran the mini dinos up my leg as he growled. "Rawr! I will kill you human!"

"No!" I whimpered, playing along as Devin cast us an amused look. "Don't hurt me, velociraptor!"

He froze, pinning me with an annoyed glare. "This is a tyrannosaurus rex, Trice! You're a grownup, you should be smarter than that."

"Ouch." I said. "That hurts my feelings, Mikey."

He ignored me, resuming his dino tirade on my leg.

"Hey!" Devin called.

Michael looked up at his serious stare. "What?"

Devin shifted to adjust the sleeping Yvonne on his arm before addressing the little boy. "That was rude, yo. Apologize to Trice."

"No." He grumbled petulantly as he crossed his arms. "I don't wanna."

"Mikey," Devin warned. "What did I tell you about saying things that hurt people's feelings?"

Tears poured down Michael's reddening face. "But I didn't do anything wrong, Devin! She should be smarter."

"So what?" He shot back. "Apologize. Now. You hurt my friend's feelings."

I expected the bloodcurdling scream and stomping to come when he usually was disciplined by Helen or Quincy, but that didn't happen.

Michael's eyes fluttered shut as he swallowed huge gulps of air, his small chest heaving. His even chocolate skin boiled an even brighter red before Devin assisted. "Remember what I taught you? Good job, bro. You're doing good just breathe."

Michael visibly calmed when he opened his eyes.

"See?" Devin said, his voice gentle. "Everything's okay. You just gotta breathe like I taught you when you get mad."

Michael nodded, his eyes still tearstained as he wrapped his arms around me.

"I'm sorry, Trice." He murmured in my ear.

I squeezed him tight, my heart lifting at the progress of Michael's emotional regulation. Mike had been getting into more fights at school and was currently serving a suspension sentence because of it. Looking back, Devin was the parent both of them needed, relied on, as it was mostly his responsibility to tend to their wellbeing since he refused the nanny Quincy offered to hire.

"Oh, Mikey." I whispered, my voice thick with emotion. "Thank you, I feel better. Can you please show me some more dinosaurs? Tell me how the t-rex gets his teeth so sharp!"

I knew that would be enough for a mood change, as he launched into another monologue about the history and physiology of reptilian beings. God, he was so intelligent. A kid genius even, and I looked on with amazement at the bright prospects for his future.

Except, the future never would come.

Sweet, chatty Michael would forever be silenced by that monster's actions. I knew Kale took his father's sins to heart by shouldering the blame of what happened.

I tried, I did, truly, to pull him from that darkness. I wiped the stray tear that slipped from my eye as I regarded his still sleep form on the couch. I had to help him...but how? He told me, warned me, to stay away. I figured the best I could do for him was to respect his wishes by avoiding him, but the closer I examined the bruises on his face and arms made me reconsider some things.

He was broken.

I remembered Jen mentioning she'd arrive shortly, and I really should leave. I really should. Kale was no child, or invalid. In all honesty, he was fully capable of caring for himself. I understood that at some point he'd awaken and wash his face, shower, and make some food like any other teen would. But I couldn't help it, couldn't control the legs pulling me forward into the large kitchen. Or the arms that fetched the fresh veggies Jen gardened in the fridge to begin the preparations for a thick beef and veggie stew. I couldn't tame the heart that refused to quit thudding at the prospect of nourishing Kale. I knew this stew wouldn't make up for my shitty friendship skills, but it didn't hurt either. And Kale really needed to eat.

The chirp from his phone brought me out of my reverie as I stirred the large pot filled with potatoes, celery, leftover steak, and beef broth. I knew he'd love this dish, as his intense love for red meat and potatoes flooded my mind, causing me to smile. A slow heat rose from my spine as I imagined him taking slow bites of the stew, a slow trail of broth dribbling down his square jaw before he flashed that thousand watt smile I melted over.

Calm down, Trice. I chided my insane hormones. Yeah, that was it. The pregnancy hormones hijacked my reason and made me hunger for something meatier than this stew.

I was fanning my heated face by the time his phone chirped again from the living room. A thought made me pause as I regarded the nearly done stew. A good friend would check his phone, ensure his affairs were in order. Perhaps it was Jen texting to check on him, right? Right.

Taking a deep breath, I left the kitchen to see Kale on the living room couch in the same contended slumber.

I searched the room again, locating his phone. I remembered resting it on the entertainment center. I studied the screen for several seconds before swiping up to access his lockless phone. How odd of him not to protect his phone with a lock screen. My finger hovered over the green message icon glowing with a red dot, indicating he received some unread messages.

"No." I muttered, slamming the phone back on the entertainment center. This wasn't right, and I knew it, but my stupid desperation for the briefest peak into Kale's world was so tantalizing I threw all pretense of morals away. My thoughts skittered back to Jen's greeting earlier, when she thought me someone else.

Who the hell was Scarlet? His girlfriend? Someone he had routine fuck sessions with, same as I did with my gangbanging boyfriend?

As silly as the thought was, it still pissed me off. The idea of my sweet camera man undressing another chick made me want to scream and hunt. Scream at the injustice and hunt the bitch who dared touch him.

Calm it down, Trice. Again, I had to scold this unexpected possessiveness that took residence in my heart. Besides, there were still ways to satisfy my curiosity while not crossing any severe boundaries. I knew just where to snoop.

I eyed Kale for a long moment before dashing, quietly, up the steps. I thanked the heavens the steps were carpeted, so as to swallow my foot noise as I ascended to scout for Kale's bedroom.

I remembered the room at the end of the hall where I spent so many lazy afternoons chatting and vibing with the Irish prince, the one who showed me so much light in the aftermath of Dark Devin.

The bare, sky-blue wall I anticipated walking into was long gone. Was this even the same room? I gawked in abject horror at the mess of photos that lined the floors. His collection of expensive digital cameras he once took so much pride in, were thrown haphazardly in the corner of the room, some even chipped broken in half. The bed, no surprise, was disheveled and unmade. There were empty liquor bottles...everywhere. This was not Kale's room, but the mess of a man downstairs. How on earth could he have drank all that alcohol without succumbing to poisoning or, worse, death?

I crouched down to sort through the images. Most were landscapes I recognized as D.C., of different lakes and downtown eateries I never visited. There were documents on the floor with scribbled handwriting I recognized as Kale's, with scattered phrases on each. One paper had one word on it, written plainly and causing me to frown at its meaning.

Monster. It read. I grabbed another, uncrumpling it and reciting the phrase aloud: "She takes it all. She can have it all. No more feelings. It is numb, but it hurts."

Determined to uncover the hidden meaning behind the cryptic scrawling, I kept digging deeper into the crumpled pile. Another phrase: "Paleontologist. Short walks. Fresh air. Riding his bike. Jurassic Park."

An eerie pang of awareness, one I wasn't prepared to face, rings loudly in my mind. Instinct tells me to search the pile, to keep digging through the hurt and mysterious writings until I feel the lump. I gulped before uncovering it, the small green and yellowish reptilian toy making my heart hurt. This wasn't what I thought it was. It couldn't be.

I didn't want it to be.

A semi-crumpled paper on his bedside table attracts me. All the pictures on the floor are printed in greyscale, as if reflecting the numbness in his soul. But the bright yellow on this paper makes me walk over to straighten it.

I gasp at the image. It was the picture he took of me that day in the hallway, just before we attended that dreadful drama class that marked the beginning of the end of our closeness. In the photo, I'm smiling and I'm reminded of Kale's words right then. That he loved witnessing me mid-laugh. This was the only photo that colored his bland bedroom where joy once lived, and I wept silently as I hugged it and the dinosaur figurine to my chest.

"Michael..." I blubbered in agony, falling to the bed. "Kale...I'm so sorry." Those were the last words I remembered uttering before a sullen sleep claimed me.

***

I woke up to a strong pair of arms squeezing me protectively to a hard body. Jack, I thought lazily, as I considered the breakfast I'd prepare when I went downstairs. I wondered if Aunt Patty would join me in the dining room for breakfast, as I was developing a new closeness to my previously estranged aunt. Strange, the forlorn whimpers from Busta didn't wake me up this morning as usual. The scents were all wrong, too, as Jack smelled only of Vici, an expensive Italian cologne he bragged about. This was different, though, as a faint trace of Axe Body spray and sweat filled the air.

I felt around my bed for the familiar fur ball that nestled my feet in the night and froze. Froze all over.

Instead of the warm thatch of fur I expected to feel, a soft piece of flesh filled my palm. Needing to be sure, I squeezed the appendage, which woke to life in seconds, hardening and elongating under my touch.

I screamed.

We both jerked and jumped in the darkness that shrouded the room. Where was I?

"Who are you?" I yelled, scrambling off of the bed and shakily to my feet.

A pained groan sounded before he slurred. "Come lay with me, Sunshine. What are you doing screaming like that?"

A naked man. An Irish accent. This could only be Kale.

"Did you follow me up here?" I asked, disoriented.

He groaned and reached out for me. "Patrice, lay with me."

The evening shadows prevented me from seeing him, but I was able to dodge his outstretched arms from a glint of light that shone through the blinds.

"Kale." I chuffed. "Get some rest. You're in bad shape."

Somehow he became lucid enough to climb up to his room, but he still sounded kind of sloshed.

"Not drunk." He garbled. "Miss my Trice."

I stilled at that, shaking my head to clear it. "Shut up, Kale. You don't know what you're saying." I patted around, finding the thick comforter and pulling it over his nude body with military quickness.

Before I could pull back, he fisted my wrist and yanked me into his hard chest.

"Kale!" I exclaimed, my voice little more than an exasperated whisper.

"Not. Drunk." He muttered huskily, his lips dangerously close to mine. "My Trice. Smell so good."

"Stop it." I pushed against him to no avail, despite the amount of definition he lost he was still so strong. "Dude, this isn't fair. Just let me go."

His entire body froze at my last words. "No! Can't let go. Need you with me. Promised him. Keep you safe."

Before I had time to ponder the manic words that mirrored the tortured scribblings on those pages I discovered earlier, his lips crushed against mine.

My previous resolve I relied on to get me out of this situation melted away as I molded my prone body to his nakedly hard one. His lips were so soft, and his embrace was so warm. God, I missed this.

I nearly drowned in that kiss until the smell of liquor wafted from his breath. That jerked me right back into reality, that I was lip locking the very man who cursed me out of his life. The one I failed.

I ripped my mouth away from his, pretending to ignore the protruding length stabbing into my belly.

"I can't do this, Kale. Gosh what am I doing?" I wasn't quite sure who that last question was intended for.

"Patrice..." He rasped dreamily. "Smell so good. Tastes so good."

At the mention of taste, memory assailed me. I could barely make out his outline in the dark room as the realization of what happened dawned on me. Shit! I must have fallen asleep after sorting through those photos. Fuck, fuck, fuck!

"My stew!" I screeched, panicked that I'd actually burned the kitchen down in my negligent snoopy behavior. This was just what I deserved for my birthday, I chastised as I bolted to the kitchen, a burned house and a lawsuit.

"Thank goodness!" I breathed in relief when I noted the stew set to the 'keep warm' setting. I could at least cross the lawsuit off my list of birthday punishments. I crossed into the living room and collapsed onto the sofa Kale abandoned earlier. My heart was set on a race so fast I thought I'd convulse or pass out from the thudding pressure in my chest.

More panic soon rushed in the minute another thought hit me. Except, fear accompanied the dread in my heart at the memory of Jack's note of instructions. Oh no, I fumed and slightly cowered at the menace guaranteed to come at the thought of missing our "date."

I recalled being in such a frenzy to ensure Kale was alive that I abandoned my cell and Gucci mini in my car. It was so dark in the living room, I had to feel my way around the furniture to find a path to the entertainment center. I patted down the lengthy shelf, running my hands along the wooden edges until I found it.

Kale's phone. Yes!

I only needed to check the time, no more snooping. Snooping and sneaking got me into this mess and now I was paying for it in missed "dates" and hard dicks.

The screen relayed what my heart intuited to be true, confirming my worst fears at the danger I was sure to confront at disobeying Jack's demand to meet him promptly at four.

Five-thirty. Kill. Me. Now!

Before I could drop the phone back in its place, a text message came in. I admit, this time I was not snooping. At least, that's what I told myself upon caving and opening the messages icon that listed the thirty-six unread texts.

Was there a fire setting somewhere or maybe he had a job? I scanned through the messages and saw that most were from Jen, demanding he text her back to make sure he's all right. Another from her mentioned that her boss was making her stay late to finish some last minute presentation and not to wait up.

The thought of worrying her for any reason when it pertained to her son's safety made me wince.

Resolving myself, I clicked on the text thread he shared with his mother to respond and confirm his well being when another text came through.

This was from an unsaved number, one from an area code I distinguished was from New Jersey as it began with an 856. Abandoning the mom thread, I chanced a glimpse at the message. Or, should I say, messages. Whoever this person, left Kale a whopping thirty or so messages. All of them in some sort of weird code. The last text iced my blood as I read it, and reread it to make sure I accurately comprehended it.

"At S-H in NJ. Wire the funds. Getting late. Coop." I recited the words through a shaky breath, my mind reeling at all the new stress it had woken up to. While I understood the danger that I'd be walking into once I left Kale's home, no way could I just sit on this. No way did I want to believe the words my heart and mind knew were true.

With trembling fingers, I tapped the phone icon at the top right of the text thread Kale shared with Mr. Unknown.

Please let this be my paranoia. I prayed as the line trilled twice before a coarse male voice spoke.

"Safe word?" He commanded in an angry whisper.

I cupped my hand over my mouth to tamp down the furious screech that wanted to unleash from my lips. Though time passed, and his voice was deeper and deadpan, I knew it. I knew this voice. The identity of Mr. Unknown was–

"Kale?" He asked. "Tell me the safe word so I know it's you. Or I'm ending the call. Ten seconds."

Ten seconds zoomed by without me saying much of anything beyond horrified gasps.

"Devin...tell me this isn't you. Please." I plead, my chest doing unnatural up and down motions as I fought to gather my breath.

"Shit. Trice, that you?" Devin sneered, panicked, and confirming his identity. "How'd you get this number? Where is Kale? Fuck!"

"Where are you?" I fought, so hard, to summon my bad girl alter, praying boss bitch Trice's strength would shine through and take over. Only, it didn't. There was only numbness, fear, and awe.

I fell to my knees as I listened to his breathing hitch on the opposite end of the call.

"We're compromised." He hissed, to himself I guessed. "Trice, fuck, this wasn't supposed to happen. Is Kale alive?"

I wheezed at the thought, my disbelief turning into rage. "You bastard! How the fuck dare you leave me without a word and have the nerve to interrogate me?"

"Trice, please, I don't got time for this shit. Is Kale alive? Is he there with you?"

A moment passed before I spoke again. "He's alive, Devin. Gosh, the fucking nerve. Where are you?" I repeated.

He either misheard me or ignored my demand, as he answered, "Do me a favor and throw that phone away, okay? I'm sorry about this. *Fuck*, man!"

He ended the call, leaving me standing there, utterly speechless on what was sure to be the worst birthday ever.

24

Sinking ships into space

I tried in earnest to block out the shrill voice of alarm in my head as I doggedly sped home. The saner, more reasonable side of my brain didn't appear to be operational as I made the short drive to the towering Newbern abode. There was just so much going on in my heart and head, I needed a place to run and hide and lick my freshly reopened wounds. I didn't dare check the several messages on my phone until I pulled into the empty driveway at home.

Empty? This was unusual.

My mother's black Hyundai typically occupied the first portion of the long driveway while dad's car remained parked on the street, since he left home so often. However, neither mom nor dad's vehicles were in sight this night which seemed to add coals to the flames of my panic. Where were they? Maybe Manny would know, I gathered as I grabbed my purse and phone to begin the short jog to the front door.

Darkness shrouded the normally lively lit foyer and living room area. The pitter patter of several feet also rang clearer the longer I stood in the foyer.

Busta leaped onto my front, his paws easily reaching my shoulders as he lapped at my face.

"Good boy," I cooed, attempting to calm his frantic affection. "Where's Mom?" I asked him as if he were able to respond.

Once he calmed, he circled my body, a gesture he did when he was distressed and I crouched to pet him. I swallowed the concern that loomed over me as I sank to the floor and fished out my cell. Busta collapsed beside me as I took a deep breath to prepare for my next actions.

Two voicemails and two text messages were left unchecked on my phone, from both my mother and Jack.

I didn't want to face the repercussions of missing Jack's birthday "surprise" so saving that message for last seemed the best choice.

I braced myself as I listened to the first half of the voicemails.

"Sweetie, I don't want you to panic, but we're at the hospital with Aunt Patty." My mother's stricken voice echoed in the empty room as I listened on speaker-phone.

"Don't panic." She repeated. "She's with the doctor now, and is conscious. Just give me a call when you receive this to let me know you're all right. I love you."

I hyperventilated as I replayed the message, unable to comprehend what was happening. Unable to process the reason behind my entire family's disappearance tonight. I remembered Mom telling me about Aunt Patty's host of medical conditions she fared alone in Harlem, and guilt tore through me.

I should have been here, I thought miserably, here with my family where I belonged instead of caring for the drunken Irish Prince. I fought to resist the urge to nibble on my lip, remembering his lips. I'd chastise myself later about making out with a drunk man, however, as the realization of the dangerous messages from Jack called for my attention.

I clicked through the screen to listen to the final unread voicemail on speaker.

"I told you not to be late." Jack's hard voice penetrated the empty air, making me squirm as I listened. "Call me when you get this. Your birthday surprise won't be completely ruined if you call back tonight."

To the average listener, this sounded like a normal reminder, but to me, there was a darker promise that lingered behind his words.

I placed a protective palm on my belly, praying for the events before us to be a safe one. After checking my text message inbox, a single message from Jack existed.

An address.

The place he instructed me to meet him from that menacing note this morning.

Time to pony up, Trice. I chanted this encouragement over and over as I stood up against the pitiful whimpers from Busta.

I smiled sadly at the sweet canine who brought so much joy to my life. "I'll be back, buddy. I promise. Okay?"

As if in full comprehension, he reared up again to lick my face agreeably.

I took the deepest breath of my life before stepping back out into the warm summer night to face my dangerous baby daddy. With a heavy heart, I opened the door to leave. Except, there stood a tall black man in a black hoodie and jeans. He stared down at me with cold, piercing eyes.

I screamed.

25

Building her millions

He grabbed my arm and dragged me to the black SUV parked on the curb in front of my house. This was it, I thought frantically as he shoved me into the backseat, this was how I died.

"Chill out." He growled from the driver seat.

"Chill out?" I spat, attempting to steady myself as he made rapid jerks and turns speeding down the street. "How do you suggest I do that? Huh?"

"Patrice, right? That your name?" The man responded evenly to my manic shouts. "Everything's okay. You'll see Jack soon."

I stiffened, a tingling sensation covering me as familiarity did. It took me a moment, but I hustled the courage somewhere within me to ask, "Luther?"

He chuckled as he sped through a yellow light. "Yep. Nice to see you remember me."

So Jack sent Luther as my escort for tonight. Where was Nino?

Nora's news of Luther joining the 590's floated back to my brain as I squinted to study the boy's face in the dark of night. I noted his blemish-free coffee colored skin and white teeth. He didn't have so much as a scar on any visible inch on him, which sparked an ugly feeling in me. If he actually got "jumped in" to the gang, then there would be no way this dude could walk, much less operate a car. This just didn't make sense, and I wondered further if Nora had lied to me again, in spite of our "no bullshit" truce to be the truest fake friends possible.

I recalled Jack's reaction when I posed the question on Luther's initiation and cringed. He was so angry, and treated me with a hostility I never witnessed before. And then there was the discovery of the pregnancy test, and that note...

"Luther." I blurted.

"Yeah?"

"Were you...were you..." I trailed off, fear gripping my throat.

"Am I what? Go on, spit it out." He encouraged in a coaxing tone not befitting a newly recruited gang member.

I inhaled. Then exhaled. Then spoke. "Were you jumped in? I mean, are you a 590, now?"

He drew in a deep breath and slowed the car to a stop. "Not my place to tell you, sweetness. Talk to Burn Man."

I pursed my lips. "Right. Burn Man."

"You feeling okay?" He inquired, now staring at me through the rearview mirror.

Again, the unprecedented friendliness caught me off guard. Was this what Nora saw in him? His ability to be calm and sweet as a cucumber in the face of danger.

I nodded. "Where are we?"

"It's your birthday, ain't it?" He said pointedly as I took in the abandoned warehouse we stopped at. An ominous street light shone near it, making all that existed beyond its illumination an abyss.

I swallowed before meeting his eyes. "Um, yeah. How do you know that?"

He gave a hearty laugh as he shrank into the seat. "How else would I know that? Girl, you're funny."

"Ha ha." I mocked lamely. Another thought struck me then. "Jack usually sends Nino to drive me places. Where is he?"

"Nino?" Luther asked. "Spanish dude, right?"

"Yeah, I believe he's Mexican."

He laughed again. "This is gonna be one happy birthday, Patrice."

"What kind of answer is that?" I said, annoyance replacing the fear in me.

Before he could give another one of those mocking laughs, a vehicle pulled up beside us. Its lights bright-ened the dark SUV Luther and I occupied, granting me access to his face fully. His grin disappeared as he studied the car.

"Showtime." He mumbled. "Come on, Patrice. Get out."

I did as he instructed, not realizing how my hands found their way to seize my belly protectively. Please, please, let no harm come to us, I inwardly prayed as I watched the figure exit the similar sized car beside us.

It was a man.

He walked the short distance to Luther and I, and my breath caught when Jack's unsmiling face came into view.

"Burn Man." Luther called, dapping my dangerous boyfriend. "Peace brother."

"Peace, bro." Jack said as they pulled apart from their hug. "She give you any trouble on the way here?"

He indicated my still form as he spoke.

Luther fanned a hand. "Nah, bro. She's cool as hell, you got a good one."

They dapped again. "Well, we'll see." Jack said, his voice deepening a few octaves.

"You still want me to drive y'all out there?"

"Yeah, man." Jack affirmed, giving my body an appreciative once over. "Trice and me are gonna do a little pregaming in the back."

Luther guffawed at that, taking the keys from Jack. "That's wassup. I hope she enjoy the show tonight."

"She should." His eyes lingered on my cupped belly, a cold look settling on him. "But the choice is in her hands."

My mind lingered on that strange statement as I stared dejectedly out the window of the Ford Flex. Just what the hell was going on? Luther took the wheel, and the car seemed to be in motion for over an hour.

I felt the familiar pulls of sleep drag me down into a fretful slumber I couldn't fight.

"Get some sleep, babe." Jack encouraged me as I slumped into his shoulder.

"I'm..." I slurred, exhaustion hot on my heels from the stress of the day and night. "...awake."

He placed the briefest of kisses on my forehead before the world blackened.

***

"You scared?" Jack asked me from the far end of the right seat he occupied. I wasn't sure how much time had passed, but as I glanced out the window I took note of a town that looked unfamiliar to me. My head throbbed from the discomfort of the position I was in. I sat slumped against Jack's shoulder with spittle dripping from my mouth. The odd question disoriented me as I rose.

"Huh?"

"Let me rephrase." He said. "Am I frightening you?"

I shook my head frantically against the grog. "Oh, no." I continued. "Not at all. But I am wondering about what this birthday show could be."

Jack nodded, a neutral expression on his face as the street lights illuminated him in flickering intervals.

"You never told me about that conference." He stated.

I gulped, the events from that visit slamming into me with juggernaut force. "I did, remember? It was long and boring, super tedious."

"Is that right?"

"Yep." I squeaked, my mind fully alert now. "Mom got an award and gave a speech, too."

"Hmm." He vocalized. "About how long was the drive from D.C.?"

I considered it. "About five hours, give or take."

"Okay." He seemed to accept my answer. "Where were you this evening? I thought I said to meet me at four."

Lie, Trice. I thought, my brain wracking itself for a convenient excuse besides telling him I spent the day with Kale.

I adjusted myself before speaking. "I had a thing with my aunt."

"Your aunt?"

"Yeah, um, my Aunt Patty. We went for milk tea, my favorite." I lied lamely, but I hoped effectively.

"Okay," he repeated passively.

His stony expression and grilling questions un-nerved me, but to my surprise, he ceased talking and opted for staring out the window. I'm not sure why, but the silence that stretch before us caused me even more discomfort. It felt like the quiet housed all the secrets I kept from him, just threatening to spill out if given enough light.

"So." I hedged. "Where are we going?"

"New York." He supplied.

Astonishment entered my heart and mind at this information. I gawked stupidly at him for a long time before shouting, "What?"

"Hey!" He growled, grabbing my wrist in his vice-like hold. "Watch the tone."

I gentled my tone and averted my gaze. "But, babe, it's like seven o' clock on a Wednesday. My parents will ask questions about where I am."

"Not my problem." His tone was glacial as he re-leased me.

"Not your problem?" I repeated in awe. "A notice would have been much appreciated. I mean, what are we even seeing in New York anyway, a play?"

He looked away. "Something like that."

"Something like what? Just tell me!"

"Trice..." He began in warning, but I kept on.

"No, Jack. Listen. We need to talk about things. About the elephant in the room."

"The elephant in the room?" He bit out, his eyes manically searching mine as he cornered me.

"Y-Yes!" I stammered, afraid. "You found the test. Let's talk about this. I'm pregnant, there's no denying that. We should just talk and sort this–"

His hand tightened around my throat, cutting off my nervous words.

"You want to talk about the elephant in the room?" He sneered as I suffocated. "The only elephant in this bitch is you. And the lies. Stop fucking lying to me, Trice. I don't wanna have to hurt you!"

"J-Jack...!" I choked, feeling the color drain from my face.

He gave another hard look before releasing me.

I coughed, spat, and scrambled away from the maniac I once thought a protector. About another thirty minutes passed before he spoke into the dark silence.

"I'm sorry, baby." He whispered tenderly.

Tears stream down my face as I folded my arms over my belly. I had to play this sick game if it meant getting out here, out of this car and away from this jilted maniac for good.

"Don't mention it." I grumbled.

He studied me for a long moment. "I thought you flew Delta. To Queens, I mean."

I bit my lip, wanting to kick myself for walking right into his trap earlier when he asked about the drive to New York.

I remained silent as I met his piercing blue eyes.

"Here's how this is gonna go." He began. "You're gonna tell me the truth from here on out, capiche?"

"How can you be sure I won't be lying to you?" I couldn't help but rasp the question.

He smirked. "Well, then you're joining the show."

The show was beginning to sound ominous, like a sight I knew for the life of me I'd never wish to see. Whatever remnants of challenge I had left me, as the desire to see the next day reared up. I had to do this for me, I thought, and for my baby. Whatever this weird game was, I needed to ensure the outcome involved holding my precious child eight months from now. For her, or him, I did this.

"We drove my mom's Hyundai to Queens. And to my aunt's house in Harlem." I revealed.

"Good." He uttered approvingly. "Anything happened there?"

"Well..." I hesitated, thinking of Quincy's ragged face in the corner store. He looked so tired and stressed that I barely recognized him. I hated betraying him and Devin, but I did what I had to do. "I saw someone. Quincy Masters."

He scooted closer to me. "That Devin's dad?"

I nodded, a tear sliding down my cheek. "Yes. His stepdad."

"Why did you keep this from me?" He asked.

"To protect Devin." I replied, the answer was the truest thing my heart felt.

He shook his head. "Not that. I figured that. I mean, why did you keep the details of how you traveled there from me?"

Saint's menacing promise and smile crept its way to my mind, making me shudder in terror. I shook my head.

Jack caressed a hand to my back. "Trice, baby, come on. Don't lie to me sweetness, you don't want me to be angry again. Tell me."

I couldn't utter the words, couldn't tell him the truth for the fear of what would happen. Saint always made good on a promise, or threat, as that's what made him one of the most ruthless in the game. Even as crazy as Jack became, I didn't wish to unleash the brunt of that punishment on him.

"Trice..." he warned, his hand stopping to clutch the nape of my neck. "Please, sweetness. Tell me."

"I can't." I sobbed.

"You can." Jack urged. "You will. Tell me, love."

"He'll hurt you, Jack." I whimpered.

"Who will?"

I gulped, preparing for the inevitable. "Saint. Saint will kill you! He told me to report back if I saw anything strange in New York, but I never did. He even sent Felix to survey us the entire trip. I noticed him everywhere."

This was it, I thought. I sealed his fate at my admission, knowing this would get back to Saint and dredging the inevitable blowback from my stupidity.

I failed Jack, now, too.

I threw myself into his arms as I sobbed. He wrapped his arms around me and squeezed tight. "I'm sorry, Jack!"

"Hey, hey." He cooed. "It's all right, baby."

"It's not!" I sniveled into his chest. "He's going to hurt you! I know it. He told me not to tell you, and I disobeyed him."

"Hey," he grabbed my chin and guided my eyes to his. "Don't you worry about me, my loyal Trice. I love you now, more than ever. Thanks for telling me the truth. You'll always be safe with me, remember that."

I nodded, internally confused by the tenderness. "How can you be sure? I did such an awful thing. I lied! And Saint is crazy."

"There'll be no comebacks." He said evenly, reaching for the bag I just now noticed at his feet. "Look through these."

"What's this?" I asked, opening the small blue backpack. There was a single folder.

"Proof." He answered. "Open it up."

I obeyed, and gasped at the stack of photos. Photos of me. There were several photos captured of me from the conference as I smiled at the stage when mom received her reward, another photo from the Luxe Hotel of me studying the vending machine I visited to get mom a chocolate bar. Horror blazed through me as I noted the additional photos, one of Aunt Patty's house and of her dog, as well as the image of me embracing my cousin Angie when she visited.

My hands trembled as I uncovered the unthinkable; there I stood, staring in open shock at the man at the checkout counter of the grocery store.

The confrontation with Quincy.

There were so many more my mind reeled from them, some not even New York related, such as a picture of my frightened face trudging behind Nino that day Saint sent for me to divulge to him info on the APA trip. A photo of Nora and I in the food court yesterday came to the forefront, as well as the image of me studying the pregnancy test box I eventually stolen in secret.

Or so I thought.

There looked to be nothing kept from Jack. The huge stack of photos uncovered the truth, that after all this time, there were never any secrets between us. He knew all. There seemed to be a photo accounting for every private moment I thought I had in public.

He knew, I thought in dismay, he knew it all. All of my secrets. There was never any escape or respite from the truth.

"You knew...everything?" I breathed in horror. In disgust. This entire relationship seemed to be nothing but a huge surveillance scheme, one that violated me in every single way.

Jack nodded. "I did."

"Did this relationship mean anything to you?" I whispered, my voice rather hollow.

"Of course."

I threw the folder, the photos scattering in the air. He sighed, shoving them back into the bag as he spoke. "You want to know why I joined the 590's, Trice?"

"I don't care." I said, so hurt I was barely managing words at that point.

"I saw it as an opportunity." He continued as if I hadn't spoken. "I wanted money. A lot of it. And I wanted power, influence. College would never get me the amount of money and respect this path does. When Coop left town with that huge bag, I saw it as the opportunity I needed to get the money. The influence. The power I needed to climb the ranks and run this shit how I want."

"Why involve me in this, Jack?" I snapped.

"Because, I knew keeping you near me and alive would draw Devin out. And it did. Took nearly two years, but it did. Remember, Trice, I still had a debt to repay on your behalf with the 590's. You were my greatest asset and liability, worth more alive to me than dead. So I kept you around."

The car came to a stop, the suddenness of it making me shiver. I had no idea what time it was, as the hours ticked by after my nap in haste as we were enveloped in our heated discussion.

"Where are we?" I demanded weakly, studying Jack now with suspicion as Luther exited the car.

"My Trice." Jack said, smiling. "It's your birthday, remember? It's time for the show."

"What show?" I squealed, losing my breath.

Luther opened my door. "Come on, princess. Time for the show." He extended his hand to me.

I stared at it with blank trepidation.

"Let's go, Trice." He said with the same silly calm from before.

Jack had long since exited the car and now stood beside Luther.

"Come on sweetness," Jack muttered. "Don't you want to find out the surprise? I promise you won't forget it."

Staring beyond them, I noticed we stopped at another warehouse. This time, however, only an open field outlined the space around it instead of adjacent buildings like before. I stared into the expectant gazes from the men, and prayed for strength an safety as I grabbed Luther's hand to the unknown evil that was my birthday show.

Luther handed me off to Jack, where he looped his arm through mine as the three of us walked to the entrance of the abandoned warehouse. My heart pounded, sweat poured down my neck and face and back as my mouth dried with indecision.

We stopped in front of the place where Jack squeezed my arm. "You ready for the show?"

Was I? I asked myself as I looked up into the blue eyes I once trusted.

"Luther." Jack nodded to the dude who stood like a soldier at the door. At the command, he released the entrance gate.

Once it finally rolled up, I shrieked at the horror before me.

"No!" I bellowed out into the warm winds, my legs giving out beneath me.

Jack held me up and spoke casually as he dragged me closer to the bloody scene. "This is the show, Patrice. This is where you make your choice, sweetness."

Three chairs lined the dark room, but the car lights illuminated the space enough so that I could make out the identities of the three men who occupied them:

Nino.

Quincy Masters.

And, perhaps the most shocking, Saint Milliard sat bound, tortured, and bloody with gags in their mouths.

26

Nobody gonna call you now

"Jack!" I cried, tears spilling freely. "What the fuck is this?"

"This." He mentioned, nodding in their direction. "Is your gift. The show I promised. The debt you need to pay in order to make up for Devin's crime."

"What?"

"It's politics, Trice." He stated matter-of-factly as he dragged me closer to the men. They each looked to be unconscious and badly bruised. "Turns out, our buddy Saint and Quincy were working together the whole time. I had one of my guys tail Saint's every move for the past year. Looks like it was him and Quincy who'd repocketed the money the 590's made through our prostitution ring out east. Saint ran the soldiers, the soldiers brought the money to Quincy, where he'd wash it through his businesses and split the lion share of the earnings with him. Both of them were fucking rats." Jack spat the words.

I trembled all over from the implication, from the story being unfolded in front of me. I also thought of those photos of me in that folder. "Who was your tail?" I found myself asking.

"Huh?" Jack asked confusedly. "Oh, Felix was my inside guy. I had him tail both you and Saint the past year."

So Felix the Terrible worked for Jack this whole time? I recounted his chilling words from the hotel, saying that the boss was keeping an eye on me. All this time, I thought he referred to Saint, but now I knew. Knew who was really running things from the shadows.

I eyed Nino, the Mexican thug who chauffeured me exclusively the past few months.

"He's a rat, too." Jack answered my terrified stare at the bloody Mexican man. Nino gained consciousness and glowered at us through seething swollen eyes. He jerked and mumbled expletives against his restraints. Luther walked up to the man and punched him. Nino fell out cold from the impact.

"Been reporting my every move to that bitch, Saint. He's no more than his drug-running dog."

I shrieked again from the violence and blood spewing from the punch. I couldn't take this. I had to get out of there.

I turned in Jack's embrace. "I have to go."

"No, Trice." He said, dragging me back to him. "Don't you see what this means?"

"No!"

"It means I can trust you, babe. You've passed every test thrown your way. For example, I had Nora cook up that little lie about Luther being jumped into the 590's. I told her, if you said you knew about it, then to tell me immediately, since at that point that would have confirmed you were loyal to Saint. Nobody would have known Saint had planned to initiate Luther except me, Saint, Luther, and whoever Saint's bitch is. I now know that bitch ain't you. Good job, sweetness."

Nora's words came back to me as I twisted in his embrace, fighting against the blockade of his arms. I sensed something amiss in what she told me about abandoning choice. It didn't sound like her to dissuade me from independence or logic. Now I knew. Jack manipulated her, too.

I shook my head, so disgusted I wanted to spit at him. "No, Jack. I'm not your bitch, either. Let me go!"

He chuckled and tightened himself around me, further molding in place.

"Don't you get what this means?" He asked, a crazed glint shining in his eyes. "It means Devin is safe."

My entire body froze, my mind not quite understanding his words. "Wait...what? Devin is safe?"

He nodded, smiling. "Yep. Devin only took orders to deliver the bag to Quincy from Saint. He didn't sell or steal anything. Poor guy was just a pawn in his greedy stepdaddy's game, a mere delivery boy who took the fall on Quincy's behalf. I have proof of that."

Warmth washed over my being I didn't know I needed. Devin wasn't involved in this? He didn't leave me on purpose that day? This also meant he truly left to keep me safe from Saint's insane rule.

I dared not to hope, however, knowing the ins and outs of gang life too well at this point.

"You haven't hurt him?"

Jack studied my face for a long moment. "No. And I won't, so long as you make your decisions wisely tonight."

"Why am I here?" I demanded, still attempting to struggle out of his hold.

"You passed another unexpected test, too. By telling me about the encounter you had with Quincy in Harlem, I knew you weren't secretly taking his side in all this either. You came through, every time I tested your loyalty, sweetness. For that, I'm giving you a choice of how this all ends since I'm now the head of the 590's."

My mouth gaped in horror as I waited for the choices he laid out. The choices, I knew, would rob me of everything in the long run.

"You can stay with me, as my loyal girl, where no harm will ever come to you. Or, you can leave. Walk away from all of this, and me, but at a cost. This is still politics baby, so Devin will have to pay in some way. I have an appointment scheduled for you tomorrow in the city."

I stared at him quizzically. "Why? Where?"

"At Planned Parenthood."

I sorted through my thoughts a moment before understanding came. I nearly collapsed again at what he was suggesting. "Jack...please...no!"

"This is how it has to be. To walk away from this, completely free and without comebacks, you'll need to get that abortion. Getting the abortion saves your life, and killing these men by your own hand, saves Devin's. This is the final test of loyalty. This is how it has to be."

"And if I say no? To all of this, including the abortion?" I hissed through anguished tears.

"Well, then we kick it old school. The only way out, then, is in a box, Trice."

"Not our baby..." my voice trembled as I wrapped both arms around my middle. I thought of the vow I made to myself earlier, the one that involved making the choice to see my baby's face in eight months.

"That thing," Jack snarled as he regarded me clutching my belly. "Was a mistake. One I can't let go unpunished or unclaimed. If you want to keep it, Trice, then you know what you gotta do. Stay mine. But think, is it worth letting Devin die over?"

"Jack!" I plead, dropping to my knees. "Please don't make me do this. I'll do anything else but that. I can't bear anybody else getting hurt because of me!"

He crouched low, on his knees to caress my chin in his hands. "Baby, this is a very generous thing I'm doing for you. You shoot these guys, go to that appointment tomorrow, and walk away from all of this with Devin alive. Or don't; you stay my top girl, and I'll even let you keep that little mistake of ours, but Devin will have to be dealt with. Come on, don't let your birthday be your death day, too. Lieutenant."

"Got it, boss." Luther answered him, materializing and extending the slim gun to me equipped with a silencer nozzle on its end.

"What's it gonna be?"

Part Four

Supernova

27

freedom

Sophomore Year

I squeezed my mother's hand in mine like a vice, my nerves going haywire. It felt like the air I inhaled was filled with lead, as it became increasingly difficult as the minutes ticked by to steady my breathing.

"Trice, relax." Mom whispered beside me. "You got this. You're gonna ace this!"

"What if I don't?" I asked in dread and hyperventilating. "What if I fail this? What if I'm not ready? Or they don't accept it?"

"Patrice!" Mom clasped both my hands in hers as she twisted in her seat to face me. "Honey, everything will be all right. Visualize the outcome you want, and it will happen for you. I guarantee it. You've been working so hard this past year."

I nodded, my heart and mind losing their accord from the consternation. She and I occupied the reception area outside the counselors office where my presentation would soon occur. This was it, I thought as the lump in my throat lodged. And Mom was right. I did work on this secret project, this EGP, too long and too hard for this not to work out.

"You're right." I affirmed gently. "I got this. I'm gonna crush this presentation."

Mom did a little dance that lifted my spirits. "That's my Poo. Yay! Best of luck in there."

My phone's vibrations interrupted the quippy response I'd prepared just then. I fished the small device out of my pocket and studied the screen, angling slightly out of Mom's field of vision as the text from my best friend brought about another smile from me.

> **KALE**: Good luck on your presentation today, Trice. Knock 'em dead! Not really, though.

I couldn't resist the blush that warmed my face as I typed back.

> **ME**: Roger that. Thank you, Irish Prince!

I giggled in spite of myself and the odd look my mother tossed me at his anticipated response to the new nickname I assigned to him since we reconnected last month.

> **KALE**: Stop calling me that, Patrice Anika Newbern.

> **ME**: Using my middle name is a no-fly zone and you know it!

> **KALE**: So long as you learn your lesson in comparing me to the likes of royalty. No-fly zone.

Gales of laughter ripped my sides by the time I felt a familiar jab at my arm.

"Ouch!" I said on a wince, looking at my mother as if she lost her mind. "What?"

"Trice," She said my name carefully, the same way she had been since adopting my otherworld nickname full time. "Stay focused. One of the biggest presentations you'll ever make is happening any minute now. We've got to get you in the mind for college next year, remember?"

I rolled my eyes before tucking my phone back inside my power suit pants. "Please, stop it with this! We were having such a good time, waiting for the counselor to arrive before this."

"What did I do?"

"Seriously?" I snapped.

"Trice, I don't mean to pressure you–"

"Well, you are!" I interrupted her usual inculpable comeback. "I was just texting a friend, that's it. You're making this such a big deal."

A tic set in her jaw before she spoke. "Mind your tone, daughter-of-mine. You can disagree with me, but you will respect me as your mother. All I'm saying is to keep the phone away until after your presentation. Stay battle ready. Stay focused. Remember what happened...what we talked about? No boys."

I froze. Of course I remembered. The blood...there was so much of it. What Jack put me through was more than enough for me not to fight Mom's decision for me to stay away from boys.

However, it was clear Aunt Patty was leaving an impression on my mother. Yeah, she was usually pretty stern, but with Aunt Patty's permanent fear-me-now presence in our house, it was obvious she was turning into her sister-mom.

I flinched from the memories. "Chill out. There are no boys. Or girls. Or anyone. I'm practically friendless, okay?"

"Poo, listen, that's not what I meant! I just want the best for you. I want you to do this presentation so you can be on track for graduating this year. Besides, you can make as many friends as you want next year at Yale."

She didn't get me, I realized as a nervous flutter swam around my tummy.

"Mom, this presentation is for me. I'm doing this for me. There's nothing else to say about this. So, after today, please butt out. You go your way, and I'll go mine."

Before we could relaunch into another heated, hushed argument, a knock sounded from the counselor's door. We stilled, shooting wary expressions at each other.

"Yes?" Mom called awkwardly. It was sort of strange for the counselor to knock to usher us inside her office.

The tall, curvy, black woman exited the confines of her small office wearing a black pantsuit and wry smile.

"Hello, Patrice. This your Mom?"

We stood, meeting her face-to-face.

"That's me." Mom said before sharing a brief handshake with the nervous looking woman.

She pursed her lips before concentrating on me. "Patrice, Mrs. Newbern, we've encountered a minor issue with the presentation today."

My heart sank, mouth dried, and...well, everything sort of went dark as I listened to the news.

"Excuse me?" Mom probed in concern. "What does this mean? What issue?"

"It seems Principal Hammin had a family emergency to attend, and will not be able to be present at your presentation."

"So?" Mom shot back. I was grateful for her, because I could barely manage words through the haze I was in. "We can present it to you, right? And maybe you can pass him the message or record it, or–"

"Ma'am." Counselor Jones interrupted with her hand. "I apologize, but Patrice will need to reschedule her presentation for a later date."

A beat passed before I could find my words. "No. I have to present today, Ms. Jones."

"Sorry," she said mournfully. "I've already considered all other options, and this is the best one. We've already rescheduled you for the end of November."

"What?!" Mom and I shouted, getting all up in her face.

"That's like two months from now!" I screeched.

"What's she supposed to do until then, huh?" Mom added, cornering the thin woman.

"Look," she started, straightening. "That's the earliest I could schedule your Early Graduation Presentation with the board. That's your only option, Patrice. However, due to the inconvenience, the board was pleased to grant you access to use the seminar room in the event you'd like to invite a large party for viewing. That sound all right?"

"Is there absolutely no other option we can pursue?" Mom asked before releasing an exaggerated breath.

"I apologize, ladies." Counselor Jones answered, chagrinned.

"Don't worry sweetie," Mom said to me during the car ride home. "You can take this time to fine-tune your presentation, you know, iron out the imperfections. Right?"

I sighed. I dedicated so much to that damn EGP, or Early Graduation Presentation project. I barely left my room last summer to focus on the eight full length essays, historical reports, mathematics booklets, and science projects compiled into one mondo project. That project was my magnum opus, my masterpiece and the very thing that kept hope alive when it came to facing the tortures of high school. So much I had at Easton was loved, then lost, including my former self. The girl who enjoyed life and living amongst the stars. The girl who believed she could do anything, be anything so long as the moon hung in the night sky. But not now. That girl, that protostar, was dead.

Same as my presentation.

"Sure, whatever." I retorted, slinking back into the passenger seat and wrapping my arms around my middle. I allowed my mind to drift as I half-listened to Mom's encouragements during the drive...

***

"Come here, sweet girl." Aunt Patty called to my depleted form at her bedroom door. A full twenty-four hours ticked by since the gravity of my birthday show. The murder show, more like it. My heart raced at the memory of holding the slim firearm, then subsequently dropping it as I attempted to shoot one of the bloodied men.

It was Quincy. He ordered me to shoot and kill Devin's stepdad first to prove my loyalty and secure Devin's safety. How was I supposed to do that? Just...how? My mind screamed in agony at the thought. But I was grateful. Grateful for the unexpected mercy from the new 590 Boss. When I dropped the gun, his reverberating words still rang in my ears as I sank to Aunt Patty's floor.

"You're fucking useless, Trice. This gets it done. Makes it square. See?"

A painful roar wracked my chest, tears poured in buckets down my eyes, and the world darkened after witnessing Jack shoot them, clean and precise, in their heads.

I woke up the next day on a plush bed. The smell of cigarettes and cheap liquor filled the air, alerting me that this bed was not my own. A hotel. I woke up in a hotel, totally alone.

Jack and Luther returned before too much time would pass. I didn't protest as Jack dragged my limp body into the slate black SUV or gripped me vice-tight as we entered the crowded abortion clinic. I remembered voices, people speaking to me, concerned stares, a firm shake as the nurse inquired about my mental state and medical information. Something about if I had any illnesses or needed to contact my guardian. No, I say, there's nothing left. No one left. No one to come and rescue me from this hell of a life. My baby is gone. My baby would be leaving me. Taken, like Michael, from the chance of a future. Jack! I scream at the man with cold hard eyes, but my voice is mute. No sound leaves my mouth as I scream and protest against the man who whispers something to the nurses before I'm escorted to an exam room. I lay there, I think, or perhaps I'm floating as the nurse asks me more questions. I answer. I don't see him, but feel his energy. Feel his presence in the recesses of my brain and room as my legs are parted. Probing, stabbing, God it hurts! My face is wet. A warm hand, the nurse's hand, pats my thigh as more wetness forms on my face and suddenly there are cramps.

And blood.

I am still cramping and bleeding as I regard my ghostly-looking aunt from her door frame.

"Patrice?" She calls again when I don't heed her summoning. She stands up. "If you won't come to me, guess I'll go to you."

"Yara…"

Aunt Patty is standing in front of me, Busta and Rhymes at her side. The trio sink to the floor as my unfocused stare looks beyond them.

"What you say?" My aunt asks, more than a little concerned now as she shakes my shoulders.

"Yara…"

"Who is 'Yara?'" She demands. "Patrice, are you okay? What's going on?"

"Gone." I feel my head shake.

She casts me a furious, but worried, glare. "The fuck? What happened? Where are you coming from?"

I was vaguely present during the car ride back to D.C.. Only mildly aware of Luther gently depositing me on the front porch of my home. No cars in the driveway, I noticed, as I fumbled inside and dragged myself to Aunt Patty's basement bedroom.

The room spun in looming circles as I tried to get the words out. Something felt warm, like a slow fire, in my pants. I tried my best to talk, react, and think past the cotton in my head.

"My baby...gone. No more." My jaw worked overtime to form the broken words. Everything was kind of hazy after that.

A slow realization dawned on my aunt as she assessed me. "That baby. Don't tell me you– Patrice!"

She hollered. Why are you hollering? I thought I asked aloud, but noticed the lack of movement from my mouth. That warm feeling spread from my crotch to my inner thigh. Mmm. I thought dreamily. So warm. I just want to lay here. Lay here with the warm in case Yara comes back, asking for me. She'll come back, I knew it.

"Monica!" Aunt Patty screeches into a phone somewhere in the distance. "Come get your child. Yeah, she finally came home. Send for an ambulance!"

A brief pause, and I can almost hear my mother's panicky demands about what's going on. I'm fine, Mom. It's super warm here...

The warmth turns into heat as I vaguely listen in on what Aunt Patty says.

"She's bleeding, Monica! I know you're with new clients, but come home. Tell Patrick to meet us at the ER. Yeah, there's a lot of blood showing on her pants. She's acting funny and not responding to my questions."

So warm, I think dreamily as a bright light assails me. So, so warm...

***

"Wake up, honey."

I jump to the sound of my mother's voice. My chest flutters with anxiety for a brief minute as my eyes work diligently to piece together my surroundings. The driveway. We were home. It was only a dream.

I slink back into my seat as relief floods me. "Oh, we're home. How long was I out?"

A troubled expression haunts her face as she regards me. "About twenty minutes."

I tried, but failed, to ignore the tense silence that ensues between us.

"What?" I wiped my mouth. "Am I drooling or something?"

"No drool. But you kept repeating 'Yara,' over and over again."

I don't say anything. What else is there to say? All I could do was sit there numbly as I recall the dream that wasn't really a dream at all. It was a memory. An awful memory that haunts all of my sleeps.

Mom squeezes my hand. "It never happened, okay? Just keep repeating this until you know it in your heart as true."

I fight to blink back the tears that threaten to fall. "I don't want to talk about it."

She nods, like usual, retreating from the topic of my nearly fatal abortion. Ever since I woke up in the hospital that day, I learned I suffered from a hemorrhage shortly after the procedure. The doctor said it was extremely rare, but that I could have, in fact, died if the ambulance weren't called at the appropriate time.

"Not a word of this to your father, you hear me?" Mom coached me after I was discharged from the hospital. "He's already under enough stress from work. We don't need him knowing this, too."

Just like now, I didn't supply that frigid warning with a response.

28

Stay twinkling

I tried in earnest to resist the eye-roll as I woke up Saturday morning to the familiar chirp from my phone. Somehow, I knew the exact identity of the texter before I even spared a glance at the cell on my nightstand.

> **NORA:** Good morning, Trice. I hope you slept good and have a great rest of the day. I'm always here for you. I miss you.

This was routine since July. Each day, Nora sent a single text message with various meanings and phrases, but each ended with the signature 'I'm always here for you. I miss you.' Per routine, I deleted the heartwarming text thread with efforts to forget about her. I wasn't avoiding her like I usually did my problems. No, this time, I realized just how toxic– just how dangerous– she and I were for each other. It seemed like all the mess with Jack and the 590's would forever be the bane of our relationship as the truest fakest friends. Regardless, I was tired of the show, of the effort it took to keep her arms length so as not to get hurt or hurt her. In the end, I couldn't protect her. Not when Jack used both she and I from the very beginning as if we were marionettes on his gang string. This was the logical next step, I decided when I awakened in the hospital from my nearly fatal abortion. I decided to put more effort in keeping people safe, and being honest. The lies and actions done under the cloak of night only exploded when forced into the light. From now on, I'd be true to me.

I cuddled Rhymes to my chest, savoring the moments of comfort her affection always brought on before facing my day. Looking back, I should have noted this clear indicator of my pregnancy. Rhymes was usually cuddly and sweet, but she refused to leave my side after I found out about my precious baby I nicknamed Yara. I wasn't entirely sure if she was a girl or not, but my heart resonated with that name, like the universe picked it out just for her.

I allowed those memories to wreak havoc as I clutched my empty womb with a free hand. Maybe I'll do as Mom insists, to just try to forget. Try and forget the little blessing that could have been smiling up at me a mere six months from now.

No, Trice. I chastised those haunting thoughts and desires as I descended the steps, Rhymes in arm. Keep going, try to forget, hold it in. I chant this to myself as I reappear at Aunt Patty's door this morning. She's sitting up, as usual, with Busta occupying the left side of the bed as Maury blasts through the room.

This was our morning routine; I wake up, get dressed, and hang with my aunt. She and Manny are the only ones I associate my company with since...Yara.

At the sight of her favorite companion, Rhymes darts out of my arms and hops onto the queen bed. The calico kneads Busta's tail before circling and snuggling into him.

"Good morning, Aunt Patty." I greeted, standing beside her bed and catching glimpses of the TV.

She smiles warmly at me. "If it isn't my favorite grandbaby, praise the lord."

I grinned at the new nickname. After I corrected her in the hospital after the incident, she grunted, "Now you know your momma is my spiritual daughter anyway— so that makes you my cherished granddaughter. Don't you forget it, damn it."

Chuckling at the memory, I answered, "Hey, hey. What are you feeling for breakfast today?"

"Hmm. Can you fry up some of those hot links in the freezer? I think your momma bought some waffles too."

I nodded. "Eggs, too?"

She giggled, the sight still awed me. "Can't forget the eggs!"

"I'm on it." I agreed dutifully.

"Good morning, Trice." Mom greeted warmly as I entered the kitchen. She sat at the dining room table, sipping on a cup of coffee as she completed her morning crossword. A loaded plate of bacon sat in front of her.

"Hello." I offer her a stiff response as I fry up the hot links.

"You, know. There's bacon here, if you want it. I made extra this morning for you and Mama Pat."

"Nope. No, thanks." I said, starting on the scrambled eggs. A few silent minutes tick by. The sizzle of the eggs the only sound penetrating the tension crackling between us.

"You're not still mad at me about yesterday, are you?" She said gingerly.

"Nope." I retort, plating the completed food on both my aunt's and my plates. I turned to leave.

"Trice!" Mom called, jumping up from her seat.

"Yes?"

"Um," she hesitated. "I...I'm sorry you got upset about our conversation the other day."

I gulped in restraint as hot fury heated my veins. "That's not a real apology. You're an actual, board certified psychologist and you don't even know how to apologize properly?"

She crossed the room to confront me. "I am apologizing! You've been acting so strange lately, icing me out all the time, like you're just tolerating me. Can we just talk about this?"

Fucking narcissist. The wrathful words hum in my mind before I can stop them. She truly was full of herself if she thought blaming me would suffice as an apology.

"What you say?" She reared back, appalled.

Dread formed in the pit of my stomach as the realization that I voiced those words out loud dawned on me. Shit.

I sighed, turning to face her fully with both plates in my hands. "Nothing, forget it."

She jabbed angry hands at her hips. "I was wrong. A bitch. That's what you've become since July. Here."

She stomped to the dining room table where her purse was place. After digging through it, she fished out a white rectangular bag and practically threw it at me. "I wanted to ease you into this discussion, but here."

I focused aggrieved eyes on the bag. "A prescription?"

She nodded, her face hard and glacial as she regarded me. "Birth control. It's my fault you got yourself in trouble the first time. I won't make the same mistake again. Take those every day."

My lip trembled as I turned my back on her. There was that wall again, heightening itself between us. "Fucking narcissist." I whispered, loud enough for her to hear.

She grunts. "Take those every day." She over-enunciates the words as I walk away. "Or you have no home here! I won't have a loose jezebel living under this roof...!"

Keep going, try to forget, hold it in. I chant this to myself again as her cold voice tapers off when I descend the steps to Aunt Patty's room.

"Here you go, aunty." I said once I reached my Aunt Patty's excited expression.

"Ooohhhwee!" She jeers as I situate the eating tray before her. "I'm about to fuck this up! Thanks, Patrice."

I offer a weak smile in response as I climb onto the bed beside her, the animals between us. This gave me comfort, sitting beside Aunt Patty as we nibbled on a breakfast of champions each morning. Sometimes we talked, about trivial things like whatever show she was watching or about stuff happening in the news, and sometimes we said nothing at all. The quiet with her was a comforting one, however, none like the impenetrable silence that existed as a barrier between Mom and I.

"Your mom talking evil again?" She asked during a commercial break.

I coughed. "What?"

"She's not exactly quiet, you know." She said plaintively.

"Yeah." I whispered, rather broken. "Called me a jezebel and threw a packet of birth control at me. I can't believe her."

Her eyes close briefly as she sets her tray aside. "She's still processing. Just give her some time. She'll come around. That doesn't excuse her behavior though. If you ask me, she needs an ass whooping for talking to you like that."

I chuckle, though I know it doesn't reach my eyes. "Thanks, aunty. I just wished she understood me, you know?"

"She should." She hisses. "Especially after what she went through as a teen. I hate her judging you like that. You couldn't have expected to nearly bleed to death after something like that."

"I didn't. Trust me, I didn't." I reply in a quavering voice. "The decision wasn't really mine."

She pinned a hard stare at me. "Patrice Junior. Don't tell me that. You know I would have supported you if you kept Yara."

At the sound of my would-be daughter's name on my aunt's lips I smiled. I loved that she acknowledged my precious baby, honored her memory by name instead of Mom's insistence on calling her "your mistake."

I didn't dare tell her about the truth behind what I meant when I said the decision was out of my hands. I couldn't tell her that it wasn't fear that brought me to that clinic, but Jack Burn, the cruel 590 boss.

"It's really my fault, you know." She uttered in a tone so light I barely understood her.

I twist in my seat, my food long abandoned. "What? No it isn't aunty."

"It is!" She groused, her gray afro bouncing as she shook her head. "I should have been more of a parent to Monica, raised her more softly. Maybe not yell so much and talk to her like I did. That Jezebel line sounds familiar."

I search my soul for the old hate that lived there for my formerly infuriating aunt. I find none as I regard her with sorrowful eyes.

"Aunty, listen, you didn't make her call me a Jezebel. You didn't make her force me into secrecy about my pregnancy towards dad knowing. He still doesn't know because of her. She's a grownup. A full adult. She knows how much her words hurt."

"Does she?" She asks, haunted. "I taught her purity. To never associate with loose women growing up."

"Aunt Patty, she threatened to kick me out!"

A bout of silence ensued before she spoke. "I wish the fuck she would kick you out of this house. She'll have to go through me."

I grinned at her, feeling so grateful for her support for me. "What can you do if she kicks me out, Aunt Patty?"

"Give her hell, is what!" She shouts. "You're not loose. You're my granddaughter. How dare she?"

I nodded wryly. "I know. I don't know how to deal with her, aunty."

"She's my fault." She whooshed out hurriedly, almost as if talking to herself.

"Aunt Patty?" I ask in concern. "What do you mean? You couldn't be–"

"Don't talk me out of this guilt, girl. I know I was a piece of shit parent. I know it's too late for Monica. But know this."

She pinned me with a look so filled with tenderness it made me cringe.

"You are my pride and joy, my junior. I...um." She scratched her head, the way she usually does when she attempts to comfort me. "Well, I love the shit outta you, granddaughter. There. I said it."

I fight the lopsided smile that forms on my face and lose, throwing my arms around her. "I fuckin' love you, too. You're my favorite grandma."

Another light giggle escapes her as she meets my hug with her fleshy arms. "Damn, right."

Busta and Rhymes stir as we cry and laugh together.

A knock sounds at the front door three hours after my heartfelt breakfast with Aunt Patty. I apparently fell asleep some time after Forensic Files aired. I giggled as I awakened in Aunt Patty's bed at the sight of both animals snuggled between us as if they belonged.

My mouth hangs open in shock at the sight of the couple on the front porch.

"Hey, P!" Cousin Angie sings, pulling me into her arms. "How are you doing!"

I blinked a few times to make sure her appearance wasn't some crazily concocted dream.

"I'm all right." I answered as I welcomed her, Ricky, and an unfamiliar little girl inside. She looked to be about three or four years old. "I didn't know you were visiting."

"What? I'd never miss out on your big day! Monica told me about your presentation. I'm so proud of you!" She squealed. I noted the several things:

Ricky, her dangerously handsome husband, is holding a caramel skinned infant in his arms. That's what was different, I thought as my gaze lingered on the precious sight. Angie's belly shrank since the last time we were in contact.

"You had the baby?" I whispered, my voice tortured for a reason unknown to me.

After hanging her coat, she returned to her husband's side. "Surprise! Little Emma Chartreuse made her appearance last month. We figured a surprise visit would be the best, especially since your presentation was coming up!"

I feel an odd cocktail of emotions at once. Angie had her baby. I was happy for my favorite cousin. Happy for the little family that treated me to nothing but kindness during our stay in New York all those months ago. But the sight of her perfect family and perfectly alive baby girl makes me wallow in self pity.

"Sorry if it's an inconvenience." Ricky said boyishly on a wince as he juggled the sleeping baby girl.

His words snap me back into the present. "Oh, um, nonsense! You guys have a seat and I'll go get Mom. I think she's finishing up with a client."

"Hola!" The toddler I forgot about chirps from below. We all stare at her extended hand to me. "I'm Yazzy."

Ricky laughs adoringly at her. "Patrice, this is my niece, Jasmine. My sister needed us to babysit at the last minute. I hope it's not a problem we brought her with us."

I remembered the kind Latina I met in NYC who visited Angie and Ricky when I stayed the night at their place during the New York visit. She came bursting in, annoyed with Ricky about finding some old marijuana joints in the trash can. Apparently, Ricky and the girl's fiancé, Ross, snuck away to smoke weed from time to time when Ricky visited his favorite cafe, which Ross's family conveniently owned.

"Oh, hey, sorry!" She apologized once she noticed my half-sleep form on the living room couch. "I'm Reina. Don't mind me. Just came to kill my brother."

We ended up hitting it off right away, however, with the night ending with the both of us chatting the night away about our pasts and exchanging numbers.

"Not a problem at all." I replied to Ricky, dropping to the toddler's level to shake her hand. "Hello, gorgeous. My name is Trice."

Jasmine stared at me with eyes the same as her mother's, widening in delight.

To my surprise, she threw her arms around my neck and whispered in my ear. "Hermosa."

I gulp down the shock and ask, "Hermosa?"

She pulled away from me and hugged Ricky's leg. She wore the cutest pair of jeans with a unicorn stitch on the pocket, paired with a dark blue sweatshirt. Her pigtails bounced as she buried her face into Ricky's pant leg.

He reached down to tousle her hair. "Is that what she said to you?" He asked.

I nodded. "Yes."

"Beautiful." Angie chimed in. "She called you beautiful, in Spanish."

"Oh." I said in mild surprise. My heart fluttered as I looked at the gorgeous toddler clinging to Ricky's leg. "Thank you, Jasmine."

"You're welcome, miss." She mumbles sheepishly, her face flushing.

We've now moved to the living room where Ricky, Angie, and Jasmine occupy the plush brown luxurious sofa my mother guilted Dad into buying. I remained standing as I regarded them awkwardly.

"My presentation was yesterday." I speak into the expectant silence.

Angie's face fell. "Oh, no! I must have mixed the dates around. I'm so sorry, P. Um, I can gift you some money? Let me get my purse–"

"No, no!" I interrupted her with my hand as she attempted to stand. "It's all right. The presentation got pushed back due to a scheduling conflict anyways. The new date is in November."

"Oh, no they didn't!" Angie muttered saucily. "How dare they do that to you? I mean, I'm happy we'll be able to attend the presentation, but annoyed with their incompetence. I'll complain to the board!"

"Baby," Ricky cut in. "It's all right. Patrice said we have another chance to see her presentation in November. As long as she presents, that's all that should matter right?"

His voice seemed to calm my irate cousin. She sank back into the seat like a petulant child. "Fine. I hate it when you're right."

A mischievous twinkle lit in his eyes. "Aren't I always?"

They break into a lighthearted argument when I decide to make a run for it.

I make a beeline for my mother's office before I have to suffer through another question from my spirited cousin. I loved her, but no way did I feel like divulging my secrets from the past year out to her. To anyone.

Mom's office was on the first floor at the back of the house. She chose that room because it faced the sun and allowed plenty of extra light in, and she claimed the sunshine was good for the mental state of her clients. I tiptoed to the little room and peered in on her session. She spoke in hushed tones, like a heated whisper, making me curious about which patient she was giving a tongue lashing.

My eyes searched for the client she was speaking to, but after several scans I realized she was alone. Talking on the phone, nonetheless.

"Helen, girl, please come in for a session." She reasoned with the unknown entity. "I know you need a listening ear. I'm here for you."

I frowned as my mind sorted through the meaning of her words. I knew that name. Before I could piece it together, her next words chill my blood.

"Oh, don't give me that! Per the conditions of your rehabilitation plan, you need to see a therapist. That can be me. I miss you, girl, I'm worried about you. Plus, I know you just got custody of your kids again. That's a lot to take on for someone in your condition. How are you handling that?"

If her words were accurate, and my mind was clear, then that could only mean one thing:

Devin was back.

29

The words of a love song

I take the deepest breath of my life before raising a shaky hand to knock on the thick wooden door. It had been quite a while since I visited this place. The place I once knew as my second home, a sanctuary away from my parent's strict rules. I took in the sights and smells of the lush landscaping, inhaling the fragrant rose bushes in efforts to distract myself from the thudding of my heart.

The door swung open to reveal...him. The man who answered the door was taller than I remembered. His five o' clock shadow was gone and the familiar bags disappeared from under his eyes. Instead of the stench of liquor, a faint trace of something expensive smelling radiated off his half naked body in waves. I licked my lips, an intense desire slamming into me at the sight of him.

Kale. The Irish Prince.

His brows crinkle when he looks down at me. "Trice? What are you doing here?"

So many words and phrases swirl in my head at that inquiry. It was a reasonable question, really, considering I showed up here after offering up my bedroom to our guests for three days. I grit my teeth in heated restraint as the visions of a few minutes ago float to the surface of my mother's face. Dad came home, a rare sight these days, and I offered for Angie's little family to take up temporary residence in my room for the duration of their stay. Mom protested, of course, but conceded when I threatened to tell Dad about the incident she coached me to "forget until my heart believes it true." After packing an overnight bag and falsely reassuring my parent's that I'd spend the three days at Nora's, I set off.

Then I ended up here.

But I wouldn't confess this to Kale.

I open my mouth to provide the carefully curated response for my presence when the direct opposite rushes out of me.

"Who the hell is Scarlet?"

An amused smile crooks his lips. "What's this now?"

I cupped a hand to my mouth in horror at the jealous counter. Fighting for a semblance of brevity, I straighten and face him. "The last time I was here...your mom mentioned something about a girl named Scarlet. Tell me, is she your girlfriend?"

Silence passes before he bursts, and I mean bursts, into laughter.

My cheeks burn as I glare at him. "Never mind! Forget what I asked."

"Trice." He says between howls of laughter. "What in the world is wrong with you, girl? Are you...jealous right now?"

"Shut up!" I sneer petulantly, crossing my arms the same way I recalled Mikey doing mid-tantrum.

"Patrice Anika Newbern," he smirks at me, making my cheeks burn all the brighter. "What are you doing here?"

I want to scold him for using my dreaded full name, I really do, but his final question drags reality back to me.

I cast my gaze away. "I...I have nowhere else to go."

"Are you in trouble?" He asks, his voice and eyes now hard as he assesses my body.

"No, no!" I groan. "Just need a place to crash for the next three days and...I don't know...I want to be near you."

He eyes me suspiciously before asking, "Do you?"

Though he makes an honest effort at masking it, his Irish accent slips with his words.

I nod, still not meeting his gaze.

He takes my chin in his hand and thrusts it up, forcing me to meet his ocean blue eyes. "I'm no good for you, Trice. You shouldn't be here."

"What do you mean you're no good for me?"

"I mean what I said. After what you saw last time you were here, of me..." He chases the words before he settles on, "a drunken mess. That was such a shitty way for you to spend your birthday, and I hate that I'm the one responsible for putting you through that."

I recount the dreadful events of that day, how the promise of threat in Jack's note loomed over me. How he blackballed my bestie from spending time with me, and then the...procedure that nearly took my life. My sixteenth birthday was postmarked with so much pain, and the only light through that dark day existed when I nurtured Kale. How could he have thought I held anything against him?

"Kale." I choked out, placing my hands on his bare chest. "Stop it. Stop all of this blaming yourself. It's not your job to take care of me. Besides, I'm the one who failed you! When all of that happened with Devin's little brother, I..."

He tightens calloused hands around mine. "Trice, stop it."

"I should have been there for you!" I shout as hot tears spike my eyes. "You turned into a hermit, and I should've fought you more. Fought to be by your side. Fought to stay the friend you needed through that. I'm so worthless!"

"Quiet." Kale demands as his cold blue eyes pierce mine. For a moment, time stills as we stare into each other, our souls seeking the elixir for our shared pain.

I feel slight tremors rocketing through his touch as he squeezes my hand to his chest.

"Aunt Scarlet!" He calls over his shoulder as a gust of wind whips between us.

"Yes, Kale? Do we have a visitor?" The soft voice emanates from the living room, I guess, but the lady makes no moves to come to the door when called.

Kale's eyes return to mine, and my breath hitches as they drop to study my nose, then mouth.

"Yes." He answers Aunt Scarlet after a time, eyes lasering into me. "For a couple of days. Get her some dinner, will you?"

"No worries!" I call into the house to the woman I came over here so jealous over. "I don't want to bother–"

Before I can finish my objection, Kale pulls me into the warm house. There's no sight of the Aunt Scarlet he was speaking to a moment ago as he drags me upstairs and into his bedroom.

"We've only been texting since July, when I last saw you." He stated as if piecing together some mystery as he paced. "Now you show up, out of the blue. I have a feeling this visit has nothing to do with the Early Grad Presentation you gave yesterday."

Again, not a question, but I shake my head. "No. It isn't."

"I know there's a lot between us, Trice. A lot we need to talk about if we're meant to truly be friends this time around."

I nod, my spirits lifting. "I know. I want to open up, Kale. Tell you everything because you've been the only light in all this darkness these past few months. I'm here to put up a fight."

He quirks a brow at that, pausing. "To fight?"

"Yep." I say resolutely, approaching him until our chests touch. "To be by your side. To stay there, where I always belonged."

A haunted look passes in his eyes as he regards me. "No, Trice. I've done so much wrong. I'm not worthy. I'm so fucked in the head, Jen keeps me on round-the-clock watch whenever she's not home. Like Aunt Scarlet."

I grimace as the memory and comprehension of Jen's question resurfaces when I find him drunk and unconscious.

I grab his chin, forcing him to meet my eyes. "You stop it. You are worthy. And I'm here. I'm here."

His tortured face meets mine, and we stare at each other in silence for a beat before he pulls me roughly into his chest and his lips crash onto mine. The kiss, like before, is demanding yet soft. Except, there's no alcohol smells radiating off his breath or through his pores. Oh no. This Kale is totally sober. And from the insistent flesh that hardens beneath his sweatpants and stabs my belly, he's totally in his right mind.

"Now." He whispers, a faint trace of humor and challenge in his tone. "Tell me why you're really here."

I recount the events of this morning, of the heated encounter between Mom and I before she threw the white package at me. The hate in her eyes I saw there transformed her. Made me shiver from the intensity, but also awakened a defiant piece of Trice from the ashes. Like a phoenix rising, I strengthen my back to mimic the strength I needed to get through this next part. To voice the shameful desire and ache that lived in my heart that could, very well, be my downfall.

I take another deep breath before staring him dead in his suspicious ocean blues. "I want a baby."

30

A quarter for your thoughts

A knock sounds at his bedroom door after I blurt my confession as if on cue. Kale's eyes saucer and I feel his absence immediately when he jerks away.

"No need to come downstairs, honey." Aunt Scarlet calls beyond the door. "I left your plate out here. Grab the tray when you're ready and call me if you want dessert. I made cheesecake."

"Thank you," Kale responds to her, the terror on his face and in his voice matching.

His legs wobble violently as he stumbles back onto the queen-sized mattress I remembered making out with him on. In fact, they shake so bad concern replaces the fear of his rejection for a moment as I close the distance between us.

"Stay back." He barks, throwing a hand up. "Th-this happens from time to time. I just need a minute."

I remain silent as I wait for the go-ahead to breathe again. Once his breathing evens and his body steadies, he collapses onto the bed.

I tiptoe toward him until I'm fully seated adjacent to his sweaty body.

"Permission to speak?" I chirp, a lame attempt at humor.

He gives a wry chuckle. "You've said plenty. Always finding new ways to throw me off my feet, huh?"

"I don't mean to," I chortle, falling beside him and into his open arms.

He encircles his arms around me before crooning, "Looks like we've both got some explaining to do, eh?"

I inhale sharply before speaking. "I want to tell you everything, Kale. I think it's time."

He stares into the empty air only nodding.

And so, after a few hesitations and inward battling, I tell him. Tell him everything. About the havoc Devin wreaked with his disappearance, my newfound then lost friendship with Nora, specific details I never expressed regarding the EGP, as well as the ordeal with Jack Burn.

Hours pass by, and after polishing off the delicious meal Aunt Scarlet prepared for me, I exhale a large whoosh of air.

"I nicknamed her Yara," I whispered, squeezing my eyes shut at the memory of the baby taken from me.

Kale remained silent as I regaled my secrets, told him all the tales I'd previously suffered through alone.

My chest is tight, I realize, as the burden of those events created a prison around my lungs and heart, making life so much more challenging enduring them alone.

"Why tell me that?" Kale's words leak cold menace, confusing me. "You're telling me that bastard forced you to get an abortion by threatening your life? Is that what you're saying to me?"

We're now sitting pretzel style on the floor, facing each other as we talk in silence.

I avert my eyes away from his intensity. "I had to. I didn't want anyone else to get hurt because of me. I only remember fragments of it, to be honest. He threatened to hurt me and Devin if I didn't."

"That's not the fucking point, Trice!" He growls. "He threatened your life. Violated your body in such an unforgivable way, then forced you to go through it alone. I'll kill him!"

"Kale, listen—"

"All this time!" He roared, punching the wall beside the bed. Unlike last time at Nora's party, the wall doesn't give, but I notice the bright red blood splash across his knuckles when he pulls back. "All this time...I thought you got involved with Burn because you were naive, a silly girl following him like a lost puppy in Devin's absence."

"Hey." I croon, chasing his eyes until they meet mine. "I'll be okay. Me and Jack are done. I'd never go back to that psycho...if only that were the worst of it. There's still so much awful he'd put me through."

"You did what you felt you had to. To survive." He stated plainly, wrapping his arms around me.

I return the hug, and speak into his shoulder. "I did. I needed to be sure there were no comebacks on me or Devin or anyone else I love. But I gotta know."

"Yeah?" He asks huskily.

"Why did you send us those nasty text messages? To Jack and I, I mean."

A minute ticks by before he answers, still holding me. "Devin asked me to keep you safe before he...left. I had to think of some way to keep you away from that gang shit, because he knew you'd dig deeper and get involved with that if it came to it. I, um, figured those texts would scare you away from the whole ordeal, so I bought a burner phone and sent you both those text messages. Then I saw you went to Jack, the same dude who'd I seen more than a time or two hanging out with Latisha or slipping drugs to certain students in the halls. It didn't take a rocket scientist to see that he'd gotten in deep with the 590's. I failed though. I failed you and Devin."

"Sweetie," I breathed, squeezing him tight before pulling apart to meet him squarely. "You did what you had to, too. And you're right. I love Devin. There was no force in hell that would have stopped me from helping him. Approaching Jack was my choice, though, Kale. If anything, I failed you! Remember, I abandoned you during a time you needed a friend the most. After Clifford did what he did...you shrank away from me. I felt the distance grow between us, but felt it wasn't my place to try to heal you. You completely iced me out..." My words taper off due to the lump of pain that forms in my throat. I remembered those cold nights, laying awake and praying for his welfare.

"I, uh, was in therapy." He muttered dreadfully into my neck. "Those pages you saw in my room that night were exercises my shrink taught me to familiarize myself with the victims. She recommended I write notes, descriptions, and details about them in order to honor them in some way. I felt like, still feel, it was all my fault it happened. After it happened, I visited Michael's elementary school pretending to be his relative. I knew his teacher saw through the bullshit, that me and him looked nothing alike, but I think she took pity on me. She probably noticed me from the news as the monster's spawn, but still gave me the details of the kid's funeral, told me about what kind of person he was. She said he loved dinosaurs, science, and playing outside. I happened to show up when she was cleaning out his cubby to prepare to turn over to his family, and she insisted I take one of his favorite toys. I accepted the green t-rex, and try to keep it with me always to remind myself of who I am. Of who he was: a person, with dreams and hopes. I keep that toy to stay accountable. To remind myself that, even though that monster's long gone, I'll forever pay for his sins, all because of the blood we share."

I remember Michael's huge grin and the pride he took in his knowledge of dinosaurs, and my heart aches, but I don't dare interrupt him.

"I was able to track Devin down eventually. I got his number from Ty, and began texting him. We kept in contact while he was on the run, and I wanted to be there for him as a friend, like my therapist said, to atone. He ignored my messages for the first few months, but responded when I offered him money."

"Money?"

"Yeah," He choked out. "Clifford was killed in prison a few months into his confinement. Apparently, one of his cellmates shivved him after he started bragging about his kills, of his need to kill again. His cellmate lost a child in a similar way that landed Cliff in there, so he dealt with him and gladly accepted the additional charges on his life sentence. His life insurance company called Jen and informed us that he left a policy open on his own behalf to be paid out to her. Twenty thousand dollars. Jen told me to do with it what I wanted, so I sent every dime of it to Devin. In no way does it atone for the monster's crime, but I figured helping him in some way would still matter. Little by little, he'd move to a different safe house, and I'd send him some cash to the bank account of his choice."

He shifts in his seat before continuing, as if the words caused physical pain as he spoke.

"I...I can't explain the relief that hit me when the prison told us the news. I cried for two days straight. You have no idea how good it felt to not have to keep looking over my shoulder. Fearing his return even though it was a legal impossibility. That's how fear gets you, there's no logic to it. No rationale. Hey, hey, no crying baby."

I don't realize I'm crying until my chest quakes from the sobs that threatened me since the start of our conversation. The wetness drenches his naked shoulder, causing him to pull us apart.

"I'm crying because I know that pain. I know that fear. I live with it every day since what happened that night. That birthday show, he called it. I'm so fucking scared and tired of looking over my shoulder. I have nightmares of him reappearing, in my window demanding I give him my body or some other part of my soul. To know that you deal with these same feelings..."

He places a gentle peck on my forehead. Then nose. Then hovers his lips before mine as he murmurs. "Let it out, Sunshine. I see that you've held a lot of this inside for a long time. I want you to release it. But don't cry for me. It kills me to see you shed tears over me."

Almost as if it needed permission, my body broke down completely. There are so many things I want to tell him. I want to tell him how much I care for him, value his presence, and devotion to my wellbeing in spite of all that transpired. I want to thank him for bearing his emotional baggage, same as me, and listening without judgment as my soul works itself out. There's still so much I need him to know, but in the end, all I can manage is, "Thank you." before curling into his arms.

The glimmers of dawn shines through the window, but we lay down as if finally being able to rest with our secrets in the ether. We drift into a peaceful sleep in each other's arms. I'm so comfortable, and emotionally sated that I barely realize that our clothes have disappeared. We spoon, flesh against flesh, and surrender our bodies, minds, and hearts to the much needed sleep.

I have the most erotic dream, however. I imagine Kale on top of me, rubbing his hard chest into my small, budding breasts. My nipples tighten and an unknown wave of wetness floods my lower channel at the slight pressure rubbing against my slit. He growls, low and promising and the rumbling sends delicious vibrations through my womb. My pussy is a sopping wet mess when he rears up and stares into my eyes.

"I miss you, Sunshine." He rasps, his eyes and face darkened with desire.

Another slide against my clit forces me into reality. This was no dream.

The afternoon sun shines brightly through the blinds, illuminating the space enough for me to grasp the full scene in front of me. Or, rather, on top of me.

Kale, the real Kale, covers my body with his, staring down at me through stormy blue eyes and fisting his flesh between our legs.

"Kale...what is..." I moan, barely able to tamp down the desire and butterflies in my belly from the anticipation.

He nudges his head inside my core again, making me shiver and squeal. "I accept." Is all he says.

I frown, trying to hold on to the remaining strains of reason between the lust fog. "What? Accept...what?"

"I will give you a baby. I accept your offer." He rubs against my clit again, sending rivers of desire through me and a fresh wave of desire to my clenching pussy.

My mind fights to remember, to force reason into the conversation, until the previous night's events float back. The memory of me standing at the Irish Prince's front door demanding he put a baby in me.

Before embarrassment assails me, he strokes my clit with one of those long fingers of his.

"Kale!" I wail as lust grips my insides.

"Shhh." He lulls. "If the offer is still on the table, guide me. Guide me in you."

"No," I whine in desperation. "Just stick it in!"

He growls again, and I feel his dick twitch at my words. He holds back, however, going very still.

"I won't do that. I'll give you this baby, Trice, but this needs to be your choice, too. Let me know you choose this, with me, and guide me in."

A pained tear rolls down my face from the frustration, but also from the tenderness in his voice. I hear his love for me, the love he always harbored for me even when I didn't love myself. This reminds me of my own strength as I gather my resolve.

With a fretful hand, I grab his dick.

"Hey," he says, clasping his hand over mine. "I'm not Jack. Remember, you have the power. You have a choice. You'll always have a choice with me, lovely."

His words, his coaxing love spell, jolts my eyes open. The fear melts away as I guide his hard length into my warm sheath, my mind reeling from the fullness of him once he's fully seated in me.

"We fit." Kale mutters sharply, stilling inside instead of rutting the same way Jack did when we had sex.

"Thank you, Kale." I moan, my voice thick with emotion as he begins a slow grind within me.

"Thank you, Patrice. I love you to death. Please keep me here."

I don't have to ask him to explain that last statement, because my heart understands it perfectly. I'd always love him, heal him, same as he did me. For a change, we both held each other, keeping our hearts close together and loving in the light instead of from the shadows our secrets were bred.

31

Highway to hate

Three days pass without a hitch. They're so seamless, in fact, that I find myself sulking as Kale packs the rest of my overnight belongings into my pleather tote bag.

"You could help, you know?" He teases before chucking a Slipknot t-shirt I thrifted into the bag.

I stood up from the bed that got plenty of use for the duration of my visit to wrap my arms around him. "Oh, but then it wouldn't be as fun to watch. Not every day a girl gets a handsome Irish Prince to fold and pack her laundry."

"Super logical." He twists in my arms to return my hug and plant a savory kiss on my forehead. "I wish we could just skip school today."

"I know." I acquiesce, ignoring the flames his tender gesture ignited in my belly. "But, I've already blown my mom off enough the past few days. Don't want to add fuel to the fire by skipping school, too."

He groans. "You need to keep perfect attendance for your graduation program, too, right?"

It was my turn to groan. He was right. Since my presentation was pushed to November, I was under heavy scrutiny from the board, as perfect attendance was factored into their decision to permit my early graduation or not. Looking back, I remembered the shock I experienced when Counselor Jones summoned me and three other underclassmen to her office. Being as I sought to avoid the attention trouble attracted, the summons terrified me. Instead of the punishment I expected, she informed us that the school selected the three of us to participate in an Early Graduation Program that, if completed within the given timeframe and the standards strictly adhered to, awarded us the opportunity to graduate with full honors by the end of sophomore year. Another appealing award included two full years of college funded through the EGP board upon graduation. The offer was too tempting to overlook, and my parent's all but threw me into the program last year.

So, unfortunately, Kale was right. I needed perfect attendance this year to break free from the Newbern house way sooner than later.

I wince as reality creeps back into my mind. "You're right." I pull away from him, my sticky body yearning for the elixir of a hot shower.

"Where ya off to, Sunshine?" He drawls in that accent he frequently tries to hide. What a weird thing,

I think as I assess his curious blue eyes. I have half a mind to question him about it before he yanks me into his bare chest.

"I...um," I began, breathless. "I was just catching a quick shower before we headed out."

"Unacceptable." He rasps mirthlessly, hovering his lips a hair's breadth of a distance from mine.

"What? Why?"

A rakish grin curls his perfect face as he leans in close to my ear, nibbles on a lobe, and breathes, "Not without me."

I giggle, twisting out of his arms. "Kale, come on, we need to really get ready to head out or else we'll be late for homeroom."

I don't realize myself inching away from him until he stalks me into the door.

"So now you're interested in going to school?"

My back slams against the door with a sharp thud, knocking the wind out of me. He looked every bit the rakish prince I joked him to be, the hard set of his jaw and regained muscle definition that didn't exist there a couple of months prior when he lay in a drunken stupor.

"Isn't Jen home by now? Won't she care?" My voice is strangled and my throat dry as I take him in.

"She won't care." He answers, unflinchingly meeting my gaze and pinning me to the door. "Plus, she thinks you're good for me. I'll tell her it's part of my therapy."

Now that pisses me off. I don't join Kale in laughter, but punch him in the shoulder.

"The hell was that for, woman?" He demands, rubbing the affected flesh.

"You," I jab an accusatory finger at him. "Don't joke about that. Therapy is serious. It plays a serious stake in your mental welfare and could be the difference in healing you."

He retreats a step, and I notice the slight tremor that rocks through much more clearly now that he's naked. "Healing me? Trice, it's not chlamydia I'm suffering from. You can't just pop a pill and get rid of it. Besides, I can manage just fine on my own."

A pit forms in my stomach from the abrupt turn in the conversation. The previously hard piece of flesh now reduced to a limp mop string. "But you don't have to go it alone. Not anymore. You have me!"

"You don't get it, Trice. What could you know anyways?" He spits, fisting his dark hair.

"Excuse me?" I retort, affronted.

"You don't know shit about the kind of agony I suffer through. What it takes to wake up and face my day. Not everyone is privileged enough to grow up in the luxurious Newbern castle."

I gasp, covering my nude body from the onslaught of his ugly words and feeling too exposed all of a sudden. Anger, so raw and powerful, surges through me as I stomp toward him.

"Privileged? Castle? You think I don't know a thing about suffering? About loss? Huh?!" I'm screeching at him.

"Trice—"

"Shut up!" I roar, now backing him into a corner as I watch his face change from red and furious to pale and apologetic. He must realize the implications of his actions, because he reaches out to pull me into his embrace.

"No!" I slap his hands away. "It's time you understand where I'm coming from, Kale."

"Trice, I'm so sorry. I was just angry when I said the whole thing about loss and—"

I can barely contain the hot tears that slip down my cheeks as I fan his apologies away. "I told you my story, of the hell Jack put me through these past few years, and I'm sorry. Sorry for all the wrong life has done to you, but don't you dare compare. I thank you for offering this baby to me, truly I do, but hear me out. I will not be intimidated by another guy, or anyone else, ever again. I became a slave to my love for you and Devin before I could realize I was in a self-esteem drought. I want to be by your side, and I love you all the same, but I won't tolerate being on the receiving end of your wrath towards your dad. If that's gonna be the case," I stalk towards the open tote bag and begin throwing clothes inside it furiously. "I'll be on my way."

His hand shoots out to cuff my wrist.

"Kale…" I growl.

"Trice, fuck, I'm sorry. I'm always fucking things up."

"Get off of me, Kale." I yank at his hand confinement to no avail. "Seriously dude. I'm not here to be your punching bag."

Stunning me, Kale sinks to his knees. He wraps his arms around my middle where I feel the dampness of his face against my belly.

"Please, don't go." He pleads miserably.

"Kale–"

"You're right!" He interjects sharply. "I'm taking this anger out on you when I should be dealing with it. Sorry to toy with your feelings and insinuate you don't know loss. You do, Sunshine, and I'm the dick who used that against you. Just," his voice hitches, "please don't walk out of here angry. Don't leave."

***

We do end up showering together, but it's an honest one. The steamy shower sex I envisioned us having like the ones in the movies straight up doesn't happen. It's more along the lines of a tender scrub of each other's obvious parts before we exit, dry off, and dress. We're completely silent as we get into my yellow beetle car.

"Did you want to drive us?" I ask, breaking the quiet and casting hopeful eyes on the stoic prince in the passenger seat.

He winces before responding. "Um, I just got my license back, so technically I can. Took a joyride with a gut full of pale ale last year and..." His regretful voice trails off as I piece together the meaning there. "Jen nor my therapist think it wise for me to operate a vehicle right now."

"Okay," I mutter before starting the ignition.

There's an unexpected rush of morning traffic as we merge onto the highway leading to Easton. Hating the strain of the awkward silence tugging between us, I lurch for the radio dial and sigh in relief as Lil Wayne's throwback, "How to Love," fills the car. The traffic eases some and I resume the mindless route to our high school. I'm barely able to see the parking lot clearly due to the tears streaming down my eyes as I listen to Lil Wayne serenade the ambitious woman with broken dreams turned stripper.

Kale and I only sit there, as the song continues, silent and unmovable stones in the emotionally charged car. Sobs wrack my chest by the time the rapper gets to, "you deserve the best, you're beautiful."

"Trice." Kale breathes in an anguished tone as he clasps my hand in his.

The song fades out, leaving us to ponder the lyrics and argument preceding it. I'm tired, I think, so tired of being angry. Of looking over my shoulder to prepare for the next fight that awaited me the next day. I look at Kale, and his face is just as weary as mine as he meets my gaze.

"Trice," he repeats. "I love you. And I'm sorry. Let me show you."

I frown at him, confused, as he brings my hand up to his lips. "I promise to try to be worthy of your love, okay?"

I gulp, my heart aching from his words. "Oh, sweet-ie."

I melt when he plants smoldering kisses on each of my fingers. "I refuse to be one of those crooks, abusing your love and treating you like shit. I'll be better."

Light fills my heart as his rendition of Lil Wayne's song brings an inevitable smile from me. I lean across the arm rest, hovering my lips in front of his same as he often did with me.

"Be mine." I say, low and sultry.

This was what he needed. I understood now that after all this time he was the one loving me from the shadows while I chased after Dark Devin, the guy I thought the impossible dream and Jack, the ruthless, power-hungry, gangbanger. Kale has, and always had, love me for the nerdy tomboy I was at heart. But I never chose him, like he did me. Another level of comprehension seizes me when I recall his words the other night, him atop my body and imploring me to choose this life with him.

"Yours?" He questioned, bewildered.

He says something else, but I don't hear it as I exit the car. I noticed students piling into the building, but the school entrance remained as crowded as usual due to the morning rush.

I take in an apprehensive breath, not from fear of other's opinions of this next action, but from Kale's reaction. Of his rejection.

I open the passenger seat door and stare down at him with watery eyes. "Come on, let's go."

He still looks slightly confused as he grabs my extended hand and exits the car fully.

"Yours?" He repeats.

I nod, grabbing hold of his hands for dear life and love for him. "Yes. Be my boyfriend. I chose you. Like I should have done two years ago, but was too afraid."

He goes ramrod stiff as he focuses tortured eyes onto the ground. "Are you serious?" He asks gravely.

I squeeze his shaking hand, to steady him and holding it as an anchor amidst the sea of anxiety swirling through me. Students are open-mouth staring at us at this point.

"I am." I confirm.

We're tardy at this point, but I'm not concerned in the least, because the small smile he gives me makes it worth it. A single tear slides down his face for a second. He wipes it and pulls me into him.

After a kiss that makes me drunk with ecstasy, we enter Easton Rogue High School, hand-in-hand as boyfriend and girlfriend, boldly imprinting our status and love for each other on full display.

I spot several eyes on us as Kale escorts me to home-room, which I'm super late for at this point. Tyrone Zelman and Sasha Kersey, who were engaged in an intense lip locking session against the lockers, stare in open shock at Jack's old girl and the reticent, ostra-cized, loner. There's a few others I notice before we reach the classroom, including Mike Lakewood, star quarterback, and Pilar Daniels, a third of the eligible EGP participants alongside me and another nerdy kid, Sorin Dempsey. None of their stares, however, are a match for the one that chills my blood as they cross the hall past us.

Latisha Millard glowers directly at me, looking just as regal as her late brother and namesake. A long arm wrapped around her shoulders, one I know all too well, prompts my eyes to glide up towards the man, the devil, who took everything from me.

Jack keeps his stony eyes on me as he leans down to deliver an overly-indulgent kiss to Latisha. Sympathy flickers in my chest for the girl, as I remembered the confinement of those strong arms slung possessively over me. I remember Jack, a non-student, making a point to walk me to my first period class every day last year, same as he did now with Latisha. I thought it was loving protectiveness, the reason he escorted me to and from school, but now I knew better. Knew the surveillance scheme that was the reality of our entire relationship. He needed to keep a constant eye on me for his plans to work. Was Latisha in trouble? I flinch at the memory of her brother in that chair, bloody and near-death and pleading for his life just as Jack took it from him.

I don't register how I appear until I feel Kale's hand on my shoulder.

"You okay?" He asks, following my mortified gaze to the 590 royal couple face-fuck each other a few feet from us. "Want me to talk to him?"

"No!" I yelp, scaring the students lingering around us. I clear my throat and force a smile I don't feel. "It's fine, babe. He's nobody. Not even worth the time to acknowledge. Just...can we pretend he doesn't exist?"

Kale trains a hard glare on Jack before speaking. "All right, Sunshine. I'll come find you after homeroom, okay? Text me if anything goes sideways."

I grab his chin, forcing him to meet my eyes before kissing him. "Thank you, my love. See you at lunch?"

"Sure thing." He kisses my forehead. "Now, go do great things."

I can almost feel Jack's icy glare in my back when I turn to enter the classroom.

32

Looming in midnight

My mind wanders during my final period, Spanish, as the images of Jack's cold hating eyes return to my memory. He agreed to let me walk away from his insipid dominion over my life, that my relationship and former status as his top girl in the gang was dissolved since I proved my "loyalty" to him. I was no idiot, however, and I watched my back closely knowing there really was no way to escape the lethal 590's. Every day I woke up, I awaited another menacing text from him, telling me to go outside and bend to whatever request. When no text came, I'd sigh in relief, but was mindful to not get too comfortable. Spending that time with Kale was the safest I'd felt in the two years since Devin's departure.

A pang of pressure presses into my bladder as I wait for a gap in between Ms. Sanchez's lecture to raise my hand. She's one of those really insistent teachers that, once they got on a roll with a lecture there was no stopping them.

I sink back into my chair dejectedly chiding myself for my negligence. I held my bladder since I last saw Kale at lunch an hour ago, where he insisted I drink all of my fluids to support our soon-to-be baby's development. That launched into a playful back-and-forth about his lack of prenatal knowledge and female physiology that consumed the rest of our lunch hour I'd planned to squeeze in a pee break.

Unable to deny the call of nature, I creep out of the room once Ms. Sanchez turns her back to us to discuss complex compound sentences.

"You are excused, señorita Patrice." She calls in amusement as I tiptoe into the hall.

I flash an apologetic grin and a *"Lo siento,"* as I sprint to the girls restroom. Judging from the laughter in her tone, I figured she took a comical pity on my pee-pee dance and let me go.

Crazy girl, I berate myself as I damn-near fly down the hall and around the corner to the blessed place. Relief was so close...

Once I reach the bathrooms across campus near the janitors closet known for being the cleanest, I lunge for the door knob.

Only to stop short when I get a glimpse at the unthinkable.

My eyes work overtime to process the sight a mere four or five feet from me. The painful sting of my

bladder is drowned out from the disbelief and astonishment as I study the tall, tan skinned boy leaving the
adjacent boys' restroom.

My throat dries as a wash of repressed emotions
surge to the forefront. Confusion. Wonder. Curiosity.
Rage. So much rage, but also relief to witness him
alive and intact.

His brown eyes size me up innocently, recognition
not yet hitting him as instantaneously as it did me. I
assume he realizes who I am from my petrified state
and horrified eyes I felt saucering as they examined
his shorter braids.

"Trice?" Devin croaks, wincing down at me.

"Devin?" I parroted, tightening my thighs to hold
the urine in.

"That really you? You're going to Easton, too?" He
asks, a tortured expression on his perfect face.

God, how many times, how many nights, did I pray
to see this face? Pray to every god in the sky to protect
him on his escape? Unshed tears blur my eyes as I clear
my throat to answer him.

"It's me, yeah. I...what...how are you here?" I end up
stuttering.

Michael's miserable face materializes just then; I
recognize the deep red flush of anger and frustration
fill his tan cheeks, his knuckles clench and unclench
in unchecked fury. His body quakes before the inevitable tantrum consumes him, and I half expect

him to faint and convulse his rage in lieu of verbally communicating his feelings.

However, the boy in front of me isn't Michael Masters.

It's Devin Cooper, looking every bit as distressed as his late baby brother mid-tantrum.

I blink in sheer surprise at the sight of the tears that pour down his face. I'm not sure what I expected from him, but it sure wasn't this.

"Trice..." he croaks between sobs. "I'm so fucking glad you're okay."

He reaches out for me, and the Trice who would have leapt into his waiting arms is long gone. Instead, I dodge his extended arms as if he was contagious.

"Of course, I'm okay." I respond, cold, clipped, and inwardly coaching myself to keep cool. "No thanks to you."

"I know." He agrees, "I always knew Kale was the man for the job. I knew he'd keep you safe from the shit I started."

"You're wrong!" I growl, stomping into his personal space. "I'm perfectly safe because of *me!* I'm so sick of everyone thinking I'm this princess who needs protecting. After all this time, it's been me taking care of myself. Get the fuck out of my way."

I try to push his massive frame away from the restroom door, but he doesn't budge. Only straightens and zeroes mournful eyes on me.

"My tough girl. Of course you don't need protection. My bad for that." He admired.

I have to chase the easy feelings away as I listen to
him. It's easy to smile stupidly at his possessive use
of "my girl." All too easy to throw myself into his long
arms and stay there. Somewhere in the recesses of my
unconscious mind where logic lived, I knew we were
no good for each other. A bitter thought churns my
stomach when I consider my body's reaction to him.
This was conditioning. An unconscious Pavlovian response to poisonous stimuli.

"How am I supposed to respond to that?" I snort.

And queue the infamous Cooper smile. I can't help
but squirm under his dark stare.

"Today's my first day. Just needed to use the bathroom before going to my last class." He says in a
hushed tone.

"What class you got?"

"Spanish. With that sexy ass Ms. Sanchez."

I roll my eyes at the return of the perpetual playboy.
"Still the same old Devin, I see. Smooth as ever."

His lazy smile morphs into a grimace at that. He
scratches his braids nervously. "No. That Devin's
dead."

At the haunted look on his face, I stop to study him
beyond the dazzling pretty boy smile. I notice he's
sporting a plain white t-shirt, baggy blue jeans, and a
pair of worn Timberlands. He appeared a stark con-

trast from the privileged pretty boy I grew to adore a short time ago.

He shifts the weight from one foot to another and leans his back against the restroom door.

"What happened to you, Devin?" My voice trembles with the question. "While you were gone, I mean."

"I ain't telling you about that. It's...not something I want to remember. But I am sorry to put you through that shit, for real, Trice. I may not give a fuck 'bout what happens to me, but I do care about you. You're the best thing that's happened to me."

I flush bright red, averting my eyes to hide the emotion that surged behind them. I don't want to go down this road, I ruminate, as I search desperately for a subject change.

"You guys living in the same house?"

"Uh, yeah. Just the three of us now. Me, Vonnie, and Helen. But we won't be staying there too much longer." He grumbles.

"Why not?"

"Not a good environment for Yvonne. I'm trying to get her back to herself. She ain't been the same since...everything. I catch her zoning out a lot, not really focusing on anything. She lost so much. First Mikey, now Quin..."

He starts and breaks off, speaking of the man I remembered being fatally shot in an abandoned warehouse. Guilt and utter disgust hits me full force at the memory, at what Jack wanted me to do. I was the reason he was back, here in his hometown but without his stepfather. Tragedy taking another chunk from his family.

"We moved around a lot, but ended up at my Uncle Troy's house in Jersey. Quincy, uh, ain't around no more. Lung cancer."

My heart clenches at the lie, and it makes me wonder if it was he who discovered Quincy's body. "I'm so sorry, Dev."

"Don't wanna talk about it. Don't really wanna go there. All you need to know is this." He leans down and swoops me into his arms. My hard nipples scrape his hard chest, making me swoon a bit. "You're mine."

"Huh? Stop talking nonsense, dude." The instant mood change makes my head swim.

The lazy grin returned as he tightened his arms around me. "Really, Trice. You can't see us together? I think we was always meant to do this shit together."

"What shit?" I ask suspiciously.

"Life." He sighs, then kisses my forehead. "Mami, come on. I'm back now, for good. Let me make you feel good."

I'm on fire everywhere by the time our lips meet. There it is again, I chide, that pavlovian response in me that exists to give in to him. The Dark Devin that helped me build Trice, the confident alter ego I lived by and often consulted in situations like this.

"D-Devin…" The whisper comes off more throaty than I intend. "Stop."

One instant, his hands were all over me, exploring regions of my body I promised to Kale mere hours ago. The next, his arms fall at his sides and he retreats a step.

"I know you want this." He stated. "Know you need this. After all the pain I drug you through, I think you deserve to feel good. But I ain't gonna force you. I seen real monsters, and I ain't that. If you want this, want me to give you the loving you deserve from me," He squints his mahogany eyes and licks his lips as he regards me. "You need to choose me."

I blink a few times to clear my head and process his statement and jump away from him. "Devin, I love you, but–"

"But you don't trust me." He cut in. "I'll earn it. For real, Trice." The bell shrills, robbing me of any chance to respond before kids pour into the thin hallways and creating a distance between us.

"Wait!" I call out for him as he begins to retreat down the hall. "This isn't fair!"

He was long gone before I could protest any further. Fuck. This truly wasn't fair. For Devin to just reenter my life and turn it upside down with the words I craved to hear a while ago. My secret longing for a love and fulfilling life with the darkly damaged boy outweighed everything at one point, but this wasn't right. Not with the pledge I made to Kale, the other love of my life and potential baby daddy.

I ran to the toilet, my bladder reaching a dangerous level of pain as I flopped onto the cool porcelain.

My logical mind knew it was wrong to enjoy that traitorous kiss. It also knew I needed some advice, someone to vent these feelings that choked me with their intensity.

I fished around my pocket and brandished my yellow iPhone. Since we hadn't spoken since July, I was not aware of her current class schedule, but I knew she was probably on her way home after that dismissal bell rang. I prayed silently as the line trilled to hear the calm voice of my Beach.

"Nora?" I called, my heart lifting at the prospect of reconnecting with my abandoned bestie. "Let me just start off by saying–"

"Who this?" A gruff male voice demanded from the opposite end of the line. Tortured whimpers in the background came into audible range on his end of the call. "Who the fuck is this calling my bitch's phone?"

I squeaked in fright before disconnecting the call. Fear invaded my body like warm acid as I worked to match the face and mocking laughter to that voice. The 590 lieutenant.

Luther Noonan.

***

"Get the *fuck* out of this house!" A shrill familiar voice yells as I pull into the driveway. After dropping Kale off at home with promises to see each other later for a dinner date at Jin-Tama, I finally pull myself together to make the short drive home.

I'm greeted with chaos, however, as the voice is so sharp and so piercing I can make out the threat clearly from inside my car. My breath catches at the voice, or voices, that I hear intersecting each other in the raucous argument from within the Newbern house.

It's Mom.

Panic laces through my veins at the prospect of danger. Was it Jack? His haunting image, smiling menacingly as he throws a possessive arm around Latisha assails my mind. Was that a threat? A promise of danger to come to me or my family if I crossed him? Or maybe a random intruder decided to hit my family in the late evening. This idea gave way to no comfort as I sprinted dumbly into the house. I raised my fist to the unknown threat, but paused when I caught sight of the scene in the living room.

My heart sinks.

It's Mom and Dad standing at the bottom of the staircase. Mom is roaring expletives and threats to someone at the upper floor. Dad is silent, but his arms are crossed and he's probably sporting the same glare as Mom.

"What's going on?" I shout.

Neither turn to me when Mom answers. "Your brother seems to think he can bring that sinful shit into this house! The Lord knows your crimes and will rejoice in your repentance. It's not too late." I fear she's half talking to me, half hurling the ugly words to Manny.

Manny appears then, a large suitcase in his arms. "I'll be gone by the end of the day." Is all he says, numbly and matter-of-fact as he stomps down the steps.

"Good deal," Dad warns ominously as he brushes by him. "I can't believe you'd have the nerve to bring that fagottry into this family. I always suspected something wasn't right with you coming up. Now I know."

Manny's jaw flexes at Dad's insults, but he remains quiet as he walks towards me. "I knew this was a bad idea, but I tried." He uttered in defeat, a sad smile on his face as Mom and Dad berated him from the staircase. "I tried to be brave like you and stay here for your sake."

"Manny!" I whimper, tears flowing freely as the agony set in. I hugged him tight. "Please don't go...forget them!"

He ruffles my hair like used to do when we were kids just then. "I'll be all right. I was waiting for you to get home before saying goodbye. Try to take care of yourself for me, okay?"

Though I hate it, the situation as well as our spiteful parents in that moment, I knew I had to do this. Had to let him walk out with whatever dignity left that Mom and Dad sought to destroy.

I nod and place a brief kiss on his cheek. "Okay, but where will you go?"

"To hell if he doesn't pray for forgiveness!" Mom shrieks behind us.

My brother, being the mature guy they'd groomed him to be, ignores her interjection.

"Spain. I've accepted an internship there and Bruno has family in Barcelona we'll be staying with."

"Please come back to me, Manny. Just...please." I beg, needing one of my only confidants and friends to be near.

He shakes his head, and this time, turns to our parents as he bites out, "This is the end for us. I hope, when judgment day comes, that God will take mercy on your loathsome souls. Forget I even existed, all right?"

His words freeze Mom into place, and I know this hits the target. Her eyes saucer as she shouts, "Baby, wait! Don't be angry with us!"

She's standing right behind him now, her hand on his shoulder. "I can call the pastor and see if he can stop by and talk to you. There's all kinds of special programs for boys with your sickness. You just need to be healed..."

Manny grabs Mom's hand, kisses it, and meets her eyes. "I'll be sure to send a postcard when I receive news of your deaths in the future. After all, I don't attend the funerals of strangers since that's who you'll both be to me after today. Understand?"

Mom rears back from the shock, and I flinch a little from the callousness of his tone.

"Good riddance, fairy." Dad sneers, unmoving from the staircase edge.

Manny blinks away a tear before meeting my eyes. "Take care, little sis. And thank you for making my childhood a happy one in spite of the monsters that raised us. Do me a favor, though."

"Of course," I reply.

He embraces me tight, kisses me on the forehead and whispers to me, "Carve out a little piece of whatever makes you happy in this world, and keep it. Fight for *your* own happiness, okay?"

Epilogue

Virginia - Five years later

"Mommy, can me and Busta play with the older kids?" My daughter's angelic voice cuts through my reverie as I stare out the window of our rental car.

I turn to face the honey-skinned four year old in her car seat with Busta snuggling closely at her side.

The sight fills my heart and I find myself having to hold back tears when I answer her. "If older kids are there, then yes. I don't have a problem with you and Busta playing with them. It'll have to be tomorrow though, sweetie, since it'll be night time when we get to Ms. Hattie's."

"Tomorrow?!" She whines, fisting the yellow-ish/green dinosaur figurine in her little hand. "But you said we could play when we get out of the car! Mommy!"

"Katrice." I warn, keeping my tone light as I eye her from the passenger seat. "We agreed that you'd play outside in the daytime and only if there are other children there and adults to watch after you."

She crosses her arms and grumbles something under her breath.

"I heard that," Kale warns from the driver seat. "Remember what we talked about, Katy? About how impolite it is to whisper amidst company?"

Katy remains stoic as she glares into the headrest.

"Where's my sweet girl?" Kale coaxes. "My sweet girl would never be mean to her Mommy, or keep secrets."

"Fine," she grumbles, conceding. "I said it's not fair that you and daddy get to play outside and I can't when we get there."

"Play outside?" I inquire, casting a curiously expectant look at my husband.

Kale chuckles. "The barbeque, she's referring to. Remember Mamma Dean said there's gonna be a 'big cookout' tonight to celebrate the wedding tomorrow?"

"Oh, right!" I utter, snapping my fingers in triumph as the memory of Devin's grandma's itinerary for the wedding comes back to me.

I was in the middle of a video conference when a knock came at my home office door. After excusing myself, I raced to answer it, and groaned when I witnessed the babysitter I was forced to hire last minute there.

"Sup, Tri-Tri!" Richard or "Wease," Kale's best friend, teases when I open the door. He's holding my daughter on his hip and an apron lined his front.

"Hi Mommy!" Katy greeted exuberantly.

"Hi, baby," I said to her, then turn a frown to her stubborn godfather/babysitter. "Wease, I told you not to disturb me for simple visits. My company is in the middle of a very important meeting right now, and I'm needed there to oversee it. Wait, what's that on your face?"

He giggled, wiping the white powder from his cheek. "Oh! Sorry, little Katy and I were trying to surprise you with some cupcakes."

"Uncle Wease let me eat some of the batter!" Katy squealed, putting her full checkered smile on display.

"Don't mean to interrupt, sister," Wease adds, glancing apologetically inside my office. "But Kale told us to tell you to check your phone. Said it's urgent and that he's been calling you since this morning."

A little pang of fear spikes in my chest, but I smile for Katy's sake. "Thanks, Wease. I appreciate your help today. I'll be sure to do that."

He readjusts Katy on his hip, before waving. "Oh, it's no sweat, I love hanging out with my little bud. Say bye bye to Mommy, Kate."

Without warning, Katy lurches forward and pins a kiss on my cheek. "Bye Mommy! Love you, always."

My sweet girl, I thought before kissing her cheek in response. "I love you always, too. Now go have fun with Uncle Wease, okay?"

Once they're long gone downstairs, I cross the room to where my phone rests on the windowsill charging.

Ugh, true to his word, there's eight missed calls from my persistent Irish Prince of a husband.

"Sunshine," Kale answers when I call his phone. "Where've you been? I've been trying to reach you all morning with the news."

"Sorry, babe." I lament. "The meeting ran longer than expected. It looks like they're thinking about downsizing the company and getting rid of all the Astro-physics interns. I'm arguing them down right now against letting that happen. I mean, can you imagine what all those kids are gonna do when they find out they're out of a job?"

I didn't realize how heated I was until Kale said, "I know that program means a lot to you, love. It's where you started out after you graduated high school and came to Wisconsin."

"I know right." I sulk, remembering the joyous times I spent as an undergrad intern in the aerospace department at GOzone. GOzone was the sustainability organization I only ever dreamed of interning when I started my Astronomy-Physics program at UW-Madison after running away from home. Hard work and the right amount of networking landed me the internship to fellowship track and I found myself as Manager of the Geological Conservation department upon graduating college. At twenty one, I now oversaw the very intern program I once worked at, and I hated the idea of delivering that news to the hundred-plus college interns.

"Give 'em hell." I can hear his smile through the phone and it's contagious, because it makes me grin and blush like a schoolgirl.

"I sure will, babe." I chant. "But what's this news you got?"

"Right," he clears his throat. "A lady called my office today and insisted on speaking to you."

"That doesn't sound ominous at all," I counter in wry amusement.

He doesn't laugh like I expect him to. "Um, she claims to be Devin's grandmother. She lives in Virginia. Ms. Hattie Carlson I believe she said her name was."

I gulp in utter surprise at hearing that name again after all these years.

"You there?" Kale probes in concern.

I nod. "Yes. I'm here."

"You okay?"

"I...I'm all right. What does she want?"

A pause, then he replies, "Apparently there's to be a wedding, and she wants you to be there. Said Yvonne entrusted her with sending the invitations."

I froze at that. "What? Why would Yvonne have a say in who's attending Devin's wedding?"

I hated the way my heart ached at the thought of Devin getting married.

"No, no. It's Yvonne that's getting married. Two weeks from now, in Virginia."

I can't help but perform the calculations in my head before I say, "Wait a minute. Yvonne's only eighteen, and already getting married? She's still just a kid."

A rich laugh sounds from his side. "Trice, you know we married super young, too?"

"And?" I cross my arms in righteous indignation. "Things were different for us. We'd already had a two-year-old and an apartment by that time and day-care sure wasn't paying itself!"

He's still amused when he responds. "You're right. But she's still an adult. And she's inviting you to her ceremony. I'm just calling to gauge if you're...prepared to see him again."

I know all too well who that "him" was he referred to. The dangerously dark teen who I gave my heart and body to after he made his epic return Sophomore year. Our complicated entanglement put a huge strain on my and Kale's relationship, and I squeezed my eyes together from the painful memories of everything that transpired. Kale's sudden and mysterious departure coupled with Helen delivering a nearly fatal gunshot wound to her son made my remaining days in DC hard to bear. There was only guilt, pain, and a serious feeling of forlorn when thoughts of Devin erupted in my mind.

Just like now: it was guilt's turn to rear her ugly head this time, though.

"I dunno," I breathe. "Do you think it's even right for me to attend? I'd already caused that family so much pain."

"First of all," my husband drawls in that deliberate way of his when honing in on a point. "I wouldn't let you go it alone. Both Katy and I would come with you."

I grimace. "Baby, you don't have to do that. I understand seeing him may be triggering for you, too."

"Well," he mumbled. "Maybe. But the need to support my wife outweighs any reservations I got about meeting Devin again."

The butterflies do their thing in my stomach at his sweet words.

"I'm game for whatever you choose, babe. But Ms. Hattie wants you to give her a call to discuss details further if you decide to attend. I told her—if you wanted to go—then I'd have you reach out." He informed me.

"Thanks, babe." I squeaked, uncertainty riding me hard. "I don't think I want to go, though."

"I figured you'd say that. Which makes this next part complicated, but still totally your decision, nonetheless."

"Kale McAllen," I groused. "What are you not telling me?"

A pause, then he blurts. "Ms. Hattie got my number from the website. She said she saw my photography work and wants me to shoot Yvonne's wedding."

"What?" I demand, pacing now.

Kale had done some serious growing up in the duration of our time together. He owned and operated
a very profitable photography business in Madison,
Sunshine Photography, where wealthy families and
college students made up most of his clientele base
since his office was situated in an affluent part of the
college town. His day job as Peer Support Specialist, however, consisted of providing substance abuse
counseling at an intervention program that doubled
as a homeless shelter. Quitting alcohol cold turkey
after we got married was a moving piece of his testi-
mony when he was invited to speaking events spon-
sored by Alcoholics Anonymous. He'd referred to his
drinking binges as "Hanging with Jack," referencing
the brown liquor brand he'd grown entirely too de-
pendent on.

However, pride and love, so strong, filled me now
whenever I thought of his fortitude and persistence to
end the cycle of abuse in his family. And as the years
went by, he proved to me, time and time again that
he chose me. Chose us and the little family we carved
out of survival and love.

"She offered a hefty amount to Sunshine Photography to cover the photos and videography for the
ceremony, and...I just thought you should know about
it."

I'm still stone cold silent after he finishes telling
me the insanely generous amount the kind old lady
offered.

He sighs, "I won't take the gig. Not at the expense of us. We're in this together, remember?"

"Of course I do," I take in huge gulps of air before stilling. "Can you give me her number?"

"Wait, what?" He queried in disbelief.

"This is a great opportunity for your business, babe. You're still a startup and just getting off the ground. I won't have you miss out on this because of me. So, shoot me her number and I'll keep you posted on how the conversation goes. Okay?"

Kale pauses a few analyzing seconds before my phone buzzes, alerting me of a text message.

"Sent it. But I mean it, Trice. We can simply say you're traveling or something for work and blow the whole thing off."

"I know," I muse.

"Okay," He chuffs. "Well, give her a call and tell me what happens. Later, Sunshine."

What "happens" after that phone call with Ms. Hattie, who insists we call her Mamma Dean, is a booked flight to Richmond for two weeks from then, a surprisingly cozy Airbnb, and rental car loaded to the gills with Kale's camera equipment, irate daughter, dog, and anxious AF wife sulking in the passenger seat.

I recall the cookout Ms. Hattie mentioned that would be taking place the night of our arrival and cringe. I had to remember this was for Kale, my hard working husband who outdid himself in providing for us. Booking more gigs like this one would definitely make our goal of becoming homeowners that much more real.

I feel a strong hand squeeze mine and toss a coy smile Kale's way.

"I'm all right, babe."

"Just making sure." He reassured me. "Not too late to turn around, you know?"

Now that makes me laugh. "Hell yeah it is! Don't get me wrong, I'm a little nervous, but not stupid. It'd be straight up irresponsible to turn back now after all this money we spent on flights and lodging."

"Bad word, Mommy!" Katy calls from the back. "You owe me a dollar."

I frown at her with feigned annoyance. "I owe you a dollar?"

"Yep," She nods proudly. "Daddy said I'm in charge of the swear jar this weekend."

I glare at my blushing husband. "Oh, really?"

"Yep!" She sings while toying with the green dinosaur. "He said he knew you would need it to be abosuntiful."

"Accountable," Kale corrects her, chuckling and turning to me. "And you do. You have a bad habit of cursing like a sailor when you're worked up."

I glare between the both of them, aghast. "Wow. I see you have me all figured out, huh? What if I promise to be on my best behavior the entire weekend?"

"Really?" He drawls wryly.

"You don't believe I can do it?" I muse, swatting him on the arm. "You watch, Kale McAllen. I'll be the picture of ladyhood and chaste diction."

He only shakes his head as he rounds a corner, leading to a long country road. There's a huge house at the end of it, and from where we are, there's a fire going and plenty of people in the front yard.

"Looks like we're here," Kale says as my breathing hitches.

"Fuck," I gasp, before pursing my lips and cursing myself for the action.

"That's another dollar Mommy!" I vaguely hear Katrice yip excitedly as Kale pulls the car into the line of vehicles on the property.

***

"Everybody, this here is Patrice, Kale, and their baby girl. Now, remind me again of your name, sugar?" Ms. Hattie, no—Mamma Dean, announces after she hunts us down from the car and drags us to the large crowd of extended family members standing around the fire pit.

Katy, being the shy girl she's always been, curls her face into my chest at the sudden attention.

"Her name is Katrice." I supply nervously, stroking her back in efforts to soothe her. "Sorry about that.

She's never been around this many people at once before."

Mamma Dean claps her hands excitedly. "That's all right! She's gonna get real used to the Carlson Crew soon enough. Y'all hungry?"

Kale speaks up, holding me tight against his side. "Yes, ma'am. We want to thank you for your business and opening your home to us this weekend."

"Quite the gentleman, you are!" She responds appreciatively, sizing my husband up in admiration. "As far as I'm concerned, y'all family. Come on over here let me fix y'all some food. Does baby girl like chitterlings?"

My stomach turns immediately at the southern delicacy I remembered Aunt Patty forcing me to eat with her as a kid.

I scrunch my nose at the memory and her offer. "No, sorry. She's not really a meat eater, to be honest. Are there ingredients here so that we can make her a PB&J?"

The entire Carlson Crew quiets and turns shocked stares my way. The feeling as if I'd said something gravely wrong overcomes me, and I fidget under the scrutiny.

"That baby don't eat meat?" Mamma Dean inquires, frowning in suspicion. "She allergic?"

"No." I blurt. "She's just never really taken to it, even as a baby. But pasta or something bready will do, if you have it. Or I can check her lunch bag and see if there's—"

"Nonsense," Mamma Dean persists, waving at me. "Vivian, can you fix this baby some collards and mac n' cheese?"

A rail thin white woman appears from the crowd. Her vibrant red hair makes her resemble Debra Messing.

"Sure thing," Vivian agrees. "Want me to take her? The kids are in the house having a slumber party while the adults party outside."

"Um," I utter nervously, adjusting Katy in my arms. "Would you like that, boo?" I ask her in a hushed tone.

"Can I take Busta with me?" Katy whispers in my ear.

I glance at Vivian and Mamma Dean with the silent question. Mamma Dean smiles and nods.

"Yes, sweetie, you can take him with you. Be sure to take it easy with him, though, since he's old. Okay?"

Katy springs up, a huge grin on her face as though I've told her she'd have free reign of the candy drawer I kept for her back at our rental house in Madison.

"Thanks, Mommy!" She sings, wriggling out of my arms and running over to the dog Kale has leashed beside him.

"Come on, Busta!" She says as Vivian guides her into the large farmhouse.

I feel the loss of my little girl immediately and am grateful for Kale's arm around me to serve as my anchor.

"Y'all come on and let me introduce you around," Mamma Dean declares, looping her arms in between mine and Kale's before we can protest.

In truth, I'm so exhausted from the dread of this event and interacting with demons I hadn't expected to deal with from this visit that I'm all but dragging as the eager old lady escorts us from table to table.

She introduces us to Cousin Petina, a very pregnant Hispanic woman who apparently made the potato salad, then to Cousin Dan who's something like the family mechanic and farmhand, and I'm trudging some more as she guides us to the small table crowded with teenagers. They're engaged in a heatedly hushed discussion

Out of the blue, the girl, whose hair is buzzed in a clean crew cut, slaps the guy next to her, so hard it energizes me.

"I don't want to see your fucking face tomorrow, Zay. Are we clear?" She thundered.

The guy, who's tan skin complexion and short braids remind me of a dark teen from my past, grumbles something before rising and trudging away. The group of teen males follow behind him and cast glares at the single girl at the table. She meets their glares with an even icier one before Mamma Dean clears her throat.

"Yvonne, not sure if you heard earlier, but this here is Patrice. You remember her?"

Yvonne? I freeze as I study the fully grown woman who took the place of the little shy girl I once knew in DC. No way was this right. Or perhaps my eyes were playing tricks on me.

Yvonne scans both Kale and I before scrunching her face in confusion. "Not sure I remember. Sorry."

Mamma Dean tuts. "Vonnie, you're telling me you don't remember, Patrice? I seem to recall reading something about a girl named Trice in your diary a couple weeks back. She matches the description of the girl you wrote about."

A horrified expression looms over her as she rises. "Mamma Dean! What did I tell you about going through my things?"

The old lady smiles devilishly. "Forgive me, baby. But you don't talk about any other friends in your journal from your time in DC, only stuff about your brother and his kind girlfriend named Patrice. So, after doing some digging around with sources I refuse to reveal, I hunted her down. She's here for the wedding, along with her husband and daughter. Why don't y'all get reacquainted?"

"Wait," I interrupt their heated back and forth, stepping out of Kale's arms. "Yvonne didn't actually invite us? It was really you?"

Mamma Dean chews on her lip and steps back. "Yvonne told me to manage the guest list, and manage it, I did."

Fury chases down the nice words I'd had readily prepared for this moment in my throat. I can practically feel Kale turn ghostly white behind me as the true identity of the woman in front of us is revealed.

"Why don't y'all have a little talk? Get reacquainted?" Mamma Dean suggests again.

Yvonne crosses her arms, averting her seething gaze. "I told you, old woman. I don't know her!"

"What's going on?" A soft voice probes from the shadows. Another red head woman, but younger this time, appears holding a giggling infant in her arms. The two make a striking pair, as the baby's toasted caramel skin makes an awesome juxtaposition against the alabaster complexioned thin woman holding him.

Yvonne visibly calms at the sight of her. "It's nothing, babe. Mamma Dean just being Mamma Dean."

"Kimmy!" Mamma Dean sings in excitement at the woman. "Please tell your soon-to-be wife that I only do the things I do with the best intentions. Patrice and Kale are here to have a little talk with her."

Kimmy eyes us, and I nearly gasp at how sharp green her eyes are.

"Nice to meet you," Kimmy greets smoothly with a smile.

Yvonne's eyes are glued to Kimmy, her jaw still hard set.

I step forward, extending my hand to Kimmy. "Sorry for the intrusion. I'm Patrice. You know, we have an

Airbnb in town and it's no trouble to get out of your hair—"

"Vonnie," Kimmy breathes sharply. "You're not gonna let these nice people make that treacherous trip back into town this time of night?" She flashes a wide grin at us. "Sorry about that! Please sit, get comfortable, and I hope you enjoy the food."

Yvonne rolls her eyes and re-sits herself at the picnic table. The sky is dark and there's a low rumble in the sky that promises a storm.

I grab Kale, who's just as still and ghostly, and tug him towards the picnic table. We sit down, the four of us, and squirm in the awkward silence. Mamma Dean has long since slipped back into the crowd of raucous family members.

"So," Kimmy breaks the silence. "Patrice, is it? Where are you all coming from?"

"Madison." I blurt. "Wisconsin, I mean. I work as a manager at an aerospace sustainability corporation and Kale's a Peer Support Specialist. But he also owns Sunshine Photography, his very own photography business." I clap a hand over my mouth, flushing in embarrassment. I'm mortified to have overshared so much information. What was wrong with me?

I look to Kale, who's unfocused eyes are just staring blankly into the darkness. "Babe?"

He clears his throat, returning to me. "Uh, yeah. Sunshine Photography."

"Right!" Kimmy exclaims, jostling the cute infant in her lap. "You're who Mamma Dean hired to take the wedding photos. It's nice to meet you! You have no idea how difficult it's been to find decent photographers in the area."

Kale offers a weak smile. "It's an honor."

She fans his words away. "Oh, stop it. We're the ones who are honored to have you here last minute to work this wedding for us. You must be so busy in Wisconsin."

When Kale's eyes go unfocused again, I answer. "Yeah, super busy. But we made sure to make time for this. It is so important that you two have the most magical day possible. We're happy to be a part of it."

"I didn't ask you to be a part of it." Yvonne sneered, glowering openly at me. "What's your agenda, huh?"

I rear back, aghast at the edge in her tone. "Excuse me?"

"You hear me." She squints her eyes. "What's your deal? Here to fuck with my brother's head again?"

"Vonnie!" Kimmy warns.

"No!" Yvonne barks. "She's from my old life, the one I try to forget in DC. All she did was play and betray my brother. You know, I think she's the reason he enlisted."

"What?" I thundered, thrown completely off by everything she's accusing me of. "I see something sparked your memory. Yvonne, honey, you don't know what you're talking about. Please—"

Yvonne shoots to her feet, pointing an accusatory finger at me. I fight the urge to recoil from the sheer intensity of her ferocity. "You need to leave."

"Vonnie!" Kimmy shouts. We're now causing a scene and the sky crackles and thunders some more. We're all standing squaring off at each other. "Baby, your center. Find your center, remember?"

Yvonne is trembling with unchecked rage, but at her fiancée's soothing command she closes her eyes and takes in deep breaths.

"Find my center," She quavers. "Find the beacon. The center is home."

I have no clue what those words mean, and I'm completely exhausted and confused by the situation. I'm overcome with the need to curl into a ball, snuggle with my little family until the monsters of the past are chased away. The Airbnb is sounding like a haven at this point, and with renewed resolve, I turn to Kale.

"Babe, let's go," I say to him.

He's not really focused on anything. I shake him. "Babe, come on, let's get Katy and head out. We're not meant to be here."

In place of the Irish soothing accent I expect to answer me, another deeper, darker one does.

"Vonnie?" The male voice queries as he approaches from the darkness. "What's all this yelling about? Is Zay still here?

Devin comes into view and I...I just freeze. Devin, the boy with whom I've had the most tumultuous relationship with, is now fully grown. His hair is now shaved into a military cut, and he's outfitted in a dark blue long sleeve shirt and black jeans. His arms are swollen with muscle and the beard on his face makes him that much more mature looking and appealing.

His eyes darken at the sight of Kale and I.

Yvonne storms off into the direction of the dark. What lay beyond there, I was not sure. Kale is now trembling, and I clench his hand in mine to steady him. I know this encounter was very triggering for him, and all I want now is to protect my heart and husband from this emotional torture.

"Kale? Trice?" Devin asks in astonishment. "Tell me I'm not hallucinating..."

"No." I bite out. "You're not hallucinating. We're...really here."

"Sorry, Dev." Kimmy apologizes, staring off into the same direction Yvonne ran. "I know you asked me to keep an eye on him, but I need to go check on my fiancée."

She deposits the now fussy infant in Devin's arms, then jets into the darkness.

"D-Devin." Kale stammers, shaking so violently he has to take a seat at the table again.

"Kale. Trice." He grounds out, rather awkwardly. "This is my son, Romelo."

Before I can say anything, the sky crackles as lightning lights the sky. Heavy, sudden rain pours in buckets over the now shrieking crowd.

***

It's the morning of Yvonne and Kimmy's nuptials and I awaken to a wet sensation splashing across my face. Groaning, I force my eyes open to see Busta giving me happy doggy kisses and Katy at his side.

"Mommy!" She yells on top of my covered body. "Good morning!"

I reach out to steady her insistent bouncing. "Baby, good morning. Where's daddy?"

My eyes flock to the empty warm side of the bed my husband occupied the night before. The torrential storm completely destroyed any notion of driving back to our Airbnb, and Mamma Dean insisted we spend the night in one of her many guest rooms. Kale, Katy, and me spend the night crumpled close in the small full sized bed. While cramped, I appreciated my little family's closeness after the night before.

Katy flopped onto Kale's side of the bed. "Daddy's in the kitchen, I think. He said he went to get us some food and that he'd be back in a pinch."

I smile at her use of her father's Irish phrases. "Okay, I'll go check on him."

"Mommy, wait! Can I Facetime Grammy to tell her good morning?" She pleads, and I only just now notice my iPhone in her little hands.

I know immediately who she's talking about, as she and my Aunt Patty's relationship was thick as thieves. Though they didn't see each other every day in person, she and Aunt Patty made it a habit to facetime every other day. I know we were long overdue for a visit, but she still lived with my parent's who I wanted nothing to do with after everything that happened in Wisconsin and with Manny. Aunt Patty was all the family we had, along with Angie, who we associated with.

I almost lose myself in wallowing my old family and old life, when Katy shakes me. "Mommy!"

"Yes, yes, yes, love." I say in defeat, too tired to deny her and too curious about the whereabouts of my husband. "Give her a call and tell her hi for me, okay?"

She's already dialing before I adjust myself, get out of bed, kiss her forehead, and set out to the halls to find Kale.

I find him in the kitchen, sitting at the table staring dejectedly at a plate of sandwiches and speaking to someone in a low voice.

It's Devin.

I notice Devin's camouflage attire, and realize he's wearing an Army uniform. Yvonne's spiel about me being the reason her brother enlisted rings more clear as I observe him.

I hang back, watching with bated breath from the shadows as the reliving of this nostalgic moment rides me. I recall the two of them in that gym, balling as if they were closest homies.

"Man to man," I hear Devin say. "I'm sorry for the shit that went down when I came back sophomore year. I had a feeling y'all was messing with each other, but I didn't care. Just wanted to keep her for myself."

Kale takes a steadying breath before answering. "Trice was able to take care of herself, you know. I barely had a hand in protecting, in sticking to the plan like we talked about all those years ago before you escaped. Besides, it's not my or your place to speak about her like she's chattel."

Devin gives a wry laugh, and moves to occupy the chair across from Kale at the dining room table. I wonder about the crowded houses' whereabouts in that moment before Devin scoffs. "I didn't mean it like that. Trice has her own mind, her own free will, and I would never talk about her that way. I...I won't lie to you, though, man. I was shocked as shit to see you two arrive last night. To see you two together still after all these years."

"Yeah." Kale breathed, leaning back in his chair. "We're stronger than ever. Made a beautiful little girl, too."

The warm smile that spreads across Devin's face melts me. "Yeah, she looks just like her mother. Tiny and cute as hell."

"You should see the look on her face when I tell her about the 'no candy past bedtime' rule we had to implement after catching her sneaking sweets from the kitchen at nights." Kale pouts and sputters, and I recognize the frustrated face he's mimicking of our daughter in an instant.

Devin and Kale burst into a laughter I'd assumed them previously incapable of ever doing. The two look like old friends, breaking bread and regaling tales from the past.

Devin sobers, "That's real sweet, man. I respect y'all, and the life y'all built together. It's beautiful."

"Thanks, brother." Kale offers, sobering as well. "And what of your family? Is your wife here, too?"

A tic works in Devin's jaw and I frown to see him wincing at the question. "Nah. I'm not the marrying type, you know. Plus, it's just me and Rome."

"Everything all right?"

"It's good. His mother, my girlfriend...um, died giving birth to him almost two years ago now. Been me and him ever since."

Kale claps his back in solidarity. "My bad, brother. Didn't mean to make you relive that. Sorry for asking."

I want to cry out from the injustice of his story. I hated how life had a nasty habit of treating him like shit, as it seemed Devin always collected more horrors as his life's story continued.

Feeling a renewed resolve and going against my thudding heart, I step into the kitchen.

"Baby!" Kale greets me nervously, standing up. "Good morning. I hope you slept okay?"

I cross the room to embrace him. "Yes, I'm all right. How are you feeling after...last night?"

He averts his eyes, seeming to recall the mild panic attack he suffered through during that confrontation with Yvonne.

"I'm good. Just chatting it up with Devin, here."

Devin waves at me in an awkward fashion. "Hey, Trice."

I blush. "Hey."

"I heard some of what you two were talking about earlier." I murmured. "And I just want to say, it's good to see you like this."

"Talking?" Devin inquires.

I smile at his confusion. "No. Well, yes. It's nice to see two of the men who mean so much to me on good terms. On talking terms. I hope..."

Kale chases my eyes. "Yes, Sunshine?"

"I hope this lasts. But I have no right to voice what I want. Not after all I've done. After how bad I failed you both after getting involved with Jack Burn."

A haunting silence falls between the room, as we sit and consider the words hanging in the air.

Kale speaks first. "Trice, D and me go way back, since before me and you actually met. We're just hashing some things out after all this time. The stuff with Jack—"

"Only happened because of me." Devin cuts in, his tone grave as he flexes his jaw. His arms are bulging under the military suit.

I take a tentative step towards him. "Devin, stop it. Don't try to protect me, not right now. You need to hear this from me, after all this time."

A hand slams into the table, it belongs to Devin, and Kale and I regard him with mirroring expressions of fear.

"That motherfucker!" Devin growls. "That mother-fucker is lucky prison got to him before I could. After what he did to Ty..."

My mind jumbles as I form the meaning. I'd only heard around that Jack Burn was caught on a heavy possession charge, but the later information was news to me.

"Ty?" I ask, remembering the Principal's announce-ment that morning in school.

Devin nodded, agony on his face. "Yeah. There's no proof of it, but I recognized that dude who ran out of that trap house and popped Ty. Jack was behind that shit."

My mind flits to the boy who held us at gunpoint that day, the one I heard flat out call me a ho when I went visit Devin in the hospital after Helen shot him. They hadn't known my presence then, but I was there listening desperately to the boy I'd previously failed to convince my innocence to.

I also recalled Nora, my Beach, having the hugest crush on the rugged bad boy. Of how distraught she reacted after his death.

"Devin, I can't take this anymore." I blurt, tears streaming down my face and my chest filled with the secrets of years ago.

"Patrice," Kale says softly, a warm warning against revealing the events I explained to him about that 'birthday show.' Kale was the only person I'd ever confided in about the abandoned warehouse slaughtering. We spoke and agreed before we married, to keep that only secret if ever we came across Devin again. We had a no-secrets policy which helped keep our marriage afloat, but the burden of a secret of that magnitude, admittedly, held me back all these years. It kept me afraid even after all these years of being honest and forgiving myself. I decided, in that moment, to atone for some of the failures in my past by just pushing this out.

I straighten myself and look Devin squarely in the eyes. "Devin...please don't hate me for this. I know I have no right to beg for your forgiveness, to even breathe the same air as you, but it was me! I'm the reason Quincy's dead."

Devin stills, training cold eyes beyond me. "No. Like I said, it was lung cancer that—"

"Stop the lies!" I screeched, sure I'd woken up somebody in the large house. "Jack...found out about Quincy and Saint stealing money from the gang. And he...had him dealt with. I'm so so sorry Devin!"

Kale grabs my shoulders. "Baby, calm down. You're shaking all over."

"Patrice," Devin grouses, standing up. "Listen to me–"

I run, sprint, no, straight up jet out of that emotionally tense kitchen in search of solitude and solace. I don't want to be the bad guy again. I hated being the one to deliver such horrific news to my former best friend who I seemed to keep failing, letting him know that I knew exactly what happened to his stepdad. That it was Jack who played that insane birthday game, forcing me to shoot and kill the old man whose death brought so much dysfunction to Devin and Yvonne.

There's a door down the hall, and I don't pause to consider rhyme or reason as I jiggle the knob. It opens. I hear Devin and Kale call behind me as I descend the steps to a creepily quiet basement. This room appears to be an extra bedroom in this large house filled with sleeping quarters. Devin's extended family treated Mamma Dean's farmhouse like a Bed and Breakfast, since there were so many bedrooms and a sweet older matron who didn't mind cooking and hosting any of them whenever they were in town.

I'm hyperventilating by the time I reach the heavily quilted queen sized mattress. I collapse onto it, my chest constricting at the anxiety and release of that tortuous long held secret. No more lies. No more drama. No more of this heartache that prevented me from giving my full self to the people who meant the most to me in life.

Heavy footsteps descend the stairs, and I don't bother to turn to greet the concerned faces.

"Sunshine?" Kale drawls, his tone infused with worry.

"Trice?" Devin asks behind him, and I hear them both walk over to stand before me in bed. My head is sunk into the pillow, and I'm quaking so hard from the sobs it's hard to hear them

"Hey, hey." I feel a calloused hand on my shoulder. "Baby, it's all right. Look at me."

I shake my head. "Just leave. You're gonna leave me anyways, so just...go." I say to...whoever is speaking to me.

"Sunshine." It's Kale. "Just look at me for a moment, okay?"

Groggy from sorrow, I rise up and meet the ocean blue and mahogany eyes of the men in the room. Kale is sitting on the bed with me, while Devin stands by the bed wearing a worried frown.

"Trice," Devin repeats. "You didn't let me finish."

"No!" I choke the words out around the tears, around the heartache of the inevitable thing to come. They were both gonna leave; leave me in the dark hole the secrets I kept lived in. "I keep failing you both. I don't deserve any of you...just leave me now, and get it over with. My heart can't take the waiting."

"Come here," Devin rushed me then, crouching down to sweep me in his large arms. "Baby, please stop this. I don't blame you for what happened."

I realize the very awkward position we're in, as Kale has me half cradled in his arms while Devin wraps his arms around my middle.

Kale starts. "We've got to get out of this business of failing each other. Of hiding and keeping secrets and punishing ourselves for the things we can't control."

"Yeah," Devin affirms, his warm voice reaching my ears like honey. "If you'd let me finish what I said earlier in the kitchen, me and Kale already talked this through, man to man before the house woke up. He told me everything."

I freeze, looking up at my husband. "Wait...everything as in, all of it?"

Kale nods. "Yes."

"But what happened to our promise to never tell?"

He readjusts himself to accommodate Devin's arms wrapped around my waist. "Like I said, we need to stop it with the lies. The secrets. And we got to forgive ourselves. We had no control of anything life dealt us back then. The roles we took in Helen's shooting Devin, of me discovering those bodies in my family's basement, and of you surviving Jack Burn to pay off a debt. None of this is our fault, you two. You get me?"

A stray tear runs down the course of Devin's face as he nods. "You're right. And I just came to tell you both I'm sorry. And that I forgive you, and I hope you can forgive me."

"All is forgiven, brother," Kale says. "We've already hashed that out."

"Solid." Devin agrees, and I stare at them in blanket confusion and bewilderment as they fist bump before pinning curious stares at me.

"Well?" Kale probes gently to me.

"What's it gonna be?" Devin adds, putting me in mind of Luther's terrifying question as he extended the black gun to me. "Can you forgive yourself? Forgive me? Forgive us?"

I'm just as scared as I was during that moment, as I reach for Devin. However, there's no hesitation as I pull his mouth to mine, crushing our lips against each other with a vibrating intensity.

"Trice..." He moans as he wraps his arms and squeezes me into his hard body. "Fuck..."

I rip out of his grasp just as I feel his hard length against my middle.

Kale is watching us, his eyes dark and searching, but there's no anger there as he examines us.

I cup my husband's nape, bringing him close to my mouth before I say, "I love you. I forgive you. Please understand..."

"I do and I will. Fuck, Trice, come here!" Kale's lips crush against mine with the same power as Devin's did a few seconds ago.

We're ripping each other's clothes off and my body hums with a wanton completeness I didn't expect to feel. Shirts, uniform tops, and pants fly into the heated air as we ravage each other. Devin and Kale pass me back and forth to lavish my mouth in sizzling kisses as we fall to the bed in unison.

I gasp as the feel of a hard body, I'm not sure who, looms over top of me, and I just about cry out into the dark room at the feel of the hard length nudging my clenching wet opening.

Time blurs and a wet pounding of flesh against flesh punctuated with resounding groans from the three of us penetrate the dark silence in the room, drowning all else out as we seek to ignite and heal. Together.

***

My cheeks are bright red as I recall the events from this morning, the hot desire of it making me squirm in my seat. My breath catches as I watch Kale, in all his muscle and sun kissed glory, snap photos of different people and areas of the elegantly decorated backyard. The wedding ceremony is about to begin, and is taking place, in spite of last night's storm, in the large backyard area of Carlson Farms.

My phone vibrates in my mini purse I bought specifically for this event. I sneak a glance at it, and sigh.

That's Mom's number.

This was the third time she called within thirty minutes, and I can't help the worry that fills my chest at her unusual persistence. We had a mutual understanding to never bother each other, not even for emergencies, but clearly she gave no fucks about honoring that pact. I scoff, thinking honor and Monica Newbern belonged nowhere near each other after what went down when I ran away. Of course she'd violate my boundaries, I fume as I send her fourth call to voicemail.

"Mommy?" A little voice calls, tugging on my yellow bodycon dress.

Katy is seated beside me amidst the crowd, and I have to hunch to hear her.

"Yes, baby?"

A frown mars her beautiful caramel face and she purses her lips in consternation. "Who's that man over there?"

I gulp, turning in the direction she indicated with a bob of her head. I see Devin with his infant son in his arms. A dark smile is on his face when he catches me watching him, and he starts to approach us.

My heart goes thunderous in my chest. "Oh, Katy, this is Mommy's...friend."

"Hello, beautiful." Devin flashes a luxurious Cooper grin at my daughter seated next to me. "It's nice to finally meet you."

"Do you like Mommy's dress? Yellow is her favorite color." She exclaims, and I suspect she's falling prey like I did to Devin's irresistible charm.

He gives my body a predatory and appreciative once over. "Yes, her dress is pretty, just like her."

"Mommy, your face is red. Are you sick?" Katy, my relentless four-year old, clearly doesn't realize how

awfully awkward this situation is and I inwardly want
to die a bit.

Cupping my face in my hands, I say. "Hi Devin, can
I help you with something?"

He throws his head back and laughs at my humiliation. "I just came over to ask if you wouldn't mind
watching Rome? I gotta get in position soon to walk
Vonnie down the aisle."

My heart squeezes at the reminder of his position in
the ceremony. Considering his and Yvonne's airtight
relationship, it makes sense he walk her down the
aisle. And while she hated me right now, I still had love
for the misguided girl and the hard life she's had to
live. At that moment, I decided to be happy for her
and the redhead who brings her peace.

I extend my arms. "Sure thing. Bring those chunky
cheeks here!"

Rome giggles loud and excitedly as I dance with him
in my arms. His large brown eyes are spitting images
of his rakish father's, and I melt inside as he clings
tight to my chest.

"Gosh, you're a natural." Devin breathes, as he stares
at the two of us dancing and giggling.

Kales walks up just then, and I have to gulp hard to
not drool at the handsome sight the two of them made
side-by-side. The feel of both of those hard bodies
rubbing against my enflamed one, made me–

"I know right." Kale utters proudly, interrupting my
lingering dirty thoughts. "The best mother around."

"She's my mommy!" Katy spits, her face heating with irritation. "Mine."

I turn warm eyes to her. "Katrice, of course. You're my favorite girl. Remember?"

She smiles smugly, seemingly satisfied as she sits back in her seat. The three of us laugh and soak in the merriment before the ceremony begins. Kale runs to the archway where the preacher is waiting and positions the camera in place to begin filming.

Devin disappeared, and I know the wedding is moments away from starting due to Richard Wagner's "Wedding March" song humming throughout the field.

Rome fusses as the bridesmaids work their way down the aisle. The heat seems to be exasperating him and by the time Yvonne and Devin march arm in arm down the aisle, I feel a hot wetness ooze down my leg.

"Eww, Mommy look!" Katy hisses as she points at the source of the gooey sensation.

"Oh, no!" I gasp in horror when I see it. Rome's tummy must have been irritated, because his poop is so watery it leaks through the sides of his diaper and down my leg. The smell is so putrid, it rouses some of the crowd and causes a scene.

Yvonne shoots an icy glare my way, and I fidget under the unexpected attention.

"Excuse me!" I whisper guiltily as I jet towards the house. I hate that I'm missing the best parts of the ceremony, but there's no way sitting amidst a huge crowd of people with a loud, poopy baby wouldn't detract from their special moment.

"Oh, honey." I breathe sympathetically as I assess the wreckage. I had to take him to the guest bathroom and toss his clothes, since they were completely ruined. As I'm bathing the now cheery infant, I hear my phone buzz again. I forgot that I'd taken my mini purse inside with me.

After wiping my wet hands, I reach over and search my purse on the sink.

Confusion shoots through me when I notice Aunt Patty's cell number on the screen. This was weird, I gathered, since she usually called during the early morning to check on Katy or see Busta since she'd gifted him to us a couple of months ago.

I answer what I don't realize is a FaceTime call, to see my mother's face on the opposite end. Her eyes are puffy and red, and she's sobbing.

"What, Mom?!" I snap. "Why'd you hijack Aunt Patty's phone? And what is it you have to say to me that's so important that you blow me up like this?"

Rome flinches at my elevated tone, and I smile apologetically at him.

"Patrice." She garbles. "I'm so so sorry. I hate that I have to do this."

My heart seizes. "Do what? Mom, spit it out or I'm hanging up—"

"It's Mama Pat." Her voice is trembling with sorrow as my hands freeze over the bottle of shampoo. "She passed away this morning. Baby I'm so so sorry, I know y'all were close..."

My mind numbs, heart stills, and the room closes in on me at her words. I pull Rome out of the bath and hug him tight, like an anchor, to my chest.

Somewhere in the distance, the backyard I believe, there's a loud shriek before a male's voice howls, "I object!"

Authors' Note

We thank you SO much for reading SECRETS, Book 6 in the REAL series. Trice's story rang so loudly in our ears, that it made not writing it down impossible. Please enjoy the excerpt to the next book in the series, entitled HOME.

Love always,
Laura & Laurie

Home

"I don't think you understand what you are to me."

Kimberly's small smile grew coy as she stared into my eyes. Our lips met in a kiss, so brief, so flickering, it almost felt as if it didn't happen at all. A harsh wind blew by us as Monday's moon shone brightly above our heads, the impact of the gust flushed our bodies close together, her front meeting mine.

"Ooh, s-sorry." She muttered, embarrassed by her actions.

Since we were eye level, it was no problem for me to caress her cheek with my palm.

My sweet Kimmy, I thought lovingly. God, she was all I wanted. All I needed. And the only place I ever wanted to be.

I couldn't hide the smile that tugged at my lips. "Baby doll, don't apologize. I knew you just couldn't help yourself from being as close to me as possible. I know it completes you."

Despite the wintry Virginia winds, a flash of heat surged to her pale cheeks as she slapped me playfully on my shoulder. "You complete me with your closeness? Now you're just fishing." She laughed.

I chewed on my lip as I watched her head tilt back with laughter. Gosh, I don't know what was with me tonight, but her every move seemed graceful, her every word I clung to.

I chuckled and tightened my arms around her slim frame. "Fishing? But aren't I just sooo cute?"

She smirked. "You're incorrigible."

I smiled devilishly. "And you're my everything."

Her face turned stone serious as she assessed mine. Her arms tightened round my neck as she lowered her lips close to mine. "Don't do this to me."

I frowned slightly and realized the events of the day and how much I needed her to see I now meant it.

My thick curls blew in the wind as another gust of wind blew straight through my thicker arms, and I allowed all the humor to drain from my next words.

Savoring the delight within her arms, I leaned in close to press my lips to her ear.

"Wherever you're not, my soul is lost." My words were deadpan.

She looked away, and I thought I caught a tear forming in her eyes. My hand shot out to gently grasp her chin, bringing her eyes to meet mine. No way was she running from this.

"You are everything." I whispered, falling and feeling myself become captive in her eyes and enraptured by her love. "You are HOME..."

About the author

LAURA:

Since the age of twelve, Laura could always be found writing. She writes within a wide array of genres, including paranormal, drama, slice of life, and (her favorite) romance. In her free time, if she's not writing, she's reading or listening to a steamy audio-book. Her most notable works include Something About Kyle and her ongoing, The REAL Series, which explores the narratives of various, interconnected young adults.

As an author, Laura aims to push boundaries and leave a lasting impact on her community. Her journey taught her the importance of perseverance, creativity, and staying true to one's unique vision. Support her craft by purchasing from her bookstore.

LAURIE:

An established poet, writing has been a part of Laurie's life for as long as she could remember. Growing up, she thought everyone had a ballad in their head that they couldn't get rid of unless written down. Writing means the world to her. She's always eager to share her world with those who enjoy taking the scenic route.

Other books in this series

GRAY
LIGHT
CAVE
*EDGE
HEART
SECRETS

Coming Soon
HOME

*written by Laurie Ross